Always with You

Always with You

A N D R E A H U R S T

The Sonoma County setting used in this book is mostly authentic with a few exceptions in location to move the plot forward. Some dates have been slightly changed as well. The story and characters are completely fictitious and derived from the author's imagination.

ISBN-13: 9781984399359
ISBN-10: 1984399357

Credits Revised Edition:

Cover Design: Rebecca Berus, 2MarketBooks
Developmental Editor: Cameron Chandler
Copy Editor: Audrey Mackaman

To Susan
with
Love,
Andrew
2020

Being deeply loved by someone gives you strength,
while loving someone deeply gives you courage.
~Lao Tzu

The Summer of 2017

Sonoma County, Forestville, CA

On a day like this, nothing could be wrong with the world. Cathy's rocker glided gently back and forth while the light breeze whispered across her redwood deck. Daylight illuminated the oak-lined hills, and a sparrow's song complemented the melodic sound of her wind chimes. June was a glorious month on the Russian River in Sonoma County. It had always been her favorite.

The grass blazed emerald in the sun, laying a soft carpet in front of the pink climbing roses that bordered her garden. Toys from her granddaughter's visit were scattered across the deck. They were quickly abandoned when her mother, Annie, arrived and announced that it was time to leave Grandma's house. Cathy picked up the well-loved, stuffed Velveteen Rabbit she'd given her granddaughter and hugged it to her chest. Years ago there'd been another precious little girl she'd given the same gift.

Cathy lifted a hand to block her eyes from an almost blinding flash of light. In the distance, a figure appeared to be walking toward her. She remembered a vivid dream from years ago, where a man walked ever closer, out of a misty fog, his blue eyes piercing into hers. That dream had lingered with her for all this time. The day she'd met Jamie that dream had become real, and her life had never been the same.

The man stepped through her white picket gate and proceeded up the garden path. She squinted, trying to identify him, but her aging eyes could not register his identity. Not that she was so very old, seventy at her last birthday. Her auburn hair was barely streaked with gray; her olive complexion held its own against gravity. Most never guessed her age. A slight vanity she admitted to.

Age is just a number, her husband, Alan, had taught her. Nothing scared him; life was for living to its fullest. Back when she met him, almost forty years ago, even in her broken state, he'd taken her by the hand and she never let herself look back.

The intense light was in her eyes again and she found it hard to breathe. She reached for her prescription sunglasses. Maybe they would help identify the visitor who stood in the yard looking up at her. His silver-streaked hair was illuminated by the sun, creating a halo effect. "Perhaps it is my guardian angel," she chuckled.

His jawline looked familiar, as did the slight droop of his shoulders.

Suddenly, Cathy couldn't catch her breath at all. Her heart pounded against her ribs and an intense pain gripped her chest and radiated down her arm.

"Cat," she heard the man say.

Only one person called her by that name.

Cathy wanted to run to him, but her limbs froze in place. Nothing made sense.

Jamie stood in front of her now, backlit by the brightest sun. The memory of him burned in her heart, and his eyes still held her fate.

Chapter One

June 1977

Sonoma County, Forestville, CA

Cathy steered her Honda over the familiar twists and turns of River Road as it meandered along the green waters of the Russian River. Sunlight blinded her as it leapt between the pines and flashed across her windshield. Her leisurely drive home from her shop was always hectic this time of year due to the summer tourists. It was those same tourists that kept Health & Hearth thriving, she reminded herself, for seven years now.

She looked down at the framed photo on the front seat. "Surprise!" they'd yelled before she left. "Happy seventh anniversary." Jill, her café manager, handed her the photo of 'the gang' wrapped in a gold ribbon. What would she do without them? These people were more family to her than hers had even been.

Her T-shirt stuck to her back from working in the hot kitchen all day. She wanted to get home and jump in a cool shower. Cathy lowered her visor, switched on the radio, and sang along to the Fleetwood Mac song about freedom and dreams. The words, "the sound of your own loneliness," stopped her. The chorus taunted her. "What you've lost … what you had …" That was not a place she wanted her mind to go. Not on this wonderful day. The past was hidden away; where she'd left it, and that is where it would safely stay.

Horns blasted. If this guy in front of her didn't stop slamming on his brakes, she was going to lose it. Cathy took some deep breaths. She needed to get back into yoga again. The traffic suddenly slowed, and without warning, a golden retriever sprinted out of the trees and onto the highway two cars ahead. She heard the screech of brakes, the high-pitched cry of a dog, and slammed on hers as hard as she could. Veering off to the right, she almost collided with a tall tree. Cathy jumped out of the car, and pushed through the onlookers. The dog was lying on the edge of the road, its chest heaving with every breath. Relief flooded her … it was still alive.

"I'm so sorry, so sorry," the lady with the red car kept saying. "The sun was in my eyes. I couldn't see."

Cathy moved around her and bent over the dog. He looked barely out of puppyhood. She petted his silky head and whispered, "Hang on, boy. It's going to be okay." The dog's soft, brown eyes showed signs of understanding.

Memories of Cathy's own golden dog years ago, knotted her stomach. She had to get this dog out of here now. She looked up at the crowd forming around her. "Can someone help me? Please."

No one moved. Cathy rested the dog's head in her lap. His warm breath brushed against her arm as he panted in distress. The traffic edged by with people gawking out their windows. "Just go away," she wanted to scream.

A station wagon made a sharp turn and parked beside them, blocking the road and creating a protective barricade. A man shot out of the car. Bright sunlight lit up his face as he walked briskly toward Cathy.

"Back away," he told the onlookers. "Someone go call the police."

He knelt beside her, blond hair falling into his face as his hands moved adeptly over the dog. "Is he yours?" the man asked.

Cathy looked up and nearly gasped. Those startling blue eyes had her spinning.

The man stared at her, waiting for a response.

"No, he's not mine," Cathy finally said. "I just saw him run out on the road and pulled over. Poor guy."

"Not everyone would do that. That was kind."

"Not everyone would pull over and help either," Cathy said.

He turned over the dog's tag. "Well, Charlie, it looks like you wandered from home and got into some trouble." He gently petted the dog's head looking closer at his injuries.

The dog's tail thumped against the pavement, followed by a soft whimper.

"We have to act fast," he said. "But I think he has a good chance."

Cathy looked down at the innocent, sweet dog. "He has to make it." She broke into tears.

He put his arm around her shoulder. Cathy let her head rest on his warm chest. "He'll be fine. He will," the man murmured into her hair.

Cathy wiped her tears and looked up. "Thank you." His eyes were so familiar. Suddenly she remembered her recurring dream.

He stood and reached a strong hand out to pull her up. "Let's go."

"There's a vet just down the road," she said. "You can follow me."

She lifted the dog's head from her lap, placing it gently on the ground beside her.

The man carefully picked up the retriever, folded him into his strong arms, and brought him to his car. Charlie moaned softy and made a valiant attempt to wag his tail.

The police had arrived and were directing traffic around the accident. One of them was interviewing the woman who hit the dog. An officer motioned for Cathy, with the station wagon behind her, to enter the road. Cathy led the way to the downtown Forestville vet clinic, trying not to speed. When they arrived, she held the door open while the man carried the dog in. Cathy explained what happened to the receptionist and promised to handle any vet bills if the owner did not show up. Exhausted, she sat down on the wooden bench to wait for the results. He sat beside her.

Heat radiated between them. Cathy kept her eyes on the ground. His legs were clad in khakis and his dress shoes indicated he was not on vacation. She let her eyes move up to his striped button-down shirt. His sleeves were rolled up revealing smooth, tanned arms and graceful fingers. Briefly, she glanced at his profile. The dimple in his chin, the way the light hair framed his carved face. She knew him. She knew those eyes. Just like in her dreams, where a man had walked toward her through heavy ground fog. And every time he approached, the image of his intense blue eyes boring into hers would jolt her awake, until one day his face was revealed. She'd known him somehow like a mirror reflection of a part of herself.

Who really knew what dreams meant? She knew one thing, she could not ask him to stay, for in their haste with the dog, she had not noticed what she now saw: the gold wedding band on his left hand.

"You've been so kind," Cathy said. "You don't have to wait. I'll take care of him."

The man hesitated, not taking his eyes off her. "I do have to get back to the city but …"

Just at that moment, a teary young woman ran into the vet's office. "Where's my Charlie?" she asked the receptionist. "He's my dog. He's just a puppy still, and dug himself right out from under my fence. When I got home, I heard and … is he okay?"

"I think he's doing well, let me check." The receptionist went into the back offices.

Cathy went over to the owner and helped her take a chair. "We found him and brought him here. He's a beautiful dog. I'm sure he's going to be fine."

The woman looked up with a stricken expression. "I love him so much. I feel so bad."

They sat with the woman awaiting the news. A few minutes later the vet walked out to speak with them. "Well, I'm happy to say Charlie seems only to have suffered a broken front leg. He's in shock, so I think we should keep him overnight. But he's young and healthy and should heal quickly. I'm confident he'll be going home with you tomorrow."

The woman jumped out of her seat. "Thank you, doctor! Can I see him now?"

"Of course," the vet said, leading her back.

She turned to Cathy and the helpful stranger. "I'm Paula. How can I ever thank you?"

"Just go love your dog," he said.

Cathy stood and watched Paula hurry through the doors to find her Charlie. She released her breath as the adrenalin that had been racing through her body finally subsided. Her legs were wobbly and she gripped a chair.

"Are you going to be okay?" he asked. The tenderness in his eyes almost made her cry again. The kindness of strangers, echoed through her mind. But somehow, he did not seem like a stranger, and she was reluctant to say goodbye.

He waited for her answer. What could she say? "I'm fine. Thank you for everything."

"I did what any good Samaritan would do," he said.

Cathy smiled at him "And far beyond that."

He shrugged the compliment off. "Right time, right place," he said smiling back at her.

Right man, she thought.

Cathy watched him start for the door and hesitate. Her turned back to her as if taking one last look. "Until next time," he said.

Would there be one, she wondered. Had she visited his dreams as he had hers? She moved to the doorway and watched him get in his car. Then like a white knight in a station wagon, he drove out of her life.

Chapter Two

The phone woke Cathy from a deep sleep. For a moment, she could not remember what day it was. The sun streamed in through her window and she glanced at her clock on the nightstand before grabbing the phone. And why was she still asleep at 10 a.m.?

"Cathy, it's Paula. I hope I didn't wake you."

"No, of course not," Cathy said. She sat up and shook off her drowsiness. "Is everything all right with Charlie? After the car accident about three weeks back, Paula had stopped by her shop with a bouquet of flowers and a bottle of wine from her small vineyard. She'd thanked Cathy profusely for getting Charlie to the vet and being so kind. Paula had become a regular customer for lunch and been over to the house a few times with the dog.

"I called the shop but they said you weren't in. I wanted to share the great news we just got. Charlie is doing so well, he got his cast off!"

"I am so glad to hear that," Cathy said.

"We're having a Charlie celebration tonight at the vineyard and wanted to invite you as a guest of honor."

Cathy smiled. "I'd love to come. I have company arriving tomorrow so the timing is perfect. I'll see you tonight."

She hung up the phone and got out of bed. Sleeping this late was a luxury, but they'd been so busy with summer tourists at the shop and all the extra cleaning at home for her guests had worn her out. She wandered out to her living room and stood at the picture window. It was such a glorious day with a cloudless blue sky and bright sunshine, Cathy longed to forget her responsibilities at work today, and go down to the river for a swim.

Technically, she was her own boss and could do whatever she wanted. And then there was yesterday's call, and all the adjustments she would have to make to accommodate Pam's last minute whims. After fixing tea she poured a bowl of homemade granola, sliced strawberries and bananas on top and added sunflower seeds and raw milk from the local dairy. Cathy took a seat at the dining room table. This was possibly her last day of peace in her normally quiet home.

Snowy rubbed against her leg, purring madly. Cathy petted the sweet cat. "You want to be let out girl?" she asked. She didn't blame the cat, the acres of woods and grasslands surrounding her home held many adventures for a cat. She stood and opened the front door to the porch and let Snowy out. "At least one of us can be free today," she said.

Her mind was made up. She would shower and go into work and make sure everything was in order before her company arrived and derailed her normal schedule.

After making the short drive to Health and Hearth, Cathy pulled into the parking lot behind her shop and turned off the car. She threw her bag over her shoulder and walked around the front of the store to see how the new display of natural shampoos and conditioners looked in her front window. Her shop manager, Tim, in his usual creative style, had arranged pine branches along the windowpane and a basket of peonies in the foreground. He'd lined the wood product risers with rainwater, honey, and oatmeal hair products. It looked fresh and inviting. Satisfied, Cathy opened the glass entry door and stepped inside. The pungent smell of leeks and garlic permeated the shop. Sunshine flooded the store, radiating through the display windows. A few customers lingered by the displays as her employees prepared for the day. Everything was humming along and she fell right in sync.

Behind the lunch counter, her café manager, Jill, in a flowery apron over denim cutoffs and a T-shirt, was busy at the stove prepping fresh soup for the lunch rush.

"Morning," Cathy said. She waved at Tim behind the cash register.

"Mornin'," Tim said as he counted out cash. His tight sleeveless orange T-shirt set off his bronze, muscular arms.

"Looking good." She shot him a wink.

He preened a bit. A cute guy must be coming in today. The River was a haven for Tim in the summer. Gay men swamped the place making it their summer playground.

Cathy wandered past the bulk products, vitamins, and herbs, into the eating area and behind the counter.

"You're in late. What's up, kiddo?" Jill asked.

Cathy peered into the simmering pot. The herbal scent made her taste buds perk up. She couldn't be hungry, not after that big breakfast she'd had at home.

"Everything is fine," Cathy said. "I just thought I would check in and make sure the rooms are ready for the guests tomorrow."

Jill's dark pupils, matching her raven-colored locks, looked right through Cathy.

"And?"

Jill never beat around the bush.

"Okay," Cathy said. "It seems I have company arriving later today to stay at my house."

Jill suppressed a smile. "You'll survive." She gave a crushing hug. "Russian peasant stock," Jill always said when Cathy mentioned her big-boned frame and enviable energy. Whenever Jill brought her family over for dinner, with her two young children running after the cats and raising the noise level many decibels, she always knew just when to leave by looking at Cathy's face.

Jill's warm hug never failed to make all worries go away.

"You know me too well," Cathy said. "How did I get so lucky to have you manage this place?"

"Good karma." Jill tightened her apron and started grating carrots and beets for the rainbow salad. "My family will never forget how you let us stay in the rooms upstairs until we could get on our feet again last year."

"That was nothing."

"Maybe to you it was, but to Dan and me, it meant everything," Jill said. "And by the way, I made up the rooms upstairs for the weekend guests."

"You're great."

"You could go home now," Jill said. "I don't want to say we don't need you," she grinned, teasing Cathy with her eyes. "But we don't."

"I get it," Cathy said, "but I think I'll stay a while. No rush to get home."

A customer entered, and Cathy decided to scoot upstairs and check out the guest rooms. The River View room in front was bathed in light coming through dual bay windows. Its four-poster bed was made up with a white chenille bedspread, and an antique patchwork quilt was folded at the foot. Pink and purple hydrangeas set off pale-yellow walls. Perfect.

Next, she inspected the Cozy Cottage room that faced the woods out back. The all-white cleanness of the attic bedroom with the low ceiling pulled the stress from her shoulders: white chenille spread, ash floors, lace curtains, and a milk-glass vase with artfully arranged lavender and thyme. It was a room for romance. She sighed, that was one area that had not worked well so far in her life. But for now, she was content being on her own, having a sense of control of her world, and choosing who would be in it.

Cathy peered out the open window, inhaling the summer scent of pine. Perhaps she should sleep here a few nights if her houseguests stayed a long time? How long was too long? This is ridiculous, she told herself. She had a home to go to. A garden to tend. Nice people were coming to see her. It would be fun.

End of story.

Brian's throaty laugh boomed all the way up the stairs. Cathy hoped her kitchen helper hadn't come in stoned today. He was a great kid and helped them out a lot in the summer, but he did have a few habits that didn't always mix well with work. Wasn't he supposed to be off today? She headed downstairs to see what was up.

She spotted Brian talking to Jill. He was in his usual attire of jeans with holes in them, a bright colored shirt, and a strand of puka shells circling his neck. His long, dark hair was in a ponytail down his back.

"Hi, Brian, are you scheduled for today?" she asked.

"Nope. But I can stay if you need me. I just stopped by to remind everyone I leave next Tuesday for a family backpacking trip."

Right. Now she remembered. "Would you mind working some extra hours starting today until you leave? I have company coming to visit and would like to spend some time showing them around."

"Sure thing, boss. I could use the extra hours."

Jill ladled up some of the soup and offered them all a taste. "Sounds like a fun trip," she said.

Brian shrugged. "My parents are a bit uptight, but by the time we hit Montana maybe they'll chill out."

Cathy considered whether Jill would have enough help cooking, bussing, and washing dishes when both she and Brian were gone at the same time. If the guests stayed that long. There had been no discussion of departure date. Tim could handle the store, but that kept him pretty busy. "How long will you be gone?" she asked.

He scratched his beard. "Ah, about a week." He turned to Cathy. "Mind if I scarf down a veggie burger before I start work?"

"Sure, go ahead," she said.

Jill turned to Cathy. "When was the last time you had a vacation?"

"Been a while." Cathy relented. "I get it. I'm leaving."

Cathy wasn't used to having others in her home, or a young child. She thought of her cats. They would likely retreat to the garden when the family arrived.

"Maybe I should stay and …"

Jill pointed toward the door. "Go ahead and take off. I can handle it from here."

"That's an understatement," Cathy said, waving goodbye. "I'll check in tomorrow."

It was 2 p.m., too early for wine but not for chocolate. Cathy surveyed the house again. The oak floors stretching across the living and dining rooms glowed thanks to vinegar and water. Ceramic vases filled the rooms with colorful wildflowers from her garden, and the sun shone through the freshly washed windows that faced the woods behind her home.

The last few days, she'd obsessed, trying to get the house clean enough for guests. She'd made sure everything was handled at work. And now two adults and a four-year-old child were arriving. She was used to a quiet house all to herself, but short-term company could work if she gave it a chance. It had been years since she'd last seen Pam. They'd been friends back in high school, not the closest, but thrown together by classes and circumstances. When everything had fallen apart, Pam had stuck around the longest, but Cathy was never sure why. They'd barely spoken over the last twelve years, and Cathy was surprised to hear from her now.

"Cathy," Pam said when she called. "We need a place to stay on and off while my husband interviews for jobs in the wine country up there." She'd gone on about their living situation and how they were staying with Pam's mom in Oakland until they got on their feet. With her mom's Alzheimer's, and Pam being a part-time caregiver, that must have been hard on them all. "We want our little girl to grow up in that nice environment," she'd said so sweetly.

Pam was right. Oakland was no place to raise a four-year-old girl. The orchards, open fields, river, and woods here in the country would be much better. Even though it was only about sixty miles north, Forestville was worlds away. Her husband had just graduated from a fancy culinary academy in San Francisco and hoped he'd be able to get a good job in Sonoma County as a chef.

Marriage could certainly be a challenge. Cathy knew that only too well. Marriage was the last thing on Cathy's mind. Thirty years old, and she'd already been divorced for several years. That took planning, like marrying just out of high school. Or picking the absolutely wrong guy, for all the wrong reasons, who'd then abandoned her alone, broke and pregnant. Her parents' marriage hadn't been much better.

She was happy for Pam, who'd always wanted a family of her own. Perhaps she could help Pam out, make their way a little easier.

Cathy remembered the hard road after her divorce. She'd moved to Sonoma County to start over, worked hard, buried the pain, and took charge of her own life. And now she ran a successful health food store and café. There were men in and out of her life, but she always kept it light. That handsome stranger who appeared last month to help rescue Charlie, he might make her change her mind. Those eyes ... she could look into them forever. But for now, she'd have fun dating and avoid commitment. It was safer that way.

Cathy entered her kitchen and admired the newly tiled cobalt-blue counters. They looked striking against the dark oak cabinets. She took out the bag of dark chocolate nuggets she'd bought at Organic Grocers and headed toward the front deck to enjoy the day. On a whim, she pulled her old high school yearbook off the shelf and brought it outside.

"I wonder if Pam is still as perky and blonde as she was in high school?" she said aloud to her lanky black cat, who'd followed her to the deck. Libby rubbed against her leg, purring loudly. It was hard to imagine this contented cat was once a starving feral kitten. She'd found Libby with her little sister pathetically mewing in the yard. The cat jumped up and curled into Cathy's lap. Snowy, her all-white partner in crime, was probably out somewhere stalking lizards. There must have been two different dads for that litter, she mused.

Cathy grabbed another handful of candy and savored the rich, creamy flavor. They would be here soon. Had she thought of everything? The lawn was cut. Tall pink daisies reached for the sky in her flowerbeds alongside sweet alyssum. Perhaps she should put some daisies in the little girl's room and remake the bed with rose-colored sheets?

Libby spied something in the yard and jumped off her lap, distracting Cathy from her thoughts. She stared at the high school yearbook sitting on the table next to her. Did she really want to go down that memory lane? Why not? She threw open the book and scanned the glossy pages. They were full of petite little Pam in her cheerleading outfit, all golden curls and big eyes. Cathy had been an awkward five-foot-nine as a high school freshman and one of the tallest girls. It was embarrassing then, and she'd envied Pam's small frame. Later, as years passed, people told Cathy she looked like a model. Her height and long, thick auburn hair were suddenly assets.

She turned the yellowing page. A huge photo jumped out from senior prom night. There Cathy was in her flowing, pink chiffon dress standing next to a beaming Todd, both sporting glittery crowns. "The king and queen are announced for 1965." Her hair trailed down almost to her small waist. Her classic smile was there, but the sadness in her eyes spoke the loudest. No one ever seemed to notice. Some days she wanted to scream right into the middle of the schoolyard, "I hate my father. He's not the perfect man you all think he is!" But people would have just walked away shaking their heads.

Cathy had almost forgiven herself for the bad choices she'd made back then. The pain of her father's death and the way her family fell apart was so encompassing, she'd blindly reached for anything or anyone who'd offered comfort. Even Todd. How had she been so blind? She laid the yearbook down and looked out at the lush ferns sprouting under the redwoods. The sun was moving down the sky toward the west, but the warmth of the day still lingered.

Her eyes closed for a short nap. "Very short," she murmured, drifting off.

There was ringing in the distance. It was the phone. She jumped up, hurried toward the kitchen, and lifted the avocado green receiver.

It was Pam. They were on River Road, at the phone booth by Speers Market, only minutes from Cathy's house.

"Make sure you take the left turn after the red barn and drive through the white picket gate," Cathy instructed.

Pam sounded excited, which got Cathy feeling that way too. It might be nice to have company, a cute little girl to read to, someone else cooking dinner. The cats would be happy for some extra attention when she was working at the shop.

A white Plymouth station wagon pulled in scattering dust. Libby jumped straight into the air, reaching for a colorful butterfly, then startled and ran into the woods when the tires hit the drive. The car was packed to the brim, even though the plan was for them to stay only a short while. Hollers from their little girl pierced the air with excitement. For a moment Cathy questioned her good intentions, inviting a family of three to invade her home. Then Pam, in lime-green shorts and a halter top, jumped out of the car, ran over, and threw her arms around her.

"Cathy, you look great!"

Gone were Pam's golden curls. Her hair was now pulled loosely back in a ponytail. Her petite frame had taken on a few pounds, presumably from motherhood and marital contentment. "You look happy," Cathy said. "I can't wait to catch up."

Pam shifted from one foot to the other. "Mind if I use your bathroom? Been a long ride."

"Sure. Go through the living room to the right and you'll see one."

Pam scampered up the stairs. "Be right back."

A man with sandy blond hair curling down toward his shoulders exited the car. Cathy's breath caught. He walked toward her. A squirming little girl in a pretty, yellow sundress held his hand.

"I'm Jamie." He started to offer his hand and froze in place.

Their eyes locked. Cathy had the distinct impression that time stopped. He was the white knight in the station wagon. The man who'd helped rescue the dog.

"It's you," she whispered.

"We meet again," he finally said. His warm smile revealed the dimple in his chin. He ruffled the little girl's hair. "I can't thank you enough for giving my family a place to stay."

Cathy reached out to shake his extended hand. "I'm Cathy. Stay as long as you need," she said, her hand still tingling from his touch.

Amber, a real cutie with yellow curls tied in pigtails, leaned into her daddy and gave Cathy a tentative smile.

Cathy bent down to meet her gaze. "You must be Amber. I hope you'll enjoy staying in my house for a while."

Amber rubbed her eyes.

"She's tired," Pam said, walking down the stairs. "We'll just go take a little rest." She took the little girl's hand and headed back inside.

Pam was probably exhausted from the trip. But now Jamie was left to unload what looked like a whole household of things by himself. He opened the liftback door and started pulling out small boxes and suitcases.

"Here, let me help," Cathy offered. Not that he needed it. Jamie's brown T-shirt stretched against his lean chest and revealed smooth, muscled arms. She picked up a few bags. "We can put these in your bedroom. Amber has the room next to yours."

"Thanks again. I hope we didn't bring too much stuff."

His eyes radiated sincerity, but she could see the worry lines etched around them. "No problem, I have storage space in the garage if you need it."

Relief crossed his face. "Good thing we didn't bring the Great Dane."

Cathy froze, then burst out laughing.

Jamie patted her shoulder. "Just kidding, just kidding," he said. "How is our mutual pal, Charlie, doing?

Sparks shot down her arm. His musky, familiar smell was startling. "Paula just let me know Charlie is doing great and his cast is already off. Turns out Paula owns a small vineyard near the river."

"Good to hear. Seriously," he said, stepping back. "If you need space or quiet, just let me know."

Unarmed, she stood in place while Jamie hoisted a pack over one shoulder and filled both hands with bags and suitcases. "Lead the way," he said.

Readjusting her load, Cathy forged ahead into the house. In the living room, Pam and Amber were curled up on her dark green sectional, resting. For a moment Cathy wondered what it felt like to have a husband who helped with all the work and a cute little girl to cuddle up with. She showed Jamie down the hall to their rooms and placed the suitcases by their brass bed.

"I hope you'll be comfortable here," she said.

His kind eyes reflected gratitude. Cathy fought the urge to hug him. Who was this man?

Jamie followed her back into the living room where Pam and Amber were spread across the couch. "Before I show you around the house would everyone like a little snack?" Cathy asked.

"I would, I would!" Amber said.

Cathy held out her hand. "Come with me into the kitchen, and if it's okay with your mom and dad I'll give you a treat."

ANDREA HURST

Amber looked at her curiously, and then at her daddy.

"I think that's a great idea," Jamie said as he hoisted Amber onto his shoulders. "We had a late lunch, so probably won't want any dinner."

Cathy led the way as Jamie galloped behind making horse-like sounds. Pam stood and stretched then followed.

"You've fixed the place up real nice," Pam said. "I love the oriental rugs." She pointed to the large picture window in the living room as they passed. "Did you make the stained-glass mandala?"

Cathy shook her head no. "Most of my time is spent working at my business or in the garden. There's a great pottery shop in town my friend Linda owns. You should check it out. It has some beautiful macramé pieces as well."

She opened the freezer to pull out some Barbara's Bakery ice cream bars.

"One of my favorites," Jamie said when he saw the box.

"You have good taste," Cathy said as she handed one out to everyone.

Amber, looking wide awake now, sat on a barstool licking what was left of her dripping ice cream. The little girl was cute. She looked like her mom. Between licks, Amber eyed the cats, and Cathy told her the rules. "No tail pulling, pet gently, and use a soft voice."

"I'll be gentle," Amber said.

"The cats' names are Libby and Snowy. They're really loving, but they had a rough start in life. Before you know it, they'll fall in love with you."

Amber giggled.

Maybe this was just what Cathy needed. A sweet face and warm laugh.

The whole family moved into the living room and plopped down on the couch.

Cathy snuggled into the rocker and turned on the Tiffany lamp. "I would have put you all up in the guest rooms above my health food shop, but summer is our busiest season."

"We love it here," Pam said, suppressing a yawn. "It's so fun to see you again and have you meet my family."

Cathy nodded. "It is. Why don't you all rest. I'm going to run outside for a few minutes and finish a few things in my garden before dark."

"Go ahead," Pam said. "We'll just shut our eyes and wait for you to get back."

Chapter Three

*J*amie watched Pam and Amber curl up on the couch. He was too restless from the long drive to join them. Instead, he headed into the large country kitchen. It was a good-sized space with plenty of room to prepare a meal. A collection of stainless steel pans hung over the gas stove. Over the sink, a picture window revealed a vast garden behind the house. There were raised beds of kale, tomatoes, and just-blooming snap peas. Squash flowers golden with promise stretched across the soil amidst red and orange nasturtiums. The gravel pathway wound around a flower garden filled with dahlias, lavender, and black-eyed susans. Hair glistening, bronzed by the afternoon sun, Cathy stood watering the chard stalks that reached toward the sky.

Jamie watched her lay the hose aside, bend down, and start weeding a large bed of culinary herbs. Perhaps he could help. He walked out the back door and followed the path toward the prolific rose bushes. He couldn't resist leaning over to catch their fragrance.

"Stopping to smell the roses?" Cathy said, startling him.

Her smile was as effortless as the breeze that played lightly in her long hair.

"They're amazing," he said. "This one smells spicy."

Cathy held the stem of the two-tone red and yellow rose. "It's called Double Delight."

Jamie smiled. "I can see why. And this one?" he said, pointing to a sweet-smelling yellow one.

"It's Koressia."

She knew her roses.

"Your whole garden looks like a celebration," he said.

Cathy's laugh rang out like soft bells. "Would you like a tour?"

Jamie followed her as she pointed out various areas, including her herb garden filled with rosemary, dill, tarragon, and many others. Cathy knelt in the dirt by a bed of leafy greens and looked up at him. Her jade colored eyes blended with the greens of the garden. For a moment, the image registered an overpowering feeling of déjà vu.

"I've got some stubborn weeds to deal with before nightfall," she said. "We depend on this garden for produce for the café."

He stooped down beside her. "Need some help?"

"After that long drive, you still feel like weeding?" she asked.

Jamie ran his fingers through the red soil. It was probably rich with nutrients. "Working in the garden relaxes me."

Cathy shrugged. "Then dig in."

He loved getting his hands dirty. They worked side-by-side clearing weeds and snipping off dead leaves. The sense of familiarity and timelessness struck him again. It felt like he'd worked like this in perfect sync with her many times before.

Cathy broke off a stem of dill and rubbed it between her tanned fingers before holding it out to Jamie to catch the tangy scent. He inhaled and thought of flaky trout drenched in butter and fresh dill, sizzling in a frying pan.

"The food at your café must be the freshest around with this assortment to choose from. We'll have to come over for lunch one day," Jamie said.

Her smile lit her face. "We try," she said. "Definitely come by for lunch."

Jamie picked up a bucket of weeds and the garden tools and followed Cathy to the shed. As she turned on the light, a rustling noise in the ceiling caught his attention. He looked up to identify its source but could see nothing.

Cathy's giggle left him perplexed.

"It's my summer tenants cleaning out the nest," she said.

Jamie strained his neck to get a better view. Peeking out of a well-built nest, cuddled up in a corner beam, a baby bird stared down at him.

"Hello, little guy," he said. "Welcome to the world."

Cathy inched closer, staring up at the little heads. "These barn swallows had me worried this year," she said, looking at Jamie with obvious concern. "They were almost two weeks late!"

"Do they have an arrival date?" he asked.

"In a way they do," Cathy said, looking a bit like a proud mom. "They've been coming to this same shed in the same corner and adding new bedding for many years. This was our summer house when I was little. My mom sold it to me about ten years ago." She pointed to the nest. I've watched many a generation flap their wings and fly away."

Cathy looked wistful at the thought of seeing her little ones leave home.

"Sleep well, little guys," she said. She turned off the over-head light and beckoned Jamie outside.

Grinning, he stepped softly behind her so as not to disturb the babies. He followed her back toward the house, walked inside, and the spell was broken.

Cathy walked into the kitchen, washed her hands after gardening, then offered Jamie the sink. Pam wandered over, holding Amber by the hand. "Did you two have fun in the garden? I'm not one for working out in the dirt," she said, "but as you can see, Jamie likes gardening. He's real handy too. I'm sure he'll help you out with some things."

"She has an amazing garden," Jamie said. He leaned down to Amber. "And tomorrow I will show you the baby birds."

"I think it's bedtime for this little girl," Pam said.

"But I'm not sleepy," Amber said, yawning along with her mom.

Jamie took Amber into his arms. "Come on. I'll tuck you in and sing you a lullaby." He kissed her cheek. "Time to say goodnight."

Amber rubbed her eyes. "Nighty night," she said. I want mommy to come too."

Cathy led the way to Amber's room. "Here's your very own bedroom," she said with a smile.

"What a nice room," Pam said. "And look, Amber, you have a canopy bed, and Daddy and I are right next door."

The little girl frowned and started to sniffle. "I want to sleep with you and Daddy."

Pam sighed.

Jamie laid Amber on the bed and sat beside her. "I think I might just turn in too. You two girls go on out and catch up a bit."

Back in the living room, Pam leaned back into the well-padded couch. "I don't know what I'd do without Jamie. He's such a good dad."

Cathy gazed toward the bedrooms. "He seems to be."

"Yeah," Pam said. "It's so different having a real family, a man who sticks around." Pam put her hand over her mouth. "I didn't mean to imply anything about Todd."

"It's okay," Cathy said. "We've been divorced almost ten years. I'm well over him."

"Are you dating anyone?" Pam asked. "If not, we could go out some night like we used to and scout."

Cathy was sure Pam couldn't imagine she could be happy at this age alone and childless. But most days she was relatively content and had no intention of settling down with anyone in the near future. In Cathy's memory, Pam had never been without a man at her side.

"Yes, but not really dating. His name is David, a local builder," Cathy said. "It's just casual."

Pam's face brightened like Cathy had just announced she was getting married.

She winked. "Is he cute? Why don't you invite him for dinner? Jamie can cook up one of his specialties. It would be like the old days double dating."

"Okay," Cathy muttered, not convinced anything would ever be like the old days again in regard to men. "I'll ask David and see what he says."

"Caroline's so happy with her husband, and I have Jamie. If you found someone, the old threesome would all be married. That would be to the max."

Dream on, Cathy thought. For one, she was no longer a part of that teenage threesome, nor did she want to be. She hadn't seen and hardly heard from Pam in years, and now they were best friends somehow? Pam needed to get real.

"Finding someone isn't my top priority right now."

Pam raised an eyebrow. "Really?"

"For sure."

Cathy stretched her arms in the air. "I think I'll turn in."

Pam followed her down the hall and waved goodnight as they went their separate ways.

Amber was in the oak-paneled bedroom with the frilly bedding. Pam and Jamie were in the adjacent wine-colored bedroom, Cathy's mother's idea for a vineyard-style guest room experience. Cathy lay in bed trying to sleep. Her thoughts drifted to Jamie. There was something about the way he looked at her. The sense of not being able to breathe when he moved too close. She was obviously attracted to him. She couldn't help that. But he was married to Pam and that ended that. The couple were together down the hall, under the quilts, kissing goodnight. Jamie's sandy brown hair falling into his eyes, his soft hands stroking Pam's body ... How in the world was she going to keep her mind off him for these next few days?

Jamie lay in bed next to his wife, thinking about their temporary home. It looked right out of movie set, a rambling old farmhouse, white with blue trim. A weathered rocker on the flower-lined porch faced the grassy and wooded front yard. It was peaceful enough and had plenty of room for Amber to play. Cathy's whole acre of organic garden was something out of a dream for him. He couldn't wait to get his hands in the soil again. And, cook with those amazing veggies and herbs.

Cathy.

When he'd first seen her standing in her drive earlier today, it seemed like a hallucination. The sun reflected brilliantly off Cathy's auburn hair and she'd looked like an angel. For a split second, everything else had faded from view and she alone radiated in full color. It was the woman with the dog. She'd visited his dreams after their chance encounter weeks before, and for a moment he'd not been sure he was awake. But she'd reached her hand out to him and spoken.

"I'm Cathy."

"Earth to Jamie," he'd told himself.

Jamie was back to earth now, listening to the creaking sounds of the old house as it settled into the night. Sleep seemed elusive as his mind raced over the job interviews coming up and the importance of securing his family's future. Soon. Their stay here was temporary. He would keep his mind on the goal and his feet on the ground, where they usually were.

Chapter Four

The aroma coming from her kitchen roused Cathy from sleep. She was used to getting up, grabbing an apple and green tea, and heading to the shop or the garden to pick herbs and vegetables for the café lunch specials. She was not used to the smell of cooking eggs and whole-wheat toast wafting its way into her bedroom. She nudged the cats so she could release the covers, then reached for her robe. It was a bit flimsy, but that had never been an issue before. Could she wear it out there? On second thought, she pulled on her sweats, reluctantly added a bra underneath, and made a dash for the bathroom, hopefully unseen, to brush her hair and teeth.

She heard Amber's high voice. "Juice, Daddy. Juice!"

She'd had better go out there and show them where everything was.

When she entered the kitchen, it was like stepping into a fairytale. On clean white plates were fresh berries, washed and cut, and perfectly poached eggs dusted with dill were accompanied by buttered toast. The Mr. Coffee was brewing away, and everyone was at the table waiting for her.

"Good morning! We were hoping the smells would draw you from the bed, sleepyhead," Pam said.

Cathy took a seat. "How could they not?"

Jamie was on the spot with the coffeepot filling her mug. She could get used to this.

"I hope everyone slept well," Cathy said between bites. "Jamie, these eggs are cooked to perfection. Runny center and all."

His grin lit up the room.

Cathy wiped her mouth with a napkin as this warm liquid yolk slid down her chin. "I can never get them like this."

"Happy to share my secrets with you," he said, joining them at the table. "But they cost."

Cathy smiled. Whatever the price, she was willing to pay it. She sipped her coffee and contemplated the day ahead. She would go into work and arrange for Brian to come in extra days this week so she could take off and spend time with her company.

"I love my canopy bed," Amber said between bites.

Pam took Jamie's hand. "We really needed a good night's sleep. Even with Dakota, our caretaker, helping out some, it's hard work taking care of my mom. But as soon as Jamie gets a job, Dakota will move in with my mother and work full-time."

Cathy looked around her table. This nice little family breakfast felt right somehow. Her eyes wandered over to Jamie. He dipped a corner of toast into the gooey egg on his plate and let it soak in before popping it slowly into his mouth. A little cowlick stuck up on his crown. His T-shirt clung to his muscled shoulders. He looked part little boy and part very alluring man. Those pouty lips. She tried not to look and nodded as Pam rambled on about their plans.

"Jamie has three interviews coming up, one in Sonoma, another in Glen Ellen, and one in Napa. Once they taste his food, they'll surely hire him," she said.

Cathy agreed. By next week, they should be looking for their own place.

Amber accidentally knocked over her juice. Jamie jumped up, grabbed a towel, and wiped it clean. "It's okay, little one," he said giving Amber a little kiss on her cheek.

He turned to Cathy. "So sorry."

"No problem." Cathy waved it away. His kindness took her breath away.

Cathy started clearing the table. Pam shooed her away. "We'll take care of it; you just go on with your day like we're not here."

Perfect guests. Cathy retook her seat and sipped her luke-warm coffee.

"Thanks, Pam. I really need to get into my shop today. We have lunch prep to do in the café and the two guest rooms upstairs are booked for the weekend. Perhaps we can hang out later."

"Sure thing," Pam said. "Sounds like the place is doing well for you. What's the name again?"

"Health & Hearth. Sonoma County is the perfect place for anything health-related, and tourists flock in, so yes, especially during the season. Winter can be slow, but the locals support us well."

Cathy stared at Jamie as he washed the dishes in her kitchen. She looked back to Pam. Pam was smiling like the Cheshire cat; she knew she had a good thing going with Jamie.

"He's so helpful," Pam said. She gathered the dirty dishes and joined Jamie in the kitchen. Cathy heard her talking to him about the dating idea. Whatever. David was basically an okay guy. She headed for the shower to get ready for work.

All morning at the store, it seemed like everything Cathy touched either fell from her hand or got put in the wrong place. Brian was late again, and Tim kept singing the same darn lyrics to Evergreen over and over again. Cathy loved Barbara Streisand too, but enough with the timeless love and ever, ever, green.

"Are we a little distracted this morning?" Jill asked.

Cathy startled. Could that woman ever not notice exactly what was going on with her? Sometimes Cathy just wanted to hide her discomforts. But Jill always meant well and was there to help. "Is it that noticeable?" Cathy asked.

"To me. How's it going at home with the company?"

"Oh, fine."

"And?" Jill probed.

"And what?" Cathy stopped herself. There was no need to snap at Jill. "I'm sorry. It's a little stressful."

Jill motioned to an empty booth in the back of the café area of the store. "Let's take a break. We can both use one."

Glasses of herbal iced tea in hand, they took a seat. Tim swooped over eyeing their drinks.

"Girl talk or can I join you?"

Cathy looked around the store. It was basically empty and for the afternoon lull. "C'mon in," she said.

Tim sat across from her. "So give, girl. What's going on?"

"Give me a break," Cathy said with a smile. "I can't get away with anything with you two around. It's my company."

"What about that," Jill said. "I thought you were taking time off."

Tim laughed. "Busted. Too much for you?"

"That's not it," Cathy said.

Jill cocked her neck getting a closer look at Cathy. "Then what is? You're not yourself."

Just who was she then, Cathy wondered. This person who was not herself and allowing herself to be completely thrown off by a man. A married man. Never, ever had she ventured in that direction nor did she plan to now. Not that you could plan to feel this sort of way for a person. What was she to say to her friends? There's this man staying at my house and I think he's my soul mate or something, but there is one tiny problem … he is married to an old friend. Neither of her colleagues would know what to say to that, nor did she expect them to.

Cathy sipped her peppermint laced tea. "What would I do without you two?"

"Deflecting, I see." Tim squinted his eyes looking at her as if she was a painting. "Slight flush, a bit spacey, dreamy eyed. Whose the new guy?"

She felt heat rush up to her face probably flushing her face and hinting at her secret. "You'll never know," she said coyly.

"Well," Tim replied, "I thought we knew each other's secrets. I told you about hot bartender Jim last week."

More details than Cathy had really wanted to hear. But Tim's loving heart and hysterical sense of humor always kept her amused and left her feeling cared for.

Jill stood taking her glass with her. "I can see there will be no reveal today on your mystery man," she said. "I guess I'll go back to work."

It was like Jill to recognize boundaries and respect them. But Cathy knew her friend would be watching her. And for all of their sakes, Cathy hoped there was nothing more to tell.

After counting the cash for today, Cathy left the shop and enjoyed her ride down the tree-laden River Road. She passed the spot where Charlie had been hit by the car that day, and she'd first met Jamie. The memory tugged at her and blended with the moments in the garden with him when he first arrived. Clicked, was the word that came to her mind. Everything clicked into place when they were together. For what purpose, she wondered.

She turned the car through the picket gate on to her drive. Amber was playing in the yard, sunlight bouncing off her blonde curls. Jamie tossed her a ball, and she chased it into the trees. Cathy could see the pure joy in the moment they shared. Longing crept up and forced her to heed its voice. She wanted to run in the grassy yard with them. Without thinking, she joined in their game.

Jamie threw her the ball. Amber squealed as she chased Cathy across the lawn.

"Toss it to me," Amber said.

Cathy threw the ball. "Let's hide behind a redwood so your dad won't find us."

Amber squeezed Cathy's hand and put her finger to her mouth. "Quiet," she whispered.

"Where are you two?" Jamie said in a bear-like voice. "I'm going to find you."

He pounced on them behind the tree, and they both screamed. Amber jumped up in delight and ran off with the ball. Jamie winked at Cathy, and then ran after his little girl.

Cathy's knees were weak. What was happening? Time slowed when she was around Jamie. It was as if just the two of them were suspended in the moment. She shook her head to break the spell, then waved at them and started back to the house.

"Leaving so soon?" he said, now at her side.

She stared at the ground. In his black and white high-top sneakers he stood next to her. She willed her body not to react to his closeness. Her attention focused on a furry black and orange caterpillar making its way across the grass to the bushes. If she left it there, it would surely be trampled. She gently picked the little guy up in her hand and placed it safely in the lavender plants. Cathy pinched a blossom and squeezed it between her fingers, inhaling its fragrant scent.

Looking up, his eyes met hers. He looked right through her, through her walls and disguises. "My favorite herb," she stammered, holding up the stalk of lavender.

"Mine too," Jamie said. He reached across and snipped off a fresh blossom, crushing it between his long fingers before holding it up to savor.

"Can I smell too?" Amber held her nose up to the sky. Jamie placed the sprig under it. She tilted her head sideways. "I think I like it," she said, before scampering off.

Jamie turned to follow Amber as they rushed to see who would get the ball first. For a moment, Cathy was very young, running free with her daddy, not a care in the world. A rare day in her childhood.

She closed her eyes letting the feelings move through her body. Go, her mind told her. She turned and hurried up the deck stairs into the house. It smelled of herbs and garlic. Pam was grilling some chicken on the old country stove.

"Welcome back," she said. "Everything all right at the shop?"

"Fine. I just needed to check in." Cathy walked over to take a look. Large chunks of chicken surrounded by onions and colorful vegetables were sizzling with fresh herbs in the pan. A ceramic bowl of salad greens waited on the counter for the chicken to be added.

Pam pulled silverware from the drawer. "Jamie put the salad together from your garden. Hope you don't mind. He made fresh dressing too."

"Of course not. I have plenty of extra produce every year. Help yourself." Cathy noticed her oak table was set with woven placemats and stoneware. It was like elves were in her house. She was the princess who came home to find every-thing done and waiting for her.

"He's good about that stuff." Pam tossed the chicken into the salad, dressed it, and brought it to the table. "Maybe you and I can take a walk after lunch, catch up some?"

"Sounds fun," Cathy said. For a moment, a twinge of guilt shot up her spine. She longed to be back in the yard playing with them again. Cathy took a seat at the table. She didn't want to think about what she wanted. The attraction would pass.

Pam went to the front door and yelled outside to Jamie and Amber to come in for lunch. Seconds later, they came flying through the door. The cats snoozing on the back of the sofa hunched up, hair high.

"Go wash your hands, Amber," Pam said. "And you too, Jamie."

Cathy looked down at her hands still scented with lavender. She would not wash hers.

"Lunch is exquisite," Cathy said, swallowing another savory mouthful. "I wish Jamie would cook for my shop, but of course he's out of our league for a local lunch spot."

Pam went on and on about how famous a chef Jamie would be someday. Cathy noticed the look on Jamie's face did not show the same enthusiasm.

"Pam, don't forget I have that interview at Wine and Sea tomorrow." Jamie's smooth voice brought her focus back to the table.

Cathy stuffed a large chunk of avocado from the salad into her mouth and listened to them talk about the swank restaurant in Sonoma.

"What do you think he should wear?" Pam asked.

Cathy really didn't know what to say, but both of them were looking at her like she was the expert of all Sonoma County fashion.

"Nice slacks, button-down shirt maybe?" Cathy looked at Jamie. With his tight, trim body, he would look good in anything. His eyes caught hers and both of them quickly looked away.

Cathy stood up to clear the table, but Jamie jumped up and told her to go on with her day. Cathy couldn't think of the last time any man acted like that with her. Certainly not her ex-husband, Todd. There was nothing she could do right in that marriage. Her dreams had evaporated like the illusion they were. Happy endings were not part of that story. Nor were happy beginnings. She loved it here with her café and her friends. Loneliness seeped through once in a while, but her work pushed those thoughts away.

Pam stood and announced, "Cathy and I are going for a walk. See you two later."

Outside, they threw colorful beach towels over their shoulders. Cathy rolled up her jeans. They walked down the dirt road bordering the apple orchards behind her house and down to River Road.

"Now," Cathy said when there was a slowing of cars on the highway. They jogged across the road and took the path heading down to the water. The sun was warm when they left the shaded path, and she wished they had brought their swimsuits.

Pam ran onto the sand to the river's edge, slipped off her flip-flops, hiked up her gauzy skirt, and ran in.

"Cold," she laughed and waded in deeper. Her hair curled at her shoulders. She looked like her old self now, playful and ready for anything.

Cathy kicked off her sandals, dropped the towels on the sand, and joined her. Pam splashed her and tried to run. Her tank top was wet now, but the coolness felt wonderful. She gathered handfuls of water and dumped them over her and Pam's shoulders until they were both soaked and laughing heavily.

"Let's go dry off," Cathy said, heading to shore.

Having Pam right here in front of her flooded Cathy's mind with memories. Pam's innocent brown eyes always looked like they needed something. Boys who wanted to rescue Pam, the fair damsel, were never in short supply. Even Cathy's dad said they needed to treat the lost little girl extra special after all she'd been through. Cathy used to alternate between wanting to take care of Pam and wishing her own dad would take care of her in that way.

The last time Cathy had seen Pam's eyes was not long after they'd both finished high school. They'd been filled with sympathy. Sympathy for Cathy because her husband had left her after a few short months of marriage. Pam knew all about abandonment. After her father's death, losing her family home, and her husband and their friends, Cathy knew all about abandonment too.

The old VW Pam drove was packed to leave for community college in Santa Barbara. She'd driven to the tiny apartment Cathy had moved into with Todd when they were first married, to say goodbye. Pam always was a dreamer, had expected Prince Charming to arrive any day and take her to a castle. When no white horse appeared, Pam decided college was the perfect place to meet someone.

"Oh, Cathy," Pam had said. "How awful for you things didn't work out with Todd. But I know you'll meet someone else someday. We both will. Rich ones!"

By then, Cathy didn't believe in happily ever after anymore. Not for herself at least. Love could not be trusted. Bitterness crept in to protect her vulnerable heart. Whatever it took, she did not want to be hurt like that again.

Cathy had cried on Pam's shoulder, and then together they'd finished packing her belongings to move to the Russian River. Caroline, the other musketeer in their high school threesome, was traveling in Europe with her fancy new husband at the time. No one else came to say goodbye. Not one of her many so-called friends, who now spent their time hanging out with Todd and his gang.

"Looks like you've come a long way since we waved goodbye at your old apartment," Pam said. "I hope you're not too lonely way out here by yourself."

Cathy shrugged. "I'm fine, busy, happy." Loneliness was the price she paid. There were worse things.

Pam lay back on the towel and closed her eyes. "I'm living happily ever after, just like I always dreamed of."

Pam meant well, but sometimes Cathy wondered if Pam would ever grow up. Pam wasn't the smartest girl in class, but she went after what she wanted. And really, what had Cathy's 3.9 GPA done for her? When Pam was in college, she majored in art and boys, waitressing on the side. Until she met Jamie and quit school. After that, Cathy hadn't heard much. Just how ecstatically happy she was married to Jamie. Then a baby announcement four years ago, and a note about being one little happy family. There were a few Christmas cards exchanged with scribbled notes, but that was all. Pam had what she wanted and no longer needed anything from Cathy.

"It is so good to see you," Pam said, towel-drying her hair. She threw her arms around Cathy in a tight hug. Droplets of water flew off her blonde curls and onto her wet T-shirt. She tossed her towel down, fell back on to it, and closed her eyes. "I could lie here forever."

Cathy sat beside her. After long days of work, it felt good to stop.

Pam raised her head. "Remember when the three of us smoked pot and tried to take a rowboat down the Russian River that summer before senior year?"

Cathy grinned. "We rowed in circles until we laughed so hard we fell out of the boat. I still wonder where Caroline got that strong stuff. In the 60s, all the pot was good."

"Caroline always did have the best of everything." Pam's words were tinged with envy.

"If you want," Cathy said, "I still own a rowboat."

"I don't smoke any more now, with Amber and all. But remember that time we went into San Francisco to the old Fillmore to see Jefferson Airplane? There was a lot more than pot floating around back then."

Cathy remembered all right. Grace Slick had been all in black. All the people dancing and crushing in on each other, the colors and loud music had almost been too much for her. But not for Pam; she'd been making out with some cute guy in a corner most of the night. "You know I still have the old shirt I wore with the bell sleeves back then," she said.

"Really? And it still fits?" Pam patted her stomach. "I remember when I wore bikinis." Her eyes were on Cathy. "Unfair, Cathy. Your body still looks like it did in high school. You and Caroline don't look any different."

"Neither of us has had a child," Cathy reminded her.

Pam shrugged.

"And a lot of good it does me now," Cathy continued. "The good men seem to evaporate with each year I get closer to thirty."

"The guys always loved you, Cathy."

She watched Pam's eyes glaze over.

"Oh, they loved me at first, they just didn't stay. It was the chase they loved, not me."

Pam's face looked stricken. "I'm so sorry to bring it up again, I just … ."

"It's okay," Cathy said. "You, more than anyone, know just how much Todd wanted me. We couldn't turn a corner at school without his big, pearly smile leaning in close, trying to mesmerize me with his charm."

Pam laughed. "I loved watching you rebuff him. His charm slid off you. You certainly had willpower. He was one cute boy!"

"I really didn't like him. From the moment I saw him I knew he was trouble." And she'd been more than right. If her judgment hadn't been so clouded by blinding grief, she would never had succumbed to Todd's charms. He only wanted what he couldn't have.

Cathy turned to Pam. "Thank you again for being there for me then. No one else was."

Pam gave her a puppy dog look and patted her shoulder.

"It's nice to see you happy," Cathy said.

She watched Pam's manicured toes curl in the sand. "I am, I really am, but …"

"What? You can tell me."

"Well, Jamie really wanted to move up here in the country, but you know I'm pretty much a city girl. But he promised if he gets a really good job, we can get a big house with a yard for Amber. She can have a swing set and a dog … all the things I never had."

Cathy nodded. "There are lots of new families here. It's a great place to raise kids." She imagined kids running in her own yard, picking flowers in her garden, swimming in the river with her.

Pam stared out at the water. "I know, but I'm not into planting, getting dirty, staying at home all day. Where's the nearest movie theater?"

"There's plenty to do in Santa Rosa," Cathy laughed. "We'll have a girl's day out soon and I'll show you all the great shops and bakeries."

"Sounds good. We're short on cash, but every girl needs something new now and then."

Pam's face went from smiles to a frown. She lowered her head and looked like an abandoned little child.

"Then there's my mom, not feeling well or remembering things too good. She still demands my help, like always."

Cathy took Pam's hand. "I'm really sorry. I know she's always been hard for you to deal with."

"Thanks. I've been so used to not listening to her complaints and lectures. It's hard to believe that she really does need me now."

"Does your mom enjoy having Amber around?"

"Sometimes. She never really liked kids. As least it felt that way. It's a long drive back and forth from here to Oakland. I'll be glad when Jamie gets a job."

"It's not too bad if you go when there's no traffic." Cathy shook out her wet hair in the sun.

"My mom's been nicer to me since I married Jamie. Remember how she used to tell me I better marry a rich man who could treat me like a princess?"

Cathy grinned. "You sure had your choice in high school. But none kept your interest long."

"Things change. Anyway, that's a long time ago." Pam shook off the subject and went back to being her animated self. "Tell me about David," she said with a forced smile.

"He's okay. Nice-looking, but a bit weird. He always wants to eat something just before we're going to have sex."

Pam thought this was hysterical. Cathy thought it was some phobic neurosis.

"When are we going to meet him? Why don't you invite him to dinner tomorrow?"

She felt trapped. Now she had to ask him. "Sure, I'll see if he has time," she said. "I'll call when we get back to the house and leave a message."

She was not so sure she wanted to see David. The attraction was wearing thin. As she got to know him better, it seemed that was all that was really left. He seemed to only want one thing from her and was content with the way things were. Something about being around Pam and Jamie made her want more.

The sun was drying her clothes and felt wonderful on her skin. A family draped over inner tubes floated by, laughing and waving as they coasted down the green water along the woodsy shore. Cathy brushed the drying sand from her feet. It was fun reminiscing about the old days with Pam. "When was the last time you talked to Caroline?"

"Just last week, actually," Pam said. "She called me. We talk—well, mostly I listen—about their new homes and trips to Europe and her fabulous friends."

They both giggled. Caroline, with a long "i," was always fabulous in high school. Best parties, best convertible sports car, and best boyfriends. Her wedding, a week after high school graduation, was over-the-top, and Cathy and Pam both had worn satin bridesmaids dresses that Cathy couldn't wait to take off.

"We don't talk often. Not much in common anymore," Cathy said.

"Tell me about it," Pam said. "We're lucky to make our rent some months, and she has a six-thousand-square-foot mansion in posh Santa Barbara with her fabulous husband." She hesitated and seemed to slip off into a faraway place again. "But Jamie is talented and will have a big career." She looked at Cathy. "I just know it."

Pam's eyes showed fear, no matter how positive she tried to sound. She reminded Cathy of Cinderella dreaming about the ball. For her sake, Cathy hoped the pumpkin turned into a carriage and the slipper fit.

Chapter Five

The morning was frantic. Jamie tried to get out the door to his interview amidst a child wanting attention and a wife trying a little too hard to be positive and wishing him well.

Cathy almost felt like an intruder in her own house and stayed out of the way until Jamie left. There was an edge to Pam today. It reminded Cathy of Pam's cheerleading tryouts back in high school. On the outside, Pam had smiled and waved. But as her friend, Cathy knew the fear and insecurity that ate at Pam and made her try that much harder. She'd tried to be there to root Pam on.

Jamie flew out the door at 9 a.m., and the three girls were left alone.

"Can we bake cookies today?" Amber asked her mom.

"Let's ask Auntie Cathy if it's okay."

When did she become an auntie, Cathy wondered. She liked it, but it also reminded her of a spinster aunt, the old kind no one wanted to marry. They were looking at her, waiting.

"Of course," she said. She could only imagine the mess.

"Can they be chocolate with sprinkles? Can they?" Amber pleaded.

"I'll look in my cupboard and see what I have." Cathy opened the door and found dark chocolate powder, dried cherries, almonds, and raisins. She pondered the combinations. "How about chocolate cookies with cherries on top?"

Amber clapped her hands. "Can my Madame Lexander doll bake with us?"

Cathy raised her eyebrows at Pam for clarification.

"It's a fancy Madame Alexander doll my mother ordered for her," Pam said. "We usually keep it in a safe place."

"Maybe we could put an apron on her, and she could watch us bake?"

Pam agreed. Amber ran into her room and back with her baby doll, and the baking began. After putting the doll in a safe place, Cathy slid the step stool under the counter so Amber could reach and help.

In no time, all of them were covered in flour and the counters littered with bowls and spoons. When the oven buzzer sounded, Cathy slid the first batch of heavenly smelling cookies on a plate to cool.

Cathy raised a window to tempt in the mild breeze and keep the kitchen cool. The smells brought her back to her mother's bright yellow kitchen, growing up.

As if reading her mind, Pam blurted out, "This reminds me of when we were girls baking with your mom and she'd have Frank Sinatra crooning on the record player all day long!"

"And remember the tea party and all the cucumber sandwiches we made for my seventh birthday?" What Cathy didn't say, and Pam didn't know, was how Cathy's father had come home drunk after work that day. Her birthday had been ruined.

"Those were good little treats," Pam said, running her finger along the batter bowl and popping it in her mouth. "And good times."

"Can we do a tea party?" Amber asked.

"Well, why not, little one?" Pam pinched her cheek. "Maybe for your birthday next month."

Eyes wide, she looked up at her mom. "Will we have cucumber sandwiches too? I don't think I'd like those."

Cathy intervened. "I've heard strawberry and cream cheese sandwiches are pretty and pink. Would you like those instead?"

"Mmmm. Much better."

They worked right through lunch and were too full from all the sugar to think of eating anything else. Plates of gooey cookies with cherries mashed on top cooled on the counter.

The sound of tires on the gravel drive caught their attention.

"Daddy, it's Daddy!" Amber yelled, running for the door with chocolate-covered hands.

Jamie walked in. He loosened the collar of his shirt and rolled up his sleeves. With a grand gesture, he lifted Amber up for a kiss.

"We have cookies, Daddy, with cherries on top."

Jamie pulled his button-down shirt out from his pants and wandered into the kitchen. Telltale lines of exhaustion registered in his face.

"Delicious!" he said popping a couple in his mouth. "Did you girls bake these?"

"We did," Amber said, reaching for one.

He looked around at Cathy's very messy kitchen. "I can see that."

She and Pam barely suppressed giggles.

Jamie leaned over and wiped the flour off Pam's cheek and then turned toward Cathy. She started wiping her face, hoping he wouldn't clean hers too. His hand and her face …

"Great job, girls."

"How did the interview go?" Pam asked.

With mild soap and water, Cathy washed the dough off her hands and listened.

"Well. They said my résumé was impressive and they would get back to me soon."

"One down, one tomorrow and two to go next week," Pam said, kissing his cheek. "They would be lucky to have you."

Cathy thought about them moving out next week. It surprised her that relief was not her first emotion. She told herself it was fine living here alone before they'd arrived, peaceful. She did whatever she wanted and did not hope for more. The Janis Joplin song "Me and Bobby McGee" echoed in her head. Freedom … you had it when you had nothing left to lose. Now she had something to lose. Friendship. The laughter of a child. The smile of a blue-eyed man.

Jamie went off to his room and Pam took Amber to wash up. Cathy started scrubbing cookie sheets and bowls. In a few hours she'd start thinking about dinner plans. The wall phone beside her rang. She dried her hands quickly and said hello as Pam and Amber ran back inside.

"It's for you," Cathy said. "It sounds important."

Pam took the phone, listened, murmured a few words, and finished by saying, "I'll be there in a few hours, soon as I can."

"What's wrong?" Cathy asked.

"That was Dakota, my mom's caretaker. She had a family emergency and can't watch Mom for a couple of days. She has to leave immediately this evening."

Cathy stepped over and put her arm around Amber. "Is there anything I can do? Do you need to go down to Oakland?"

Pam looked dazed. "Yes, I need to pack and go right away. My mother, her memory is so bad now. She can't be alone, and there is no one else I can call."

Cathy remembered Pam saying that phrase so many times when they were young. When something went wrong, Pam's mother was always gone somewhere and Pam had no one to call. Except Cathy.

Jamie walked in wearing jeans. He took one look at Pam and was by her side. "What's wrong?" His eyes moved to Amber assessing her first.

With a dazed look on her face, told him about her mother, and then looked to him for advice.

Jamie gave her a hug. "She needs you," he said. "Do you want me to go with you?"

Pam shook her head. "No, you have a big interview tomorrow." She hesitated trying to catch up with the situation. "But I have to take the station wagon."

"Don't worry," Cathy said. "Jamie can use my car to get to the interview."

"Really," Pam said. "You'd do that for me? I just have to go down for a night or two and then I can come right back."

"No problem. I can watch Amber," Cathy volunteered. She'd always felt so helpless to really make a difference with Pam when they were kids. After all, Cathy had been a young girl too. There'd been no one to help her when her father came home drunk and she'd hidden in the closet and held her hands tight over her ears. Everyone loved Pam. Everyone admired Cathy. She was the strong one.

Pam hesitated before answering, "It's only for a couple of days. I'll bring her with me so you can work." She took Amber's hand and walked to the bedroom. "Let's go pack a little suitcase for our trip to see Grandma."

Jamie followed them to the bedroom. Within a few minutes, he returned carrying their bag and a few toys, and took them out to the car. He kissed his girls goodbye and joined Cathy on the porch.

She watched him wave and blow sweet kisses back and forth with Amber. The car rumbled down the road, light dust in its wake. Neither she nor Jamie moved, as if they were weighted to the porch.

Chapter Six

*J*amie watched his wife and daughter drive off to Oakland. He hoped Pam would drive carefully and not rush down the freeway to the city. If he didn't have the interviews, he would never let them go alone. But getting a job was a top priority right now.

He stood on the porch motionless until the car was out of sight. Sunlight bathed the rolling green hills in the distance. After all their talk, he and his family were finally here in this beautiful country. It felt right. He shifted his weight and became aware of Cathy's presence. There was a certain awkwardness standing there alone with her, a sudden sense of being off-center. He didn't know whether to go in the house, take a walk, or what to do.

As if reading his mind, she said, "Shall we go pick some things out of the garden and figure out what to cook for dinner tonight?"

"Absolutely," he said.

He followed her across the yard and onto a path that circled the lawn to the gardens. Cathy's auburn hair trailed over her tanned shoulders and down her back. It was obvious she spent a lot of time outside.

"How about we pick some salad greens and maybe steam some of the Swiss chard with the early yellow squash?" she asked.

Jamie kneeled by the salad greens. "Perfect color and ripe for the picking."

"My thoughts exactly."

Cathy handed him a basket to fill.

Carefully, he pulled lettuce greens and then moved over to the patch of herbs. "The basil is amazing. Perhaps we should make a pesto salad dressing?"

"Mmmm, that sounds yummy," Cathy said, holding up a basketful of squash. She pointed to the rear corner of the garden. "There are some bunching onions over there that are very sweet. And fresh garlic too."

In the moment, there was no place Jamie would rather be. Sun on his shoulders, exquisite produce at his fingertips. He hoped someday soon Amber would join him in their very own garden.

Cathy snapped sugar peas off the vine, and he imagined them tasting cool and crisp.

With their baskets full of colorful nasturtium, herbs, and veggies, they made their way back into the kitchen. Cathy pulled out a large ceramic bowl for the salad and handed it to him. "I'll get some butter on a low flame and you can throw in the garlic and parsley to sauté with the chard and squash."

Heavenly smells began to fill the kitchen.

"Sure thing," he said. Jamie washed the veggies then chopped garlic and parsley. In the blender he added basil to blend with olive oil and lemon into a salad dressing.

"I made some brown rice this morning; we can heat that up. There's some creamy goat cheese we could put in the salad with toasted sunflower seeds too," Cathy said.

"Any avocado?" Jamie asked.

She smiled, as if sharing a conspiracy. "I'm never without avocado. It's one of my major weaknesses."

Jamie laughed. "A woman after my own heart."

He held his breath as their eyes met, hoping Cathy wouldn't take that statement the wrong way. At this point, his feelings weren't clear even to himself. Her face had not left his mind since the day he walked out of the vet office. And now, this slow dance of cooking together, so effortless, in perfect step, as if they'd been doing this forever.

She tossed her auburn hair and turned to the refrigerator, producing an enormous Hass avocado.

"Enough?" she asked, grinning. With that, she sent the black delicacy flying through the air to him, which he caught flawlessly, not even leaving a dent.

Jamie opened a chilled bottle of local chardonnay while Cathy set the table and retrieved wine glasses. He placed the colorful bowl of salad garnished with edible flowers in the center and a jar of creamy basil dressing next to it. Cathy followed with a platter of sautéed vegetables in butter and herbs and a bowl of warm, brown rice. Before sitting down, she placed a cassette of Bach's sonatas in the tape player. The melodic music was his favorite.

"Dinner is served," she said, taking a seat at the table.

"A toast," Jamie said holding up his glass. Cathy followed suit. "Compliments to the gardener."

Cathy clinked his glass. "And to the chef."

"Chefs!" he added.

Jamie tasted the squash, and an explosion of herby flavor burst in his mouth. He watched Cathy savoring the salad after she complimented him on the dressing.

"Did you see the flowering sweet peas? The pink ones are so healthy this year, they look ready to take over the fence," Cathy said.

Jamie sipped the pale wine. "I'd be happy to help build a trellis for them if you'd like. I'm pretty good with a hammer."

"I was thinking a trellis would be a good idea," Cathy said.

"Just let me know when and where to get the supplies."

As he ate, he tried to keep his gaze from floating back to Cathy. He could feel her eyes on him. It seemed so natural sitting here together. At the same time a heaviness weighed on his chest. Silence permeated the warm summer air, and he forced himself to think about the job interview tomorrow.

"Thank you again for offering to let me use your car tomorrow," he said.

Cathy took the wine and refilled their glasses. "Where is the interview again?"

"In a town called Jenner. I think that's down by the coast, right?" He watched her turn her wine glass in her hand as she thought.

"You know," she said, "I would be happy to drive you down there and then show you around the county a bit. We could follow the coast down to Bodega Bay and you could sample some of the freshest seafood on the west coast."

"Sounds wonderful," Jamie said. "But I don't want to impose."

"Are you kidding? A day off playing hooky along the river, a trip to the ocean, fresh fish off the boat? Sounds like torture to me!"

They laughed, and the decision was made. They would leave for the interview in the morning and do a short day trip. Jamie wanted to see everything this county had to offer. From what he'd seen so far of the open hills, towering trees, green river, and rich, red soil, it was a place he could call home.

Jamie insisted on cleaning up. As he washed and dried dishes, he saw Cathy curl up in the rocking chair by the stove. The felines jumped into her lap. She looked up at him and smiled. He dropped the soapy bowl in his hand on the counter and caught it just before it bounced to the floor. "Sorry about that."

She placed the cats on the wood floor and walked over. "Good save."

Cathy picked up a dishtowel and finished drying the plates and silverware. She leaned to put a dish away just as he turned and they collided. A current of heat passed between them leaving him breathless. Her eyes wide, Cathy backed away.

She laid down the towel; her eyes everywhere but on him. "I think I'll call it a night," she said.

Jamie wanted to say something. "Thanks for a perfect evening," sounded wrong. "Sleep well," he said.

Outside the kitchen window, a full moon illuminated the black sky and threw silver light across the garden. It would be hard to leave when the time came.

Perhaps harder than Jamie had ever imagined.

Jamie tossed and turned, finally sitting up in his bed at 4:15 a.m. Pam was in Oakland. Cathy, who he was more than aware of, was down the hall. Quietly, he slid out of bed and pulled on his 501s. No one was up, so he didn't bother about a shirt. Briefcase in hand, he walked quietly into the dining room and turned on the small lamp. He did not want to wake Cathy yet, but he was looking forward to seeing the area with her later in day.

The résumés, all neatly typed and printed by the company he'd hired in Oakland, lay in front of him. Clean white stock reflected his experience. Cordon Bleu training from the a culinary school in San Francisco. Three years at a top restaurant in Santa Barbara, where he started as a line chef and then an assistant sous chef. Eventually he'd worked his way to assistant executive chef. Still, he was worried. The job market was tight, and in the Wine Country, even the most experienced chefs coveted jobs.

What if he didn't get a job? How would he support Pam and Amber?

"Son," his father had said. "Why don't you go into something more stable? Medicine was good to me and your mom."

Jamie only stared back. Black and white: That was how his father saw everything. Good and bad, right and wrong. Being a chef was too risky now that he was a family man. Dreams were to be put aside, and the yoke of responsibility taken up.

But Jamie's soul longed for the color, texture, and taste of a finely prepared meal. Serving pleasure, tapping nature's finest and plating it like a work of art: That was his calling. He was at home in a kitchen with the sounds of sizzling oil, clanging pans, and happy customers.

Today, he would see if this training paid off. His eyes wandered out the window. A robin's song brought in the dawn through the trees. Perhaps he'd make coffee and prep for breakfast.

His father would tell him to pray. Cooking was the form of prayer he preferred.

Chapter Seven

Cathy pulled out her polka-dot sundress with the empire waist. It would keep her cool and was appropriate for wherever they stopped for lunch. She walked out and checked the vinyl record-shaped clock in the living room.

"It's almost nine," she yelled down the hall to Jamie.

He walked out in khaki pants, still tucking in a turquoise blue buttondown shirt. "Will this work?"

"Perfectly," she said.

His eyes reflected the color of his shirt. She wanted to hug him for good luck, but was afraid she couldn't stop there. Cathy imagined the feel of his strong arms around her, his lean body pressed against hers. It wasn't just that he was a good-looking man. She'd known plenty of those. It was the way she felt around him: seen, cared about, safe. She sighed and turned toward the door.

"Let's get a move on and get you that job!"

Hot air blasted through the windows as they cruised down River Road, past fields of wildflowers amidst the gnarled oaks and towering redwoods of Forestville. The river sparkled to their left as beach areas revealed themselves through the trees. Sweet summer air filled the car. Sprawling vineyards and the quaint vine-covered buildings of Korbel Winery lined the road to the right.

As they cruised into the quaint town of Guerneville, Cathy pointed out her shop, Health & Hearth.

"Jill and Brian are probably slaving away prepping for lunch now," she said. "I'll bring you in soon to meet them and see the place." She hit the gas. "But not today. Today I am on vacation! Let me know if you want to stop anywhere along the way. We're running early and have plenty of time to make your eleven o'clock interview."

"Anywhere you'd like." His eyes were glued to the scenery. "I want to see it all."

She slowed as they entered the town limits and passed under the sign announcing "Monte Rio, Vacation Wonderland." Cathy pointed out the funky metal-roofed Rio movie theater. They drove by a few shops until they were almost out of town.

"There's the turn off to the famed Village Inn Restaurant," she said, pointing to the left. "A must-come-back-for-dinner place."

Jamie hummed a few bars from "Don't Stop," a popular Fleetwood Mac song playing on the radio, and tapped his fingers on the dash to keep time. Cathy sang along. Together they managed to remember a few lyrics and create some decent harmonizing. She stole a glance at Jamie. He looked light, happy.

Just past Monte Rio, Jamie sat up and pointed out the window. "Wait, stop."

"What?" Cathy hit the brakes.

"The fruit stand. Let's see what they've got."

"You almost gave me a heart attack," she said. She pulled the car into the gravel parking area.

Inside, Jamie wandered the rows. He was amusing to watch as he held up a piece of fruit, smelled it, and ran his fingers over its surface. Gently he squeezed some nectarines, then sampled the purple grapes. He popped a grape in his mouth and tossed one in the air to her.

She caught it with her hand and tasted it. The sweet tangy juice was delicious.

His eyes were on her lips. She swallowed in nervousness, her lips parting.

"Shall we get some of these?" He started filling a bag with nectarines.

"Sure, but they're so ripe. They'll ooze everywhere after a bite!"

"The better to lick off," he said, running his tongue along his lips.

Cathy shivered. He had no idea how the sight of his tongue running across his full lips affected her. How could she not think of him licking the sweet nectar off her mouth? Was he flirting? Probably not. He was just being a little boy, excited, having fun. But the way he looked at her. That was not a place she'd allowed her thoughts to go with a married man, no matter how much he drew her. Pam was her friend. Jamie had a family that depended on him. She would not forget that.

With two bags of fruit aboard, they continued down River Road toward the town of Jenner for Jamie's interview. The morning sun played between the trees as they thinned into prairies and rolling green hills. The next curve revealed the old town of Duncans Mills. Cathy turned left off the side road to quickly show Jamie the quaint Blue Heron Café.

"This is another one of the best places on the River that serves amazing food. We'll have to try it sometime," she said.

"Mind if I jump out and peruse the menu on the door for a sec?" he said.

"Go ahead."

She watched him examine the giant blue heron statue out front. The ocean breeze, cooler now as they approached the coast, ruffled his hair as he studied the outside menu like a textbook. He leaned over and peeked through the windows.

"Totally awesome," he said as he jumped back in the car. "It's exactly the kind of place I would love to own myself someday. Wonder if they need another chef?"

"It's worth a call when we get back," she said. Cathy drove down the parking lot to show him the Country Candy store and original train cars, abandoned when the depot was still active before 1930.

"Amber would love it here. I'll have to bring her back sometime," he said.

She pointed out the rodeo grounds across the street with their bleachers and rolling green acres.

"If you're around for the Fourth of July picnic, we'll have a booth here and sell food. Lots of things for kids and families to do as well."

He shrugged his shoulders. "We'll see how the interviews go. Count us in if we're here."

Cathy wondered where Jamie and his family would be in July. He was here today, she reminded herself as she turned onto the main road. Each bend revealed another postcard picture of hills with cattle and sheep dotting the landscape among the oak trees. As they entered Jenner by the Sea, she slowed down.

"What a view," Jamie said. "The river looks like an open hand pouring out to sea."

Small homes and ranches lined the low hills that leveled out where the river flowed into the Pacific Ocean.

"I love this area. I've had fantasies of living here on the hill and watching the sunset every night over the water," said Cathy.

"Totally. It would be a great place to hole up and write a cookbook."

She could imagine him owning a classy little restaurant overlooking the ocean, a destination spot for tourists and locals. The entry way would prominently display his natural foods gourmet cookbook.

"I could see having a little place on the bluff over there."

"I was just thinking that," Cathy said.

He laughed. "You've said a few things right out of my head today too."

The road curved south at the gas station, so she veered right and the Jenner Hideaway Restaurant came into view.

"There it is," she said pointing to the wooden structure. "Inside there are high-beam ceilings and wall-size windows facing out to sea."

"Looks cool," he said as she parked the car.

He combed his hair in the rearview mirror and smoothed down his shirt.

"You look great," Cathy said. "Now go in there and ace that interview."

He stepped out and closed the door behind him, leaving her with a dazzling smile as he walked away. It would be a primo place for him to work, and they could probably find a home up River Road to live. They wouldn't be far from

her, but there wasn't much to do down here. Maybe Napa or
Sonoma would be a better choice for Pam and Amber.

She left the car and walked along the side of the building for a better view. The tide looked like it was coming in,
encroaching on the land with each new wave. She sat back on
a bench and let her thoughts drift. Seagulls shrieked as they
dive-bombed from the air. It felt good to stop, really stop. It
seemed like years since she wasn't running from or hurrying
to something. She buried her past by working hard, but she
buried herself in it as well. She had Tim and Jill, her women's
book group, and loyal customers. Dating amused her, but she
kept her heart at a distance. The men she chose seemed fine
with that.

Cathy checked her watch. Thirty minutes had gone by.
It must have been a thorough interview. She rose and walked
back to the car. Jamie stood there unbuttoning his shirt to the
T-shirt below. He rolled up his sleeves before getting back in
the car.

"How'd it go?" she asked, sliding in the driver's side.

He raised an eyebrow. "Well, let me say it wasn't a total
bummer. I got to taste the seafood chowder they were prepar-
ing for lunch."

Cathy frowned. "That bad?"

Jamie waved his hand as he imitated the voice of the restaurant manager. "We are a very conservative place. Every
recipe is made the same, no deviations."

She knew that style would kill his spirit.

"Let's split," Cathy said. "The coast is awaiting us. And a
scrumptious lunch."

Leaving the seals lounging on rocks, they sped along
the rocky shoreline of Highway 1. Cathy pointed out Goat

Rock and her favorite places to beachcomb and explore. The expansive rocky cliffs dipped into the Pacific Ocean. Clear blue water glistened in the sun as they approached Bodega Bay. Tourists were everywhere. She passed the bait shop and turned into the Tides Restaurant parking lot.

They hopped out of the car and stretched in the warm sun.

"Wow. Smell that salty air." Jamie hurried toward the fishing pier to get a better view.

Cathy followed him along the boardwalk, watching the fascinating pelicans flap their enormous wings over the tin rooftops. The scent of fish permeated the boats unloading their catches. Families passed with dripping ice cream cones and sticky kids.

"Amber would love it here," he said.

"She would." Cathy wondered if he wished he had his real family here instead of her.

"Are you hungry, Cathy? The seafood is obviously fresh off the boat."

She gave him her of-course-I'm-hungry look, and the rest was forgotten. "The shrimp cocktail is to die for too. Let's go."

They scampered up the pier into the large dining room of the rustic restaurant. After a short wait, the hostess led them to a table by the window. Jamie slid into the far side of the booth where he could watch the kitchen. Cathy glanced over the menu while Jamie scanned the wine list.

"They have the wines!" he said.

Cathy looked up. "Which ones?"

Jamie pointed to the award-winning wines on the menu. "Where have you been? Last year these wineries in Napa put California wines on the map!"

She remembered hearing about some big upset in France last year. "I kind of remember."

"Stag's Leap Wine Cellars entered their Cabernet against France's best Bordeaux. They say the French Judges were very skeptical, but it was a blind tasting. And in the end the 1973 Stag's Leap S.LV. Cabernet Sauvignon won first place along with Chateau Montelena's Chardonnay from Napa just a few miles from here!"

"That's amazing," Cathy said.

"And the winery has only been open now for seven years. These fine wines are one of the reasons I wanted to be a chef here in the Napa/Sonoma Wine Country. It's the up-and-coming food and wine destination of California." His cheeks were flushed and his eyes sparkling.

"It's not like you're excited about it or anything?"

Jamie grinned. "Sorry if I'm talking your ear off. They do have both wines though."

Cathy laid down her menu. "By all means, let's order the Chardonnay with our entrée and the Cab with dessert."

"A perfect choice, my lady. And if we have time someday, I was hoping to get over and meet Mike Grgich. He was the winemaker consultant that steered Chateau Montelena's 1973 Chardonnay from start to finish."

"No problem," Cathy said. "It's about fifty miles east of Forestville. We can all make the drive someday and check out potential restaurants to apply to as well."

The waiter appeared and placed hot sourdough bread and soft butter on the table. Jamie ordered the wine with two shrimp cocktails and looked over to her.

"Anything else?"

"Not for now," she said. Her taste buds prepared for a treat.

A few awkward moments of silence passed as they stared out the window at the glistening bay. It felt like a date, but she reminded herself it was not.

"When did you start cooking?" she asked.

He buttered his bread and took a bite, obviously assessing its flavor.

"I wanted to be a chef since I was about five years old. I'd tell my parents, 'When I grow up, I'm going to be a cook.'"

"They must have thought that was cute."

Emotions raced across his face. "They would laugh and say, 'Not with that brain you won't.'"

She watched the lines tighten around his eyes. "What did they want you to be?"

"My father was a prominent physician in San Francisco, with a PhD from Wheaton. My grandfather, a surgeon at St. Mary's. They pressured me to go to the right schools." His jaw tightened and released with a sigh. "What about you?"

She couldn't imagine his creative, free spirit trapped in a classroom, glued to rigorous studies.

"Well, I got married immediately out of high school. Real smart move."

Jamie laughed. "None of us make great decisions when we're young."

The waiter appeared with the bottle, showed them the label, uncorked it, and poured splashes of wine into both their glasses. Jamie swirled it before tasting. He let the wine open in his mouth before swallowing.

"Excellent," he said to the waiter. Jamie made a toast. "To playing hooky."

He looked more relaxed now. Cathy wanted to know everything about him but was hesitant to delve further. Between sips she rambled on about herself.

"The marriage lasted shorter than the ceremony."

He chuckled.

"It's funny now," Cathy agreed. "But it sure wasn't back then. After it was over, I packed and moved in with my mom at her country place on the Russian River. She left soon after, and here I've stayed."

Towering shrimp cocktails with celery stalks rooted like small trees were placed before them. Jamie inhaled before he took his first bite. "Awesome fare!"

As she talked, Jamie nodded, chewed, and gave her his complete attention. She wasn't used to a man really listening, much less caring what she said. Occasionally his eyes wandered to watch what was happening in the open kitchen.

She took a break from her long, sad story and bit into the crisp shrimp drenched in tangy cocktail sauce. The flavors melted in her mouth. She followed it with a sip of wine. It paired perfectly with the meal.

"During my practical stage, when I realized no one was going to take care of me," she said between bites, "I did end up going to Sonoma State, known as Granola State back then, and majored in business."

His eyes smiled back at her. He gets it, she thought.

"Where did you end up going to college?" she asked.

"Berkeley ... Berzerkeley. I majored in pre-med and hated it, spent more time getting high and throwing Frisbee in Tilden Park than going to class."

"Hey, I loved that park when we lived in Oakland. I used to hike to the lake and contemplate my life. Did you ever go over to Mt. Tamalpais?"

"Of course. Sunrise on Mt. Tam was a life-changing experience." He sipped his wine and looked out at the waves. She wondered what memories played across his mind.

"So, how did you end up in culinary school?"

Jamie laid down his fork and took a sip of wine. "My first job in college was waiting tables at Heavenly Fare. The chef noticed my interest and brought me back in the kitchen as an assistant sous chef. I learned fast. By the time I graduated college, I was the executive chef, dating a cute waitress named Pam, and had no intention of ever doing anything else. CAA was the gold choice in culinary academies and a way to progress in my career. It was the logical next step."

Jamie refilled her wine class. The warm liquid left her floating. "It must be nice to have so much passion and know exactly the direction you want to go."

"It is. But it's not always easy to go after it." He paused, his eyes almost gray. "What do you dream of, Cathy?"

His searching expression stopped her mid-bite.

"I don't dream anymore," she said. "I just go with the flow."

He studied her. "Life is hard without a dream."

"Life is hard when it turns into a nightmare."

"I had my share of those too."

She looked at him. His life seemed so perfect. Wife, child, new career. "Seems you bounced back well."

His crooked grin seemed forced.

"Looks can be deceiving." His eyes searched her face. "You look happy."

"Touché," she said. "A few years after moving up here, my mom moved to Arizona and left me the house. I finally figured out my life would be what I made of it. So I took the money I finally got from my divorce from Todd, and leased the building in Guerneville. The health food store led to adding the lunch café. Then I expanded upstairs."

He laid his fork down and wiped his face with his napkin. "Very impressive."

"Thanks," she said. "Some might say I bury myself in my work."

"Work can be healing."

Cathy couldn't pull her gaze from his. There was no judgment there, only acceptance, and something deeper. "I hope you find the kind of work you want soon too."

Cathy looked down to her food. One lone shrimp rested in the bowl, but she was full. She stared out the window. The beach looked inviting. She longed to be on the sand. She looked at her watch. It was 1:15. Jamie had agreed to call Pam in the late afternoon, so they still had some time.

"What do you say we take off our shoes and stick our toes in the sand?" he asked.

"We'd have to skip dessert," she said.

Jamie thought a minute. "We can come back another time for that."

Cathy tossed her napkin on the table. "The best beach is just a short drive north."

"North it is," Jamie said, leaving cash on the table for the waiter.

They drove back up the windy coast, green rolling hills to their right, gorgeous shoreline with raging surf to their left.

"I think we'll go here to Salmon Creek beach," Cathy said, pulling into the parking lot.

They tumbled out of the car, threw off their shoes, and raced stumbling in the sand to the water. Jamie pulled off his T-shirt, revealing his smooth chest, then rolled up his pants. Hand in hand, as if they had done this together a thousand times before, they ran into the shallow water and plunged their feet in.

"Brr," Cathy said, hopping up and down in the freezing water. Jamie wrapped his arm around her shoulders to keep her warm. She snuggled in and could feel his breath on her hair.

"Cathy," he whispered.

She looked up into those familiar eyes that had searched for her in her dreams. He stared longingly at her lips. She yearned for nothing more than a kiss. A child waving a stick ran by, kicking sand on their legs. The moment was broken and her feet were freezing. She ran to the warm sand.

"Lightweight," he said, walking out farther in the sea.

"Don't go too far, Jamie, there are riptides here."

For a second, she imagined a giant, rogue wave pulling him out and having to tell Pam, "The water just took him away." Would she believe her?

Would Cathy go in after him?

In a heartbeat.

Jamie came running out, goose bumps up his gorgeous arms, and sprayed a little icy water on her.

"No, no," she said, backing away.

A wicked smile crossed his face, and he started toward her. Cathy ran down the beach, splashing in and out of the water while he followed close behind, threatening to throw her in. Out of breath, she turned and faced his bluff.

"Do not throw me in or else."

"Or else what?" he said, inching closer.

"I'll leave you here and drive home myself!"

He scanned the surroundings. "Not a bad place to be left. I could always climb up on one of the large boulders when the tide comes in."

Not a bad image.

Rolling up in the tide, a large sand dollar bounced in the shallow wave. Cathy leaned over to pick it up. Perfect, not a crack.

"Have a look at this," she said, holding it up.

He took it, turning it in his hand. "Never saw one that big before."

"For you then." Cathy handed it to him.

"Perhaps we could find one for Amber too?"

"Great idea. You're lucky to have such a sweet little girl."

He looked out to sea, and the mood shifted with the incoming wave. "I am, very lucky," he said softly. "She's everything to me."

They walked along the wet sand, heads down, hunting for shells to bring home. Everything? Cathy wondered. It was clear Jamie adored his daughter, but he didn't talk much about Pam. Neither had she. For just this one day, they were playing hooky from life.

The sun lit on her shoulders, and the incoming foamy tide crept up her bare ankles. She was glad she'd shaved her legs this morning. After finding another perfect specimen, they stopped to look back toward the car.

The sun drifted down the horizon into some wispy clouds. They'd walked a long way. She looked at her watch. "Two forty-five p.m.," she said. "Kinda late if you want to call Pam by four."

She saw disappointment in his eyes.

"Guess we better get back," he said, more like a question than a statement.

It was quiet walk to the car except for the seagulls' endless screeching overhead. A few dogs ran along the beach, catching Frisbees and driftwood sticks.

She tossed him the keys. "Want to drive?"

"You still trust me?" he said with a devilish grin.

"So far," she said, trying to keep a straight face.

Jamie started the car. "Where to?"

Cathy thought a moment. "Why don't we take Coleman Valley Road back and stop in the town of Occidental. They have killer family Italian restaurants that make the best minestrone you've ever tasted. We can bring some back for dinner later."

Jamie perked up. "Sounds good. I can call Pam from there and see how her mother is doing too."

A narrow one-lane road, Coleman Valley wound into the hills. They had to slow down even more when they crossed cattle grates. It crisscrossed through open-range farmlands and redwoods, grasslands, and oak groves all the while displaying a breathtaking view as far east as the eye could see.

Jamie pulled the car to the side of the road and pointed out a mom and baby calf that had wandered away from the herd of cattle. They approached the car and looked at them like, "What are you two doing here?"

"They're cute," Cathy said. She wished she'd brought a camera. "When you look into their eyes up close, you can see why I chose not to eat beef."

"Something to think about," Jamie said. "I just hope they stay out of the road."

Cathy nodded. "The road is so curvy and remote, I would think most people would have the sense to go slow."

"You'd hope," Jamie said.

They pulled away and followed the road as it narrowed and the trees thickened into a canopy. After a few sharp turns, the old white church was prominently in sight through redwood forest as they entered the town of Occidental.

Driving through felt like going back in time. Little gingerbread houses filled with shops, old-fashioned bakeries with hand-carved signs and cafés everywhere made this town a tempting place to visit.

"What a cool place," Jamie said. "Where do we get the soup?"

His mind worked just like hers. "There are three Italian family restaurants to choose from," Cathy said.

"What's your favorite?" he asked.

"Negri's is fantastic. Hot bread, amazing minestrone soup and salad: a feast."

Entering the restaurant, they admired the old family portraits covering the walls. This place had been in the Negri family for almost fifty years. After going over the menu, they put in an order for minestrone soup and sourdough bread. Both would reheat well later.

While Jamie scouted for a phone booth, Cathy covered the bill since he'd paid for lunch. Bags of food in hand, she went off to find him. He was already out in the car, so she put the food in the liftback and joined him. Jamie's hands gripped the steering wheel as he started the car.

"Which way?" he said, speeding up the hill toward the stop sign.

She gave him directions back to Forestville and wondered how the phone call went. Not well, it seemed. Perhaps there was a lot more to his marriage than met the eye.

"Is everything okay with Pam's mom?"

Jamie nodded. "She's fine. Dakota will be back late tonight. Pam and Amber will be coming home tomorrow morning after the traffic."

His expression was drawn, so Cathy didn't ask anything else and just stared out the window.

"Smells awesome," Jamie finally said as he made the turn toward the river.

"Wait until you taste it."

He turned on the radio and started humming along. He must be feeling better. She noticed new color in his cheeks, probably from the sun today. This was a man with dreams and they wove so close to her own. It felt natural sitting next to him and yet surprising to find a man who was truly kind. His boyish charm was so innocent, and when they'd run along the beach his joy was evident. When she'd leaned against him, his skin felt silky. It was hard to reconcile with what her heart wanted on a day like this. Cathy wished it would never end and she'd never have to go back to reality. When she was with him, she remembered what happy felt like. They still had the evening. She had a bottle of Merlot that would go well with the soup. Maybe they could take an evening walk along the river.

What was she thinking? Could she even trust herself another night alone with him? Not with the way she was feeling.

Jamie looked over. "You okay?"

How did he know? Could he read her thoughts?

"Of course," she said.

He shrugged. "You just seemed to stop breathing."

He was right. Her shoulders were tight, and a sense of panic was building. It would be better if they were not alone again in the house. She thought about where they might end up. The feelings were too strong. They crept in and blinded her to whom Jamie belonged. What could she say to him? I'm going out without you tonight? She thought of Tim. She could call him and suggest they all go somewhere together. Not that he would be the greatest chaperone, but at least they would be out in public.

That was a better alternative.

Chapter Eight

Jamie put the food in the refrigerator and waited outside on the deck for Cathy to get out of the shower. The sand still lingered between his toes, but he was in no hurry to wash away the memories of this perfect day. It had been a long time since he completely relaxed and was able to be himself. He enjoyed being a dad and a husband, but his needs always seemed to come last. Or he let them.

Jamie watched an elegant white egret glide through the air toward the river. The magical looking bird seemed to beckon him to follow. A walk sounded nice, but the minute they walked in the house, Cathy had called Tim, her store manager. They arranged to meet him at the Highland Dell Lodge to hear the band Queen Ida play Zydeco. He was looking forward to the evening, but would have been just as happy to stay home and sit on the deck with Cathy. It was much more than her beauty, which she certainly had. It was hard not to run his hands across her smooth skin or get lost in her pale green eyes. Everything else faded away when he was with her. It was probably for the best they were going out.

The call with Pam had abruptly brought him back to everyday life. She was not happy he was an hour late calling her. Way past when she thought he should have called. It seemed to him that four o'clock fit the late afternoon she specified, but perhaps he should have called sooner. She was tense, and he felt for her having to deal with her mother. When they were first married, Jamie tried to help, but Pam and her mother were in constant conflict. He found it was best to stay out of it and give Pam plenty of space and support when she would take it.

He could understand why Pam was upset being stuck with her mother and a four-year-old in a stressful situation while Jamie galloped on the beach with Cathy. She made it real clear that she expected him to take her there as soon as they got back. Of course he agreed, but he wished it hadn't been put across as a demand.

Patience, he told himself. That is how he got through.

"The shower's all yours," he heard Cathy yell from the hall. He waited a moment so he would not catch her running from the bathroom in a towel, then took his turn. He watched the warm water send the sand down the drain and felt his heart drop. It was like watching the day wash away.

That's crazy, he thought. Sing, you idiot, before you go getting depressed. He sang James Taylor's hit, "You've Got a Friend." When he got to the lyrics about calling out someone's name, it was Cathy's he wanted to call.

Clean and dry, Jamie put on some Levis and a blue-and-red plaid button-down shirt. He rolled up the sleeves and slipped on some loafers before walking into the living room. Cathy stood in the kitchen arranging some flowers in a vase. She turned and smiled. His breath caught. Her flowing auburn hair cascaded down her shoulders across a hot-pink tank top exposing her bronze skin. She twirled, and her long skirt rose in the air circling her ankles.

"My favorite dancing skirt," she said as her translucent gauze skirt rose in the air.

"Gorgeous, my dear," he said playfully.

"You clean up pretty well too," she said. "Let's go. Tim awaits us. You're going to love him," she said as they walked to the car. "He's fun to talk to and he always keeps me laughing."

They parked in the lot across the street under the redwoods. As they walked up the stairs, they saw Tim waiting for them near the door, wearing tight bell bottom jeans and an even tighter see-through T-shirt.

"Over here, guys," he waved.

Tim gave Jamie a look up and down. Clearly his interest was men. Jamie was used to roaming male eyes from living in the Bay area, and it was no big deal to him.

Cathy gave Tim a big hug and introduced them. Jamie put out his hand but Tim hugged him instead.

"Hey, man," Tim said. "We're all friends here."

They walked through the large entry. There was a towering high-beam ceiling, wood walls, and wood floors. They took a seat close to the dance floor and stage, where the band was setting up.

"Drinks?" Tim asked. "I'm buying."

Cathy ordered a glass of wine and Jamie said ditto.

A stunning black woman in a bright red dress took the mic.

"Queen Ida is here!" she said, raising her hand in the air before starting to sing. Her band played a combo of R&B and Cajun music while she called out for everyone to dance. The dance floor filled, and the noise level limited conversation.

Tim returned with the drinks and set them on the table. "Hey, you two, what are you doing in your chairs?"

He took each of their hands and pulled them onto the dance floor. Jamie swayed with the music and tried to let loose like Tim was doing. Cathy was a sight to watch, smiling, shaking her hips, twirling over the floor. Tim winked at him and gently pushed him toward Cathy before disappearing into the crowd.

Jamie admired how free and graceful her movements were. One song ended and another slow song began. He held Cathy close as they danced, closed his eyes as they moved together in perfect sync. Every fiber of his body was aware of her. She rested her head on his shoulder and the sweet scent of chamomile lingered in her hair.

Suddenly the band broke into the song "We Will Rock You" by Queen. People flooded the floor. Sweat broke out on the back of his neck, and Jamie wanted to unbutton and discard his shirt like many of the other guys were doing. He could see Cathy's face was flushed from the heat. They headed toward the back of the room near the windows for air.

She fanned her face and leaned over, yelling into his ear. "Let's go get some air."

Jamie nodded and followed her outside on the deck over-looking the river.

"Whew," he said, "I can't remember the last time I danced like that."

Cathy laughed. "Tim drags me out dancing every so often. He insists it will enhance my social life."

"Does it?" he asked. He imagined her dancing with other men and did not like how his stomach twisted.

"Not really," she said. "Most of the time he takes me to gay bars because they have the best music."

The silent river flowed beneath and a starry sky spread over them endlessly. He rested his hand in hers.

"Found you," Tim said, throwing open the doors and joining them on the deck.

Cathy released his hand and turned. "We're not the one who went off carousing," she said. "Did you meet anyone interesting?"

Tim frowned. "Not really. I think I'll head over to Fife's. Wanna come?"

"Not tonight, I'm afraid," Cathy said. "We've had a long day and I have to go into work tomorrow."

Tim raised an eyebrow and looked at Jamie. "Do you have to work tomorrow?"

"Unfortunately, no," Jamie said. "But I do have a wife and daughter coming home in the morning."

Tim scooted them toward the door. "Well then, off you two go."

They made their way through the noisy crowd and back to the car. "Want me to drive?" Jamie asked.

"That's okay," Cathy said, getting into the driver's side.

Cathy was silent as they drove. Jamie rolled the window down and let the warm night breeze cool him. The night was coming to an end. It was time. He would go right to bed as soon as they returned. Not that he would sleep. But he would shut his door, turn off the light, and hopefully turn off the thoughts filling his mind and heart.

Chapter Nine

Cathy poured homemade granola from the Mason jar into the ceramic bowl her friend, Linda, had made. Jamie had prepared the nut, fruit, and oat mixture the day before. She covered it in milk and sliced bananas. The day was already warm, and she wanted a light breakfast. Luckily, Jamie already made the coffee, so she poured herself a cup.

Outside the window, she watched Jamie in the garden building the trellis for her flowering sweet peas. His T-shirt lay on a bench beside him. Cathy's eyes roved over his body. With each stroke of the hammer, his muscles rippled down his back and strong arms. He stopped a moment, wiped the sweat from his brow with the back of his hand, and turned back toward the house.

Cathy jumped back from the window and took a seat at the eating bar. She spooned some cereal into her mouth and gulped some coffee.

Last night. It was a good thing Tim had interrupted them when he did. When they were together, it seemed like they'd never been apart, and never would be. His hand fit perfectly in hers. His laugh lifted her heart. Why now under these circumstances?

As she watched, he finished the work and turned to come in. She hurriedly took a seat at the table. She didn't want him to find her staring.

He walked in the back door, his skin flushed with the start of a sunburn.

"I think I heard a car," he said walking toward the front door.

Amber came running in. "Daddy, we're back!" she said, flinging herself into his arms. The joy in his face was evident as he bent to hug her.

Pam was right behind. She carried a small suitcase and looked exhausted.

"Here, let me have that," Jamie said, taking it from her hand. "How'd it go?"

Pam rolled her eyes. "How do you think?" She took a deep breath and let it out with a sigh. "I'm sorry, I'm just so tired," she said, walking toward the kitchen. "It's been a long drive and we didn't have much breakfast. I'm hungry."

"Me too," Amber said.

Jamie took Amber by the hand. "Well, let's find you something to eat then, little one." He turned to Pam. "And big one."

Amber waved as she walked past. "I got to see my grandma," she said, stopping at Cathy's side while Jamie continued into the kitchen.

"How is she doing?" Cathy asked, making eye contact with Pam as well.

"She's resting," Amber said before bouncing into the kitchen to help her dad.

Pam gave Cathy an exasperated expression. "Dakota's back for as long as we need her. My mom seems a little worse, but is seeing the doctor again tomorrow."

Pam walked into the kitchen and poured everyone some lemonade, clanking each glass down on the counter. She put one at each place setting on the table and took her seat without a word. Jamie carried over granola and toast. He leaned over to kiss Pam on the cheek. She did not respond in kind.

Pam's eyes looked from Cathy to Jamie while she chewed her toast.

"Nice tan you two got yesterday while I was stuck in Oakland."

Cathy held her breath. Pam was tired and stressed. She did not want to say anything to make it worse.

For a moment, the only sounds were the clanking spoons and forks and Amber slurping milk out of the cereal bowl.

"The beach was warm, and I worked in the garden this morning," Jamie said.

"I want to go to the beach too, Daddy," Amber said.

Jamie patted Amber's cheeks with a napkin. "I'll take you and Mommy there very soon." He looked at Pam for approval.

She gulped lemonade and watched Pam's smile return. Her heart sank. The beach had been beautiful when they were there. For that one day, it was their time, their place. Pam and Amber had him for the rest of their lives.

Cathy was appalled how selfish her thoughts were. She had no right. Forcing a smile, she said, "Perhaps sometime this week you could take them to Johnson's beach on the River. It's a great family place, good for swimming. So feel free to go whenever."

"We will," Pam said.

Cathy got up and cleared dishes. She felt like banging a few plates, but thought better of it. Out the window, her garden offered solace. She could take some frustration out there.

"Off to weed," she said, heading out the back door.

She pulled off her peasant blouse to the tank top below and let sunrays play across her shoulders while she attacked the garden invaders. She wrapped her hand under the bottom leaves and yanked until their roots were free from the earth. Into the compost pile they went.

Hard labor worked wonders to ease her mind and heart. The corn was starting to get high. It would be ready to pick in a month or so. She wandered down the rows and saw the red and yellow stalks of chard shimmering in the sun. She would pick them tomorrow morning; they would be ripe and delicious in the café soup special.

Cathy laid down her tools and climbed into the hammock chair tied between two oaks. It supported her body as she gently rocked for several minutes. She needed to get things back into perspective. No matter how fast or how strong her feelings for Jamie grew, he was not available. She would get her mind back on other things and her life back on track. "Starting now," Cathy said, jumping out of the chair.

There were a few sweet strawberries left. She brought them into the house as an ice cream topping for later.

When she returned, the three of them were cuddled up on the couch and reading aloud from a picture book. A picture-perfect family.

They looked like the three bears on the couch: Papa, Mama, and Baby Bear. Who did that make her? Goldilocks intruding on their happy home?

Cathy tossed a few strawberries into her mouth. Their sweetness set off her taste buds like the succulent shrimp at lunch yesterday. She remembered the ice-cold wine, his warm

hand. Was this the same man sitting, reading in different char-
acter voices, and acting out the parts like a big kid?

"And the wolf huffed and he puffed and tried to blow the
house down!"

Amber squealed and buried her face in her mother's chest.

Cathy stood behind the couch. Out the window, the sun
dipped behind the pines, casting shadows across her lawn. She
turned back for the last words of the story:

"And he lived happily ever after."

That's why they call it a fairytale, Cathy mused. She wondered sometimes if it was such a good idea, putting these
thoughts into fertile young brains. Those expectations had not
served her well. She hoped they would for Amber.

"Time for a little nap now," Pam said to Amber.
"Tomorrow you will have a big day, going swimming with
Mommy and Daddy."

Pam looked at Cathy, all sweetness and light.

"Let's go, honey." She lifted Amber up and carried her
toward her room.

Amber reached her arms out to Jamie. "Daddy, come and
sing me a lullaby."

"Coming." He stood and his eyes met Cathy's.

"Have a good sleep, little one," Cathy said as they walked by.

She watched Jamie walk toward the bedroom, shaggy
curls over the rim of his T-shirt, faded jeans hugging his legs,
Birkenstocks flopping on the wood floor. Her heart skipped
a beat.

Cathy had planned to skip her Monday book group pot-
luck this afternoon, but now she felt like going. Some friendly
faces would be nice. She'd call her old friend, Lisa, and let
her know she was coming. Perhaps Barb from the Head Start

afterschool program could use a ride again. She'd bring the strawberries and pick up sour cream for dipping.

The afternoon was picking up. So were her spirits.

Chapter Ten

Cathy sat at her rolltop desk in her home office, paying bills and making a list of things to do when she went into the shop. Mondays were bookkeeping day, and she needed quiet time. She had shown Pam her old sewing machine and all the extra material her mom had left behind when she moved. Pam would probably be happily sewing all afternoon. Cathy would leave soon after the lunch rush was over at work.

The ringing phone startled her. Cathy picked up the receiver and heard a panicked Brian calling from the shop. She held her breath as Brian told her Jill was doubled over in pain.

"I'm taking her to the emergency room. I'll wait until her husband gets there. Okay?"

She glanced at the clock. Two o'clock. Jill must have waited until after lunch, pain and all.

"Should I come?" she said.

"Cathy, don't worry," Brian said. "Dan is on his way. Tim is manning the shop. But tomorrow I'm leaving on vacation. I'm sorry, man."

Cathy sighed. "Brian, just go. I'll take care of everything. Tell Dan to call me when they know what's wrong."

Cathy prayed it was nothing.

Having Jill manage the café and guest rooms had made everything so easy for Cathy. She opened the office door and walked into the living room, assessing all she had to do to prepare for lunch tomorrow. The guests would be arriving for the upstairs rooms too.

Pam stood in the kitchen, watching her pace. "Everything okay?" she asked.

"Yes. No."

"Can we help?"

"No. I mean yes."

Pam looked concerned. "What is it?"

Cathy started rattling, "Jill is heading for the hospital in terrible pain. It might be appendicitis. I have to shop and prep for tomorrow's lunch, handle the B&B rooms and …"

Pam stood and hugged her. "That's easy. Jamie will help you. He doesn't have another interview until next week and has nothing but time. You're letting us stay in your house, now we can help you back."

"But you guys were going swimming this week. I don't want to disrupt your plans."

Pam looked disappointed, but it passed quickly. "That's fine, we'll figure out another day to go. And besides, I'm going to use some of that way-cool material to make me, Amber, and her doll matching dresses."

"Did I hear my name?" Jamie said, coming into the room.

"Cathy needs help with the café for a few days. Jill's out sick. I told Cathy you'd be glad to help her."

"Of course," he said.

Cathy smiled. It would all work out. Brian would leave for vacation tomorrow, and hopefully Jill would be home recovering quickly. "On one condition," Cathy said.

Pam cocked her head. "What?"

Cathy continued. "Since you will be staying here longer, I'll pay for your caretaker's extra time so she can work full time with your mom while you're gone. Jamie will be working for me, so you guys don't have to drive back and forth to Oakland, and you can stay here. It's only fair."

"It's a deal," Pam said before Jamie could get in a word.

Cathy turned to Jamie. "I'm sorry to say we have to act fast. In fact, right now to make it work."

"Ready when you are," he said.

"Let's go then." Cathy led the way to the car. They got in her Honda, rolled the windows down, and headed over to Speer's Market. They could plan while they shopped and pick things up at the same time. On the way, Cathy handed Jamie one of their lunch menus she had pulled from her desk. She fidgeted as he reviewed it.

"It's very Sonoma County," she said in defense. "Mostly vegetarian with some chicken and fish."

His crooked smile reassured her. "Mind if I make a couple changes, spice things up a bit?"

"Sounds good to me, but we're known for our killer veggie burgers and soups."

In the store, Cathy watched Jamie scanning the produce, catching its scent. His fingers caressed each surface, searching for ripeness. He chose items that would complement produce he could pick in her garden, Leafy spinach, purple cabbage, shallots, and garlic began to fill the cart.

Jamie held up a package of goat cheese and handed it to her as if it were a gift. "My favorite brand. Creamy. It's packed with herbs and melts in your mouth."

She didn't know whether to squeeze it or read the label, so she did both.

"Is it worthy of your café?" he said jokingly.

She slapped him lightly on the shoulder. "I'm not that picky," she said. "Just checking it out."

She tossed it to him, and their hands brushed as he reached to grab it. His skin was warm, inviting. Their eyes met briefly, and her stomach fluttered. It felt like she was back in high school again with some boy crush. She turned and walked away.

"Do they have pine nuts here?" he yelled after her.

She turned and scowled. "What do you think? We're in the country, not on some distant planet."

Watching him in the market was like watching a grown-up version of a kid at Disneyland for the first time. Cathy's mouth watered as she thought about the possibilities piling up in their cart.

"Gazpacho, maybe pasta, and sourdough bread," he mumbled to himself.

She followed and paid even though he offered to.

Cathy opened the liftback, and they loaded the groceries. On the way to the café, Jamie discussed menu choices with her. They were in business mode now. Her mind lingered back to the touch of his hand. This was ridiculous. She would clear her head and focus on how they were going to work together. They arrived at the shop and started unloading. Jamie put the perishables in the large refrigerator. Tim had closed at five, so they were alone in the kitchen.

"Let's prep while it's fresh, okay?" he said.

"Agreed." She handed him the blackboard and some chalk to list the specials and waited for all those ingredients to spell out an amazing lunch for tomorrow.

LUNCH BOARD – DAILY SPECIALS:

Chilled Gazpacho with a sour cream dollop
Whole-wheat penne pasta with pesto
Spinach salad with goat cheese dressing
Fresh-baked sourdough dill bread with
grilled tomatoes and cheese

"I'm impressed," she said, hands on her hips. "You're hired."

"You can't afford me," he kidded. "But for now, no charge."

"I definitely got the better end of that deal."

Chapter Eleven

The alarm brought Cathy reluctantly from her dreams. She pulled the covers over her head. Why in the world …? She jumped out of bed. She didn't usually get up before 7 a.m., but today she had to go in and start cooking. Cathy pulled on her robe and headed for the bathroom. The door was shut, but ear to the door, she could hear the running water and fan. Please don't use all the hot water, was all she could think. Her toothbrush was in there and everything she needed to get ready. The other bath only had the black claw-foot tub. At least she could use the toilet in the guest bath, which was probably taken too.

Early morning was not her best time of day. Her mind raced with everything she needed to do. Tim would open the shop at nine o'clock, but soup needed to be made, salads prepped, coffee brewed, veggie burgers mixed.

Then she remembered Jamie, his adept hands choosing the produce, his menu that would bring spice to the café. All she had to do now was show up and handle the extras.

The guest bath was also taken, so she headed back, hoping the shower was vacated. She bumped into Jamie, mostly dressed, buttoning his shirt over golden skin, wet hair dripping down his neck.

"Shower's free," he grinned. "I tried to get up early and get out of your way." His sensuous lips curled in a smile that sent a jolt to the depths of her toes.

"No problem." She slid around him into the bathroom, careful not to make contact. Heat flashed between them as she passed. She shut the door and leaned against it. The futility of this attraction weighed heavy on her heart.

She pulled off her clothes and tested the water. It was still hot, so she jumped in and washed her hair. The faint scent of Irish Spring soap lingered in the shower. Jamie had been here right before her. Feet balanced on the porcelain tub, she imagined him soaping his body, slick suds easing down his chest, his legs. She dropped the shampoo bottle directly on her foot.

"Ow!" That's a karmic wake-up call, she thought.

Out of the shower, she blow-dried her hair and brushed through her long, auburn waves. If she cut this mop, it wouldn't take so long to dry. But Cathy liked it long, liked the feel of it lingering down her back.

Robe wrapped tight, she opened the door to run back to her room. Amber saw her and rushed over. "Good morning, Auntie Cathy. Do you know what Mommy's making for breakfast?"

Amber followed Cathy into the bedroom.

"No, tell me," Cathy said, squeezing into just-washed jeans.

"French toast with strawberries on top!"

4

4

4

444

44

Cathy threw on a yellow tank top and opened the door. "Yum, let's go eat."

Breakfast service was in full swing; coffee steaming in mugs and thick gooey toast covered in berries were piled high on the table.

"The cats are fed, those sweeties, so just sit down and eat," Pam said.

Cathy felt like a queen, her every need anticipated. Jamie had already eaten and was in the kitchen packing up some of his knives.

"I'm ready to cook," he said.

Ready, that was a thought. Looking at him made Cathy wonder if she would ever be ready for love again. It was not a subject she usually broached, particularly not when it was early and she had a lot to do. Scraping the last bite on her plate, she jumped up and tossed a light sweater over her shoulders and retrieved her keys.

"Let's go," she said.

Libby and Snowy followed them to the door. Jamie bent down and scratched behind Libby's ears. Snowy rubbed her face against his leg, claiming her territory.

"Bye, guys," he said, opening the screen for them to race out. "Off you go to chase lizards and things." The cats raced out the door.

"Bye, Daddy. Bye, Auntie." Amber scooted out of the kitchen chair and raced to the door. She jumped into Jamie's arms and smothered him with kisses, then turned to Cathy and reached out her arm. Cathy moved in close for a group hug. Over Jamie's shoulder, Cathy could see Pam watching intently from the kitchen.

Jamie sat Amber down and went to the kitchen to kiss Pam on the cheek. "Thanks for breakfast, hon. You girls have a fun day, okay?"

Pam's high beams were on again. "Off to work you go," she sing-songed to them.

Cathy parked in the back of the shop and led Jamie in through the kitchen.

"Good morning, Tim," she said.

Tim stopped straightening up a shelf and waved.

"Mornin', boss lady," he said. His gaze moved over to Jamie and a half-grin crossed his face. He sauntered over and put an arm around them both. "And to you, Jamie. I couldn't be more happy to see you two. I thought I was going to have to handle the whole place myself. And I am noooo chef!"

"But he makes one fab cocktail," Cathy said.

"I do have talent in some areas," he said, preening in his flared bell-bottom pants and shiny disco shirt.

"I bet he does," Jamie whispered to Cathy.

Jamie's little aside comments always made her laugh. "Back to work," she said. Cathy pulled the lunch board out and stuck it at the entrance of the café area, then joined Jamie in the kitchen for the prep.

That was the last thing she remembered until four hours later when the full lunch rush was over. Their first day of service had gone amazingly well. Jamie was a wizard in the kitchen. They worked perfectly in sync, hardly needing to say a word. A look, a point, and he knew exactly what she wanted or needed.

Like they'd spent lifetimes working together.

She snapped back into reality, at least today's reality.

"Oh, by the way," Cathy said, "tomorrow is the day I visit the Head Start program for kids after lunch. The one I told you about. I can drop you at home if you don't want to come."

"Tell me more about it again," he said.

He looked genuinely interested, so she explained how she brought over healthy sandwiches and snacks for the low-income kids. "I really want them to understand nutrition. Many of them are not learning that at home."

"I'd be happy to help. I'll bring the station wagon for extra room if you want."

"Sounds good."

Cathy headed to the back room and dialed Jill's home number. Her husband, Dan, had called last night to tell her Jill had her appendix removed and would be in bed a while.

Dan answered on the third ring.

"How's the patient?" Cathy asked.

Dan hesitated. "She's fine," he said. Then in a whisper he added, "But not having an easy time staying in bed or not helping with the kids. She wants to go back to work."

"I'll set her straight. Just tell me when it's a good time to visit."

Dan assured Cathy that in a few days Jill would be better and more settled.

"Well, tell her I send my love and will see her Thursday. Tomorrow I'll be at Head Start. And tell her to rest or else!"

Cathy leaned against the wall. There was a lot going on. She really needed a break, some time to think, a glass of wine.

She walked back into the store, where Jamie and Tim were having a quiet conversation. From the look on Jamie's face, it looked intense. Cathy walked a few steps toward them. "Hey, you two, something going on I should know about?"

Tim raised an eyebrow. "If you only knew," he said, smirking.

"Listen, I'm going to run over to Sebastian's Bar for a glass of wine. Do you think you two could finish up here?"

Jamie looked surprised. "Sure, if that's what you want."

No, it was not what Cathy wanted, but it was what she needed. She was alone. Jamie was married to Pam. "You know, I just need to clear my head."

His face looked concerned.

"No worries," she said. "Just want some alone time."

"Check ya later," Tim said. "I'll take Jamie home."

"Oh, there's a fantasy come true," she teased.

Tim was a good friend. He'd been through a lot of heart-ache, and many nights the two of them had shared their sad luck stories over a drink. He knew her well and probably felt her vibe.

"Be good, you two." Cathy waved as she walked toward the rear exit.

Jamie followed Tim to the front of the store. "Hey, thanks for offering to take me home," Jamie said, watching Cathy leave.

"Anytime," Tim said with a wink.

Jamie was quite sure that was an invitation. He certainly was not interested in men, but he could tell Tim probably knew that already.

"I'll be right back," Jamie said. "I'm going to call and let my girls know I'll be home soon."

Jamie picked up the back phone and dialed. It made him uneasy thinking about Cathy wandering off to a bar by herself.

"Hello," Pam said, her voice rising.

Jamie couldn't tell if she felt chipper or stressed. He knew Pam wanted a home, and he was trying to give it to her. But he wanted Amber to grow up with a yard to play in, open fields and trees, not some dirty city. He'd pushed hard to try the Wine Country, hoping she'd relax and find it as soothing as he did. She was a great mom to Amber, and he was sure Pam would see Sonoma was the perfect place for a kid to grow up.

"How was your day?" Jamie said. He could hear the TV in the background. Pam relayed their day sewing new clothes, making cheese sandwiches, and watching Romper Room and Captain Kangaroo.

"I'll be home to see my two girls soon," Jamie said before hanging up and returning to the front of the store. "Do you need any help with closing?" he asked Tim.

Tim opened the cash register drawer and started counting bills. He placed a stack of one-dollar bills on the counter in front of Jamie. "How are your counting skills? Are those hands as good with sorting as they are with cooking?"

Jamie shrugged. "We'll find out," he said. He sorted the bills in piles of ten, enjoying the mindless work.

"So, how do you like working at Health & Hearth so far?"

Jamie finished counting the money in front of him. "I dig it," he said. "Cathy is easy to work with, and the clientele are friendly."

"Cathy's special all right," Tim stared at Jamie.

Tim didn't miss much.

"I could see myself having a place like this someday," Jamie said. "Maybe adding an upscale dinner service too."

"Cathy might be interested in expanding. You could broach the subject with her."

Jamie let the idea run through his mind. Working with Cathy every day. He could run the dinner service and expand the menu. The two of them could really build the business. "I need to get something stable right now," Jamie finally said. "With a wife and child to support, I need to interview high end."

Tim nodded. "We can't always get what we want. Take me, for instance. Last year I fell in love with this hot guy who forgot to mention he was already married to a woman."

"I'm sorry, man," Jamie said. "That must have hurt."

"It always hurts when you can't have the one you love." A pained expression crossed Tim's face. "And he loved me too, but he couldn't leave his wife or she'd keep the child."

Jamie's stomach contracted. Was that line directed at him? He certainly felt like he was falling hard for Cathy. Falling wasn't the word, more like rolling over a cliff and having nothing to hold on to. This was not like him. His eye never strayed from the marriage.

Tim closed and locked the cash register drawer. "You ready to get truckin'?"

Jamie didn't really know what he was ready for. "Right behind you. Lead the way."

Cathy pulled into the dirt parking lot of Sebastian's Bar just off River Road. There were a few pickup trucks and an assortment of cars. It was a popular place with the locals.

The atmosphere with the high-beam ceilings, old photos, and memorabilia on the walls always felt cheery. Richard, the bartender, waved at her from behind the L-shaped oak bar. He was the owner and was almost always there with his wife, Kate, who still looked like she lived in southern California. She was young and gorgeous, with her long blonde hair and manicured nails, but she always looked a little overdressed here in the woods. The guys didn't seem to mind one bit. That was a no-brainer. As long as they didn't put the moves on her, all was fine. She was clearly off-limits.

Cathy sat up at the counter and ordered a glass of chardonnay. "Bohemian Rhapsody" was playing on the jukebox, and she caught a lyric about trying to escape from reality. She could relate. Taking a sip of wine, she surveyed the surroundings. The usual carpenter-looking guys were there in work boots, Levis, T-shirts, and flannels with the sleeves rolled up. Most straight guys on the river were carpenters, or at least trying to be. She'd dated a few. Real estate started to boom, and with all the remodels and odd jobs, there was a lot of work for craftsmen.

A couple of Cathy's regulars waved to her from the pool table. She waved back.

"Your nectar of the gods, my lady." Richard set a chilled glass before her with a mock bow.

"Where's Kate?" Cathy asked.

He started towel-drying some glasses. "She should be here any minute. I think she was working on her tan at Wohler Beach today."

Cathy raised her eyebrows. "You let her go there alone?"

"She knows the secluded places. Most of the guys down there are gay anyway." He laughed. "She knows how to protect herself just fine, and the all-over tan ..." He winked at her.

Cathy shook her head. "You men, is that all you ever think about?" She forced back a smile as Richard turned to help another customer.

Sitting to Cathy's left on a bar stool was a hunky guy. He was obviously tall, with dark hair falling around his face, and long slender fingers wrapped around a cold beer. He appeared to be in conversation with the woman on the other side of him. The woman leaned over, breasts bulging out almost in his face, and tried hard to get and keep his attention. Her eyes drifted to Cathy.

Cathy watched the woman throw her woven purse up on the bar and reach in.

What was she getting out, a sign that said, "He's mine!"

Mellow out, lady, Cathy thought.

The cutie turned toward Cathy, and she saw his eyes travel down her body and back up.

"Hello," he said. "Name's Chuck."

His front view was even better. Cathy flirted a bit, sipping her wine, fully aware that the woman on his other side was giving her dirty looks. He was very attractive, funny, and seemed nice. But what was she going to do, invite him home with company there? Or, if she didn't come home tonight they'd wonder where she was.

Her mind drifted to Jamie. Suddenly the game did not seem that interesting.

On the other side of Chuck, Miss I-Want-Your-Body pulled out a large jar of Vaseline and put it in on the bar. When Cathy started to laugh, he turned to see why.

The woman pushed the jar over in front of Chuck and gazed, most suggestively, into his eyes. Cathy watched his body freeze and couldn't wait to see what he would do next. The jukebox banged out "Love is in the Air," but in this case, love was in the Vaseline jar.

Cathy found this hilarious. Was the woman suggesting …? Of course she was!

Chuck pushed it back toward the woman. Cathy leaned over and saw her shrug, drop it back in her purse, and get up to leave. She shot Cathy one more dagger-eyed look and walked out.

Chuck turned to Cathy, and they both cracked up. "Can I buy you another glass of wine?" he asked.

Normally she would have said yes and known where the evening was headed. "Sorry, not tonight," Cathy said. "Company is waiting for me at home."

"Can I have your number?" he said, pulling a matchbox out of the dish on the bar.

She wrote down a fake one, kissed his cheek, and made her exit.

Chapter Twelve

Cathy overslept the next morning, exhausted after the day back at work and the late night at Sebastian's. Now they were running late, with no breakfast. Jamie was driving them to the shop this morning. It took a little extra time to load more produce from her garden and bring supplies for later, when they would work with the Head Start kids. Cathy's stomach growled, and she hoped he didn't hear it. She looked over at the bag of food he'd brought along and waited for him to offer. But he just kept staring straight ahead again.

He was making her ask. It was ridiculous. Was he mad at her?

"What's in the bag?" she asked.

He opened it and produced a luscious-looking scone. She reached out her hand and waited. Nothing.

"Please," she said, trying not to sound annoyed.

He handed one over with a look of victory. It was delicious, better than the ones in the shop. Another recipe she would have to ask for.

Jamie turned the corner a little fast and mumbled under his breath when a driver almost cut him off.

"Is anything wrong?" she asked.

"Just tired," he snapped. "I didn't sleep real well last night."

Cathy took another bite of the flaky scone. "Hope I didn't wake you when I came in?"

He shot her a side glance. "It *was* late."

"So?" she said. When did he become her gatekeeper?

"So, I was worried."

Cathy swallowed hard. She wasn't used to anyone caring when, or even if, she got home. Except maybe the cats. But they could go a few days as long as there was food and water. She touched his arm. "I'm sorry."

He pulled into the parking lot behind the shop, switched off the car, and turned to face her. Hurt was written across his face. "I know it's not my place. I know ..."

"Jamie, stop. Thank you for caring."

They held each other's gaze. The silent communication said all they could not voice.

Tim had just opened the shop when they arrived. Already there was a lineup for his Wednesday morning special: carrot, raisin, apple muffins with organic coffee. She doubted Jamie could top those.

"Morning, Tim, how's it going?" Jamie said, like he'd worked there forever. "Shall we show Cathy how this place should be run?"

Jamie threw her an apron.

Cathy caught it in midair. "Watch out, or I'll tie this apron around your neck and pull the strings tight." First he withholds food from her and now he knows how to run things better than her?

His grin distracted her. What time she got home was really none of his business. She could take care of herself and they had a lunch to get ready. Prep began, and soon the café was filled with the scents of fresh-baked honey bread for the curried tuna sandwich special.

Apron on, Cathy was ready to work. Jamie was at the sink, washing the leeks then chopping them with brisk, fine strokes. On the stove in a large pan, butter melted into luscious cream on one burner, and garlic and potatoes sautéed with the leeks and rosemary on another. The aromas made her mouth water.

Her hands were wrist-deep in veggie burger mix now, as she squeezed the beans, rice, veggie, and chopped nut mixture and added some fine olive oil. She could feel Jamie watching her. She was not used to this scrutiny in her own place.

"Would you like some to play with too?" she asked, holding up a handful of the mushy mixture.

Immediately she felt like an idiot. Playing with your food was not exactly his level of expertise. His frown did not help. She mixed with renewed vigor.

"We could make snowballs," he said with a wink. Now he was next to her, watching over her shoulder. She could feel sweat beading on her upper lip.

She held up her grimy hands. "May I pass to wash or …?"

"Mind if I taste it?" he said.

"It's a great recipe; everyone loves it," she snapped. She had no need to feel defensive, but he was making her nervous. "Go ahead," she said before she could dry her hands and strangle him.

His long, shapely finger dipped into the mixture and then popped into his mouth.

"Tasty. Have you thought about adding some chives and a touch of cumin?"

Cathy wanted to be mad, but his voice sounded so innocent and it was a damn good idea. "No, but that sounds good."

He dropped a bunch of chives on the cutting board next to her to chop. He must have been used to working with a sous chef who did all the prep work while he was the recipe creator. What the heck, she had time.

Jamie added the sautéed leeks into the warm creamy butter mixture and then poured half into the VitaMixer. Quick pulses blended the ingredients, and then he poured it back into the soup pot.

"Voila, cream of potato leek soup, served hot or cold." He held a spoonful to her mouth.

It was smooth, flavorful, a perfect mixture of cream soup and chunky goodness. Better than Jill made, but Cathy would not say that aloud.

"Pretty good," she said.

He glared at her, waiting. He knew just how good it was.

"Okay, great." Cathy turned to get more ingredients. She sliced tomatoes for sandwiches and stocked the salad containers, trying not to notice how efficient Jamie was. She should be happy. Customers loved his food. But what about after he left?

"So, are you going to share your recipes with us before you take off to gourmet pastures?" Cathy asked.

"Of course, but I want chef's credit," he said.

Cathy turned to give him a dirty look, but the sparkle in his eyes told her he was kidding. He knew he pushed her all-too-easy buttons. "I will name today's special after you."

He cocked his head in contemplation. "That's acceptable."

"It better be," she said, throwing a dishtowel at him.

Customers started coming in for an early lunch. A few took seats. "It's still damp and foggy out there," said a woman sitting at the counter, who worked at the Guerneville 5 & 10. She was lucky to find her way out of that store; there was so much stuff everywhere.

"Where's Jill?" Susan from the post office asked.

"Home resting," Cathy said.

She shrugged her shoulders and studied the chalkboard menu. "Is the potato leek soup any good?"

What did she think? Just because Jill wasn't there, the food wasn't good?

"Well, let's ask the chef." She turned to Jamie.

He ladled some soup in a bowl and snatched a spoon. "Now, who would like a taste?"

Charm oozed from every word. He got several takers. A middle-aged woman in a green cardigan took a sip and murmured, "Ooh." A young man with shoulder-length hair brushing over his army jacket sighed, "Wow."

Jamie looked pleased. Orders for soup poured in. Cathy ladled bowls for the customers while Jamie passed around a tray of veggie burger bites.

"If you guess the secret ingredient, your burger is free," he said.

Now he was giving away free food. Cathy was going to have to watch this guy.

The shop filled up fast with locals and tourists, and no one was leaving. Jamie knew his way around people. Cathy tasted the dressing for the grated salad that Jamie had doctored with mustard and lemon: divine.

"Hey, Cathy, the food was good before, but now it's dy-no-mite," Susan yelled from her table.

Cathy frowned. "Careful now, we don't want it to go to his head, do we?"

Jamie winked at her. "Praise where praise is due."

I guess wanting to hit him over the head is better than wanting to kiss him, she thought.

The next few hours were a whirlwind. No way she could have done it without him. The word was out about town, and all six tables, the counter, and the booths stayed full most of the afternoon. Tim scrambled in the front selling products, and Cathy looked forward to seeing the results on paper.

Jamie cleaned the kitchen while Cathy counted the tabs.

"Good draw?" he asked, sweeping the floor beside her.

"Beginner's luck." She continued rifling through the receipts. He was no beginner and that was clear, but what could she say? Thank you. You're a god in the kitchen?

Maybe she could get on her knees and beg him for the recipes. It was crazy. She didn't want to get too accustomed to having him around. Jill was golden and the business was successful before he arrived. She didn't need him. But he was a perfect fit.

Cathy turned and faced Jamie. "Thank you. I couldn't have done it without you."

"My pleasure," he said with a satisfied grin. "I'll fix something to eat now and take a break."

With the rush over, Cathy took a break too. Jamie made a veggie burger he'd doctored with guacamole, grilled chilies, and onions. A pile of his special-baked garlic fries steamed next to it. Her mouth watered. But today she was going to eat healthy. She put together a grated salad of beets, carrots, and daikon and joined him at a table. Her feet were killing her, but he didn't look a bit tired.

"Busy day," she said, spooning avocado slices drenched in Tahini dressing into her mouth. Ambrosia.

"You have a great little business here, Cat, and some loyal customers."

Cat. No one called her Cat. She kind of liked it. "Thanks."

Jamie's eyes were pale blue today and easy to get lost in. She glanced back at the salad but could feel his stare. Heat crept up her spine. She snuck a look at his fingers and remembered how perfectly they prepped the food, held the knives, held her hand. He placed a fry, smothered with roasted garlic, under her nose for a whiff.

"Tempting," she said.

He waved it in front of her. "Bite?"

She opened her mouth. Jamie placed the fry gently between her lips and watched her bite down. She could hardly breathe, much less chew. But the savory flavor of roasted garlic on the buttery potato skin was hard to resist. "Divine. We should make these a regular on the menu."

"We could call them Jamie's Fries," he said between bites.

There was that smirk of his again. She glared back with mock annoyance then continued to eat her salad. She could feel his gaze but refused to look up.

"Thanks for letting us stay with you. I'm sure I'll have a job soon."

When she looked up this time, she saw a man struggling. She could relate. It was hard for him to ask, hard for him to say thank you, and probably hard for him with his Cordon Bleu degree to work in a health food café. For free no less.

"Any restaurant would be lucky to have you," Cathy said.

His face melted into a spectacular smile. She liked the way his blond hair curled around his face and turned up in a flip at his shoulders. The way his eyelids drooped slightly like a puppy dog's.

"I have an interview tomorrow in Sonoma, but not until the afternoon. I can still help you through lunch."

Jamie's eyes flashed concern. Sonoma County had some great restaurants, and he seemed to really like it up here. But it was not like a big city with jobs everywhere.

"Good luck. They'll love you." She would hate losing him, but she meant it.

After putting away dishes, they started gathering food and supplies to bring for the kids' afterschool program. She didn't want to forget napkins this time.

"Go ahead and pack the mashed avocado and some of the leftover grated veggies," she told Jamie.

He put plastic wrap over the bowls and loaded them into an ice chest. "So, what do you usually do over there?"

"We make sandwiches, sometimes, or bake oatmeal raisin cookies."

Jamie reached for something on the back counter. "I made extra bread this morning, so we could lay out some different proteins and vegetable combinations and help them make a nutritious snack. Kids need to know these things."

"Great idea," Cathy said. "We could bring some tofu egg salad, real cheddar cheese, and nut butters. And maybe talk about how to grow sprouts in a jar."

Jamie smiled. He was obviously all over this idea. "We have lettuce and radishes from your garden. We could add them to the sandwiches.

Next he unplugged the VitaMixer. She gave him a quizzical look.

"You'll see," he said with a wink.

Good thing they'd brought the station wagon. The kids and counselors were going to love this, Cathy thought.

Jamie and Cathy drove up and parked in front of the big entry door. It was open, and they could see the kids playing pool. Other kids ran, yelling as they chased a bouncing ball. Books and games were scattered across tables, along with a TV set, and an eight-track tape player all donated by local businesses. A few of the younger kids ran to the door to greet them.

"It's the food lady," said a skinny boy with frizzy hair and a torn shirt. Cathy hoped this was not his only meal today. Larry, an older boy who'd been there a while, rode over on his skateboard and skidded to a stop in front of them. He was in his usual cutoffs and no shirt. "Got anything good in there?" he asked.

"Come on in and see," Jamie said.

They walked into the kitchen and started laying out food.

"What did you bring us today?" little Rio asked. He had just started kindergarten and was one of Cathy's biggest fans.

Jamie pulled out a box. "How do strawberry banana smoothies sound?"

Rio stared at him. "Is that like a milkshake?"

"Absolutely," Jamie said. "Only better."

They were drawing a crowd. The young boys and girls poured into the big kitchen area. Barb, Cathy's friend from the book group, was the working counselor today and followed in behind the kids.

"C'mon," she said loud enough to drown out the Raffi song on the tape player. "Who wants to see what Cathy is making today?"

After getting the youngsters' attention, Barb introduced Jamie as a gourmet chef.

"What's a gor-may?" asked Geneva, a cute little girl with long black braids.

Jamie pronounced it for her and said, "It's a fancy name for someone who went to school to learn how to cook well."

"You went to school to learn how to cook?" little red-headed Justin asked. "Anyone knows how to do that."

They all laughed. It was time to get down to business before the enrichment hour was over.

Jamie started by telling everyone, in simple language, that the government was trying to get people to eat well to stay healthy. "Not everyone agrees on what is healthy," he said. "But Cathy and I think that natural foods, foods you see in nature, are pretty good for you."

A hand shot up. "My mom makes me eat my vegetables every day. But I don't really like them."

"Me too," a few kids echoed.

Cathy brought out the fresh baked wheatberry bread and held it up. "How about sandwiches? Do you all like them?"

A resounding "yes" filled the room.

She loved volunteering here and Jamie fit right in.

Jamie unwrapped the plates with sliced vegetables, avocado, tuna, cheese, and tofu egg salad. "Why don't you all get in line? When you come by the table up here, Cathy and I will help you choose which things taste great and are good for you, too."

Barb led the way. Cathy let the kids choose their toppings and suggested a sprinkle of grated carrots or beets. Not everyone was willing, but most were interested enough to try.

"What's this yellowy white stuff?" Rio asked.

Jamie laughed. "It's tofu egg salad. Made with soy bean curd instead of eggs."

"Yuck."

Five-year-old Annie, in her faded blouse and ill-fitting shorts, tapped Rio on the arm. "Mr. Rogers says to try new things."

"Annie, that's just a TV show," he said, skipping the tofu salad and moving to the alfalfa sprouts.

Jamie stepped in. "Rio, if you eat sprouts, the Force will be with you!"

Rio's eyes opened wide.

"Like Luke Skywalker?" said one of the older boys.

Jamie nodded, keeping a straight face.

The veggies moved fast after that.

When all the kids finished the line and Jamie whipped up smoothies, they sat down at the long table to eat. Annie came and snuggled next to them. "I like my smoothie," she said. "Pink's my favorite color."

Cathy's heart went out to Annie every time she saw her. Today, Annie's hair needed washing and some tender loving care. Last week she looked like she'd slept in her clothes. But most of all it was Annie's eyes that pulled on Cathy's soul. That exact mixture of sorrow and fear reminded Cathy of herself at that age.

Jamie froze beside Cathy and stopped in mid-sentence. Cathy turned to see what was wrong. Jamie nodded his head toward Annie's arm. She was holding up the smoothie. Revealing itself under Annie's sleeve was a large bruise. It was obvious by the shape that someone had grabbed and held Annie's forearm very tight.

Cathy willed herself not to throw up. A white heat raged through her body. There had to be something they could do for this little girl.

Annie caught the stares and quickly pulled her sleeve down over the bruise. She forced a smile. "It's okay," she said. "I just fell down."

Cathy put her arm around Annie's shoulder. "I'm sorry you … fell down."

Annie shrugged. "It doesn't hurt anymore."

Larry slid his skateboard over to the table and butted in. "Annie's always falling down. No one picks her for their team either."

Jamie leaned over and met Larry eye-to-eye. "Annie would be my first pick for any team. In fact, next week she is going to be my assistant chef."

"That's not fair," Larry sneered. He picked up his skateboard and sat farther down the table.

Jamie shot a look at Cathy. She could read his thoughts. He sat down next to Annie. "Did you know strawberry smoothies help heal every hurt?" Jamie asked Annie.

Annie's eyes opened wide. "Really?"

Jamie held up his glass. "Bottoms up."

Annie giggled and gulped down some smoothie.

"You too, Cat," he said. Jamie stood. "My glass is empty. I better go pour a refill. Cat, could you come help me?"

Cathy followed him to the kitchen. She had a good idea what his real motive was.

"Why hasn't anyone done anything about Annie?" Jamie demanded.

Cathy sighed. "Barb and all the counselors are aware of this. Social Services has been notified, but they can't prove anything."

Jamie slammed his hand on the counter. "The bruises aren't enough?"

"This afterschool program is all Annie has. Her mother has threatened to pull her out of here if the counselors make any more trouble for her."

"I can't believe we're suppose just turn our heads and ignore it."

"I know. It's horrible. But for now, we just need to feed her and give her all the love we can."

Jamie wiped away a lingering tear from his cheek. "For now only."

Cathy nodded and held out her hand to shake on it. Jamie's hand in hers was warm and reassuring. Resolved, they walked back to the lunch table.

"Miss Cathy," Annie said. "Is he your boyfriend?"

"Yeah, is he your boyfriend?" Larry called out.

Everyone looked at them. Jamie grinned. Cathy's face felt like a third-degree sunburn.

"No," she said. "Jamie and I work together."

A bit of twinkle left Jamie's eyes, and the kids looked suspicious.

Cathy put her arm loosely around Jamie's shoulder. "We're friends."

The kids smiled, and eating resumed. Cathy removed her arm and sipped her smoothie, trying to cool off before they packed up and headed home. What if she'd had a champion like Jamie when she was a little girl? Someone she could show her bruises to and would take her side? Under the table, Cathy placed her hand over Jamie's and whispered, "Thank you."

He looked perplexed. "For what?"

That's easy, she thought. "For being you."

Jamie's gaze said all she needed to know.

Barb stood up and clapped her hands. "Time for everyone to start cleaning up,"

The kids picked up the plates and cups and put them in the big trash bins. Cathy and Jamie packed up their supplies.

Barb met them at the door. "Time to say thank you to Cathy and Jamie."

A big thank you resonated through the room, followed by multiple forms of goodbye.

Annie raced over and hugged Jamie. "Will I really be assistant chef next week?"

"You bet," he said. "I wouldn't want anyone else for the job."

Barb carried the blender and followed them out to the car. "Thanks again. You two are great together. The kids really enjoyed themselves."

Jamie and Cathy both said thanks at the same time.

"See you next week," Barb said, waving goodbye.

When they got home, Pam was made up like she was going to the Academy Awards. A clutter of pink makeup boxes laid open on the coffee table."

"I had the most fun today," she said. "Ellen, the Mary Kay lady from Santa Rosa, came by and did a makeover on me." She held her face up to the light. "What do you think?"

Cathy was not sure what to think. Pam looked like a little child who got into her mother's makeup.

Jamie quickly chimed in. "Attractive."

Pam puffed out her lips. "Do you like this Pink Posey lipstick? Caroline has the same shade. It stays on all day."

Their friend, Caroline, always reminded Cathy of a perfect, pretty doll with silky hair and all the right outfits. Barbie had left her mark on Caroline. But Cathy highly doubted that anyone with Caroline's tastes would buy Mary Kay. Lancôme maybe.

"And look at my fingers, Daddy!" Amber held up both hands to show off her glittery nails. They matched her sparkly T-shirt and barrettes that held back her curls.

Cathy admired her rainbow-colored nails one by one. "Gorgeous!"

"Very cool," Jamie said. "My two pretty girls had fun today, I see."

Pam held up a basket of pink-labeled products she had bought. "More than that! All of this was only twenty-five dollars to get started. Now I can be a businesswoman too."

Was that really the best choice? Cathy wondered. But then who knew what she herself would do if left home all day with a four-year-old and trying to help out? Caroline's influence was in the air. Cathy made a mental note to check her phone bill for long distance calls to Santa Barbara.

Pam rattled on about possibly becoming a Mary Kay representative and how she'd make lots of cash. She meant well, but Cathy had her doubts about success with Mary Kay on the River. Makeup was not big with most of the back-to-the-earth types here in Forestville.

"Then I can make everyone gorgeous," Pam said. "You know, Cathy was one of those pretty people in high school."

Pam looked at Jamie for a reaction. Nothing like putting him on the spot.

"Ah …" Jamie muttered. "I'm sure you both were."

Cathy felt her cheeks burn. "Not as popular as you, Pam, Miss Head Cheerleader."

Suddenly Pam was up, throwing her arms in the air, repeating an old cheer. "Hey all you in the stands, jump up and down and clap your hands! Come on, Cathy, join me."

"I … I've forgotten how. Too long ago."

Amber ran over and started kicking and jumping in the air beside her mom. Pam beamed at Jamie as she finished her cheer, slightly out of breath.

"My, my," he said. "My two beautiful girls are so talented."

Amber giggled and ran into his arms. She looked so safe and loved. Cathy wanted to run there too.

"She's definitely a daddy's girl," Pam said. "Just like you were, Cathy, when you were a kid."

Cathy froze and glared at her, willing her to shut up.

Pam's smile widened. "Cathy had the coolest dad. We all loved hanging out at her house and swimming in her Doughboy pool."

Jamie's eyes flashed to Cathy. She tried keeping her face a rigid mask. That was another lifetime ago. Her dad, who everyone thought was the most wonderful dad ever, was not the same man behind closed doors. Cathy shuddered. To the whole town he was the great guy, the people's attorney who always helped the underdog. At home, some of his inflicted bruises could be covered by clothing and makeup. But the most painful ones, on the inside, were hushed and hidden. Her mother recycled the whiskey bottles out of sight.

"Where is your dad now, Auntie Cathy?"

Amber's eyes looked so innocent. How could Cathy tell a four-year-old that his final abandonment was drinking himself to death at forty-five? That day the earth opened and took her dad, her heart, and her life with it.

But Pam always thought Cathy's dad was so great. The way she'd looked at him was heartbreaking. Pam's own dad had picked up and left them when she was only five years old. As much as Cathy needed a friend to confide secrets to, someone on her side, Pam would never have believed what Cathy's father was really like. It was lonely having a secret and no one to tell it to. She was the good girl at school. Her mother's crutch at home. A support to her poor friend Pam. But there was no one there for her.

Pam put her arm around Cathy's shoulder and squeezed. "Cathy's dad is in heaven now. Sometimes the good die young."

"Oh," Amber said. "Like our old dog, Lady?"

"Yes, honey," Jamie said. "Just like Lady."

The room became quiet. Cathy pushed the searing pain back to the dark recesses inside her, and forced a smile. She'd become a master at denial.

"Who wants some ice cream?" Cathy asked. There was nothing ice cream couldn't fix. That was what her dad said when he was in his "it's over, let's put it behind us" mode.

"Me, I do!" Amber ran ahead of Cathy to the kitchen, with her mother close on her heels.

Cathy felt a warm hand on her shoulder.

"Are you okay?" Jamie asked.

The sympathy in his eyes made her want to scream, "Don't be. Don't make me feel!" Before she could respond, Pam yelled for them to hurry up before the ice cream melts.

The Lucerne chocolate ice cream, bought as a special treat, was cool and soothing. It worked its momentary magic. Cathy took her dish and retreated to the privacy of the wing-back chair in her room. The luscious treat was gone all too soon, along with any comfort it offered. She placed the dish on the side table and leaned back, staring at the ceiling, willing her racing mind to stop.

Once stirred up, she couldn't stop the memories. Men were so good at compartmentalizing their feelings. First was her father, who saw himself through the eyes of everyone but his family. Then her ex-husband, Todd, who was a pro at ignoring the nagging voices that interfered with him doing whatever he wanted to do, no matter who got hurt. Cathy wondered if Pam's dad was like that: I want out of here, so goodbye wife, goodbye child, I'm gone.

Cathy sought out neat little cubicles in her memory to place these thoughts in permanent storage. The one for her dad was nicely decorated but mostly inaccessible. The one for her baby girl, who never saw past four months' gestation, was pink and pretty but covered with a no trespassing sign. She never wanted to go there again. The one for Todd was a dark pool where dreams went to drown.

Giggles echoed into Cathy's bedroom as Jamie, Pam, and Amber walked down the hall toward the bedrooms. Their visit had caused a fissure that rumbled through all her caves and caverns. She wanted them to leave; that was the lie she told herself.

Jamie. He broke her heart in a whole new way … with kindness and longing. The hole in her heart that she tried so hard to keep filled with work, food, friends, sleep, or anything, was preferable to these feelings that were tearing her open.

She imagined herself a lone wolf, wandering the wilderness, searching, then raising her head and releasing a piercing howl that filled the entire universe.

Wolves mated for life. Where was he? Where was the echo to her howl, her mate? Was there no other lone wolf, searching the hills for her? Was she the only one destined to cry in the night and never be heard? Never be answered? In her mind, she howled to the heavens, and mercifully, Jamie's warm laugh echoed back and filled her heart.

Chapter Thirteen

It was a good thing that the afternoon slowed at the shop. With Jamie leaving early for his interview and Brian not back yet, it could have been hectic. Cathy called Jill to confirm she was up for a visit later that afternoon. Cathy decided to stop home briefly, to see if there was any news on Jamie's interview and pick a bouquet of herbs and flowers for Jill.

At home, Pam was in the kitchen making a salad. Jamie was still at the interview. Cathy held up a bag of fresh-baked lemon cookies. Amber saw them and came running. Her golden pigtails flapped like she would take off.

"No cookies until after dinner," Pam yelled.

"When is Daddy getting home? I'm hungry," Amber said, rubbing her tummy.

Pam dried her hands and came into the living room. "Amber didn't get her nap today, so she's a little grumpy. How was your day, Cathy?"

For a moment Cathy was taken back. No one ever asked her that. Libby and Snowy just purred, if they bothered getting up at all.

"Thanks for asking," Cathy said. "It was busy, but Jamie is a great help."

Pam grinned. "Isn't he just the best?" she said, baring a full row of teeth with her smile. "We don't know what we'd do without him. Right, Amber?"

Cathy couldn't believe Pam would bring up the possibility of Jamie not being with them. What kind of image was that to put in a four-year-old's mind?

Amber's face looked worried. "Daddy's coming home soon. Right, Mommy?"

Pam hugged Amber. "Of course, of course, little one."

Cathy laid her purse and some papers on the counter. She pulled out a pitcher of iced tea and a bottle of lemonade to make an Arnold Palmer.

Pam laid two glasses on the counter. "I think I'll have one too."

"And what about you, Amber?" Cathy asked. "Would you like some lemonade?"

Amber nodded. "Can you make it a pink one?"

Pam shrugged. "A pink one?"

Cathy winked at Amber. "We mash a few strawberries in and presto, it's pink!"

"Well, you two girls do have your secrets, don't you?"

Cathy and Amber giggled.

"Come on, Amber, let's sit down with that juice."

They all took a seat at the table and sipped their cool drinks.

"Are you home for the night?" Pam asked, helping Amber into a kitchen chair.

"No, I'm heading over to Jill's house to see how she's feeling."

"Well, let us know, because Jamie may not be available much longer. And we'll have to find our own house soon."

Cathy took a deep breath. "Did he get the job?"

"We're not sure."

Cathy exhaled.

"But Jamie should be home any minute. He called after he left Sonoma Country Inn, and he sounded excited."

Cathy's stomach dropped at the thought of him getting the job. Jill was still bedridden, and there was no one to help. No one would greet her at the door, and there would be no wonderful dinners waiting when she got home. But self-pity was not her style. She learned long ago where that trail led. Cathy forced a smile. "Hope it's good news."

Jill's oldest daughter greeted her at the door and led the way to the bedroom. Dan was handy. He'd converted the thousand-square-foot, two-bedroom house into a three-bedroom by remodeling the basement into a master suite.

Looking pale after her appendectomy, Jill lounged in a red-and-white-checkered robe on the queen-size bed. A fan blew cool air from the window, ruffling the orange and brown hanging lamp at the side of the bed.

Dan, hair askew, wore a wrinkled shirt and was tripping over himself to bring Jill whatever she needed. He had already placed the flowers in a vase by Jill's bed.

The dark circles under Jill's eyes worried Cathy, but Jill was sharp and probing as always.

Jill waved Cathy over. "What's under the foil? What did you bring for me?" she asked, propping herself against the brass headboard.

"Have you been a good patient?" Cathy held the plate just out of her reach. "Dan, has she stayed in bed?"

He nodded and attempted a smile, but he looked exhausted.

"I brought enough for both of you," Cathy lifted the foil to reveal the cookies Jamie baked.

Jill picked up one and held it to her nose. "Lemon, honey, and something else." She took a bite and closed her eyes. "Lavender. Yum. Who made these?" she said, handing one to Dan.

Cathy knew she couldn't take credit because baking was not her strong suit. With salads and sandwiches she could hold her own.

"Jamie, my houseguest, baked them. He's a real help right now. So you don't have to worry. Chill."

"Like I have a choice." Jill popped another cookie in her mouth and sighed. "Lie in bed, eat, and watch stupid daytime TV for another week. I'll go crazy."

Cathy could relate. "What did the doctor tell you to do?"

Dan held up a list and started reading. "First twelve hours, stay in bed and watch for fever." He glared at Jill. "Most patients need two to three weeks of rest."

Jill sat up straight in bed. "He did say some people get better fast, after only a week."

Cathy patted her on the shoulder. "We'll see. Now lie down. I want you better!"

Jill always worked so hard that she exhausted Cathy just watching her. As an employee, she could not be replaced.

Jamie was a real lifesaver, but Jill was the heart and soul of the business.

"Dan, don't you have something to do somewhere in the house?" Jill waved him out and patted the bed beside her for Cathy to sit. "Something bothering you?"

"No, not really. I'm just worried about you getting well."

Jill stared at Cathy like the darn clairvoyant she was. Nothing got past Jill. "Tell me about Jamie."

Cathy's eyes darted around the room. She rose. "It feels a bit warm in here. Do you want me to turn up the fan?"

"Sit down, Cathy."

She sat. Sometimes she wondered just who the boss was around here.

"What, are you planning to oust me for this new chef who can bake cookies out of a dream?" Jill said.

"No, of course not."

Tears threatened. A few days with company, no, with Jamie, and she was falling apart. Cathy wasn't a crier. She wouldn't start now. What was she supposed to say? Well, you see, my best friend and her family are visiting and I'm helping them out and, oh, by the way, I'm captivated by her husband. She didn't think that was something Jill needed to think about now in her condition. And Cathy didn't want Jill to think less of her as a person either.

"Jill, no one could ever replace you."

Satisfaction spread across Jill's face. "The doctor said I might be able to work part-time in a week or two."

"Although," Cathy paused, "this baker is pretty cute."

Jill's eyes penetrated Cathy. "I knew there was something you were hiding from me. How cute? Tell me."

"You lay back down, and I'll return soon with something yummy and tell you more then."

Jill sank back into the propped pillows. Usually, deterring Jill was not so easy. She must feel lousy.

"Okay, but tomorrow I want a full description."

"Fine," Cathy said heading out the door. "Rest."

When Cathy got home, she found a note from Pam saying she and Amber had strolled down to the river for a quick swim. Cathy wanted to fall into her bed. She would hibernate like a bear in its cave before everyone descended on the house again. Even the cats were nowhere to be seen, so she shut the door and embraced slumber.

In the distance she heard a car hitting the gravel in her driveway. Half awake, she realized it was probably Jamie. Muffled sounds came from the living room. Amber screeched the cry she always did when Jamie lifted her to the ceiling.

Maybe Cathy could sleep through dinner in this nice, safe den.

As she almost drifted back to sleep, a light knock sounded at her door.

"Cathy, do you want some dinner? It's ready," Pam said.

Pam's voice brought Cathy back to her parents' house years ago. Pam was always over, especially around dinnertime. Pam's mom never felt well enough to cook, and Pam got sick of cereal.

"Your mom cooks so good," Pam would say with pleading eyes. Then Cathy invited her home with her from school. Sometimes Cathy got sick of having her there all the time and would lock herself in her room. And here she was, as an adult locking herself in her room, in her own house.

"Not now," Cathy said loud enough for Pam to hear. She covered her ears and willed herself back to sleep. She didn't want to think anymore today. Her mind raced with what-ifs. What if Jamie got that job and they left tomorrow? What if he didn't and she had to keep seeing him? Watching him work right next to her? Wanting ... wanting ... to touch his cheek, muss his hair, and feel his arms around her.

Laughter filtered in from the kitchen, and Cathy's stomach clenched. Did Jamie get the job? She wanted to pull the covers over her head and will herself to think of something else. But she knew it was futile. She wasn't a teenager. She would get up and ask.

The three of them were curled up on her couch watching TV. Libby and Snowy snuggled on Pam's lap, and for a moment Cathy felt jealous. All eyes went to her.

"You're up! Come sit with us," Pam said.

Everyone moved in closer to make room. Cathy sat next to Pam, who rested her head on Cathy's shoulder. Very cozy.

"How did the interview go?" Cathy finally asked.

Pam interrupted Jamie's response. "Great! They loved him. We'll know more tomorrow."

"Fantastic," Cathy said, a little too enthusiastically. She closed her eyes and let the white noise of the Alka-Seltzer, plop, plop, fizz, fizz TV commercial lull her. All of a sudden, the theme from *The Love Boat* blasted out all cheery and sweet. Was this what they were watching? She looked at Jamie.

He grinned. "The girls like this show."

Pam sang along about adventure and romance. Amber giggled. Pam probably liked *Fantasy Island*, too, which wasn't Cathy's kind of show. She almost never turned the set on anyway. If her mom hadn't left it behind, she wouldn't even own one.

"Do you like this show?" Pam asked.

"It's fine. Nice scenery," Cathy said.

"Jamie always watches with us. He used to like *The French Chef*, with Julia Child, but it went off the air last year." Pam patted Jamie on the back. "His idol is Alice Waters in San Francisco. I bet you wish she'd do a show."

"I'd certainly watch that!" he said.

"Me too," Cathy seconded. "She's a master at gourmet cooking."

Jamie gave Cathy a thumbs-up.

Cathy watched the big white cruise ship on the screen as it pulled into port in sunny Mexico. She would love to do some traveling. Todd promised her a honeymoon to Hawaii. Like most of his other promises, Cathy never saw the island's sunny shores. Her head rested back onto the couch as the show continued. Snowy jumped on her lap and started purring. It took so little for the cat to be content.

Chapter Fourteen

arely awake, Cathy walked into the kitchen for her first cup of morning coffee. Pam was clamoring away about Jamie possibly getting the job as assistant executive chef at Sonoma Country Inn. She stood at the kitchen counter, looking over the menu he'd brought back and reading every delectable offering.

"Duck a l'orange, lobster bisque, pan-seared trout with lemon zest. And *Black Forest cake* for dessert." She spun on her heel, holding the menu in the air. "Look at the ratings! I bet celebrities eat here. Can you imagine making a soufflé for Farrah Fawcett or even Robert Redford? Make sure you get an autograph for me!"

Cathy imagined Jamie in a black chef uniform that set off his blond highlights, sharpening knives, master of a large kitchen. Pam and Amber would live in a ranch-style home with a golden dog in the yard.

But that only happened in the movies, Cathy reminded herself. She needed to stop this. She was just fine before they got here and would be fine again when they left.

"Breakfast," Jamie announced, placing a stack of blueberry pancakes on the table. Warm butter, heated syrup, and fresh-squeezed orange juice awaited them.

"A celebratory breakfast," Pam said.

"Does that mean he already has the job?" Cathy asked, gulping some juice.

"Not yet," Jamie said, sitting down to join us. "The manager said I'd know by the end of today I gave him the number at your shop. I hope that's okay."

Cathy stuffed down another bit of the fattening meal. After they left, it would be back to granola. "Of course."

Jamie stared at her. "Cat, I might have to start next week."

"Cat," Pam rolled out the word. "You never used to let anyone call you that."

When Jamie called her Cat, it made her smile. She shook off the comment as she drowned her pancakes in more syrup. "Don't worry about helping me. Jill may be back by the time you start, and Brian will be back today or tomorrow."

"Perhaps I could help prep in the morning until Jill is on her feet? If I get the job, I would be doing dinner service only to start."

"We'll see." Cathy carried her plate to the kitchen.

Jamie followed behind with his. "I'm ready to head to work when you are," he said.

The day progressed at the café and no call came for Jamie. His shoulders drooped, and Cathy was torn between sympathy and relief. She kept her distance in the kitchen to allow him some space.

He chopped celery furiously. Then she heard him mutter, "Damn."

"Do you have a bandage?" he asked. Blood dripped from his finger. Cathy grabbed a dishtowel and wrapped it tightly around his finger. She could feel pulsing under her hand.

"Stupid move. I just wasn't paying attention," he said.

Cathy waited until the blood slowed, then hunted for a bandage in the restroom cabinet. She knew where his mind was today. As she rounded the corner to bring him the bandage, the phone rang. She froze. When she heard Tim call Jamie to the phone, her heart pounded. Standing at the edge of the kitchen, she watched Jamie's face and strained to hear.

"Sure, I understand," Jamie said. "Thank you again. Yes, please keep me in mind."

Cathy stepped back so he wouldn't know she heard the conversation and counted to ten before returning to the kitchen. "Bandage," she said, knowing it wouldn't do much good for what really ailed him.

He held out his finger. She wrapped the shiny bandage around the cut. "Good as new."

He sat down at a bar stool, elevating his finger.

"Coffee?" Cathy asked.

He looked up, but his eyes seemed far away.

Cathy poured two cups of coffee and sat down beside him. "Any news?"

"That was the Sonoma Country Inn. Their old chef came back into town, and they felt compelled to give him the job. I would have had the position otherwise."

"Tough luck," Tim said, taking the stool on the other side of Jamie.

"Luck? I'm not having much of that these days."

Tim pointed to Jamie's bandaged finger. "Hey, what's happening here? I can't stand the sight of blood," he said, covering his eyes. "And I don't want to stain my white pants."

Jamie rolled his eyes. "Don't worry, you can peek. It's under control."

Cathy stifled a laugh.

Tim flung an arm around Jamie's shoulder and gave Cathy a knowing look. "If anyone can cheer you up, it's Cathy. And if that doesn't work, I could always take you dancing again."

A customer entered the front of the store, and Tim stood to leave. "Seriously, man, if you need anything, just let me know."

Jamie slid off the stool. "Thanks, Tim. Let's get back to work. At least I can earn my keep."

Cathy stood and blocked his way. She made him look into her eyes. "Jamie, you and your family are welcome in my home as long as you want." His eyes drifted back to the floor. She wanted to hug him but touched his arm instead. "I'm the lucky one having your incredible skills to help me in the café."

"Seems you're the only one who thinks so," he said. "Here I am wanting to feed the world, and I can't even feed my family."

"Jamie, it's a small county. There aren't a lot of jobs. This is not about your skills."

He slipped back onto the stool. "All I can hear is my father's voice saying, 'I told you so.' And Pam is expecting that money and success will just roll in any day."

"At least you're following your dream, pursuing the career you really want."

"I guess so," he said. "Then why does it feel so damn bad? Maybe Pam was right about starting out in a big city first."

"Jamie," Cathy said. "Stop feeling sorry for yourself and get back in the kitchen."

He looked surprised. At least she'd gotten his attention.

She continued, "Get back where you belong, because you are the most incredible chef I've ever met."

Feelings flitted like shadows across his face before he broke out in his boyish grin.

Jamie covered Cathy's hand with his bandaged one. "Thank you."

Cathy followed him back into the kitchen and proceeded to put away the leftover veggie burgers and pull the carob chip cookies out of the oven.

"At least it's Friday," she said to Jamie. "Tomorrow Brian takes over for the Saturday lunch, and we don't serve lunch on Sunday." He kept working with his back to her. "We could all take the rowboat out and head down to the river, have a picnic."

"Amber would like that," he said, sounding better.

"Done then! We'll bring some goodies home to pack up and bring. Then we can sleep in tomorrow as late as we want."

In her mind she planned the perfect day for them. All four of them.

After putting Amber to bed, Jamie buried himself in the classified ads. Pam was curled up in the rocker in the living room, rocking back and forth. She'd been moping around all evening after the news that Jamie didn't get the job.

Cathy sat down beside her. "Would you like to talk?"

Pam stared at her. "Are you tired?"

"Not that much," Cathy said. "Why?"

"I have a little surprise and I think tonight is the night."

Cathy was not sure she was up for a surprise and Jamie looked like he was ready to fall asleep at the table.

"Tequila Sunrises! I bought all the stuff and hid it in the cupboard for a special occasion. No one can be sad with one of those."

Pam's reasoning was a bit flawed, but it sounded like a good way to drown their sorrows. "Let's do it," Cathy said.

Pam bounced up from her chair, hurried over to Jamie, and put her arms around his slouching shoulders. "Honey, do you want to join us for a Tequila Sunrise?"

"No, I'm too tired," he said. He forced a smile. "You two enjoy yourselves. I'm going to bed."

Eyes wide and her lower lip in a pout, Pam stared at him. "You sure?"

Jamie rose and tossed the paper in the trash. "Yes, I'm sure." He turned and left them standing there in the dining room.

Cathy hoped he felt better in the morning. She wished she could put her arms around him and tell him how great he was. Pam wanted to have a party to forget, like she'd seen her mother do. Fix it with a drink. What about love?

Pam turned to Cathy. "Well, why are you just standing there? Let's go make Sunrises."

The blender roared, crushing ice that was placed in tall glasses while Cathy squeezed some fresh orange juice. Pam poured a generous amount of tequila into the glasses. "Now add the sun," she said to Cathy, indicating the orange juice was next. Pam measured a teaspoon of grenadine into each and stirred. "Perfecto." They each took a glass and held it in the air. "To us!" Pam said.

Drinks in hand, they returned to the couch. Cathy had to admit the drink tasted great and the tequila was already relaxing her aching muscles.

"It's been quite a while since we did this, hasn't it?" Pam asked.

"It sure has. What, maybe ten years ago?"

Pam sighed and took a large sip of her drink. "We've known each other twenty years. Can you believe it? It makes me feel old."

"We're not that old. And look what a great life you have now," Cathy said.

"Yeah, I do. A whole lot better than when we met in sixth grade. Remember that dingy apartment I lived in with my mom? You were the only friend I ever let see the place."

Cathy remembered it well. It was up two flights of stairs. Everything seemed gray inside, except Pam's pretty mom with long blonde hair and red lipstick. But she was often resting on the couch, a drink in hand. "I do remember going there a few times, but we usually went to my house."

"That's for sure," Pam said. "You had the best parents and the best stuff. I was so jealous of your clean, white furniture and fluffy pink bedspread. We spent hours outside on the trampoline your dad set up for both us. He always included me."

To Pam he was nice, Cathy thought. To his family, not so much. Even the trampoline had been his gift for all the kids in the neighborhood. He'd made that real clear. It was for the poor kids who had nowhere to play. Cathy was not to use it unless she invited some friends who would lavish thanks on her dad. It was always about show for him. Making sure everyone knew what a great guy he was. Resentment burned in her stomach. She had to let it go.

"He was nice to my mom too," Pam said. "The good old days," she added with a wink, then snapped back to the present. "Do you want a refill?"

Cathy held up her half-full glass. "Not yet." While Pam was in the kitchen, Cathy ruminated over how her father might have been *nice* to Pam's mother. She'd never heard this before. She waited for Pam to return to her seat and drink a little more. "My dad was nice to your whole family?"

"He was," she said, her voice slightly slurred now. "Even before we moved into the school district and I met you. He helped everyone in town."

"That he did," Cathy said between clenched teeth. "You knew my dad before we met?"

"Just a little. I remember him stopping by sometimes with bags of food and stuff."

Cathy scrutinized Pam's moves. Was she telling the truth? Why now? She felt dizzy, like the room was moving, and put her glass on the table. "Did he give you any other gifts?"

"Not really, he just helped out some. Remember that crazy fashion show we did in junior high? And that creepy guy who kept wanting to wear our clothes!"

Cathy had wondered how Pam afforded the cute jacket and pleated skirt she'd worn in the fashion show. But she didn't give much mind to things like that back then. Now she probably knew.

"We did have fun, didn't we, Cathy? And then Caroline came along in high school and we were a bitchin' threesome. We ruled that school."

They were not as pleasant memories for Cathy as they obviously were for Pam. She'd never really liked Caroline, but she had to admit, they did have fun. "I haven't heard from Caroline in years."

"She's even richer now than when we were in high school. Her and Bentley travel to Europe and have this mansion in a swanky area of Santa Barbara, and her clothes!"

"She always had great clothes," Cathy said. "Remember her prom dress?"

Pam giggled. "It was miles and miles of silk organza! She looked like she belonged on the cover of *Seventeen Magazine*."

"You were the bold one wearing a miniskirt," Cathy said.

"And all the boys loved it." Her face dropped. "Except Todd. He only had eyes for you."

"I hope so. We were dating then," Cathy said.

Pam stared out to space. "I have to admit, I really wanted to be the queen. I'd look in the mirror and imagine wearing the crown and everyone clapping." She sighed and looked back at Cathy. "But you always got everything."

"That's not true," Cathy said, annoyed by the implication. "Being the high school prom queen and marrying terrible Todd, how is that everything?" Cathy took a breath. To Pam, it must have seemed like the world to be queen. But Cathy knew she'd won the vote only because she was dating the school's football star.

Pam narrowed her eyes. "Now I have almost everything I ever wanted, just like I planned."

Pam and her plans. She had what she'd always wanted. Back in school, Pam often had some devious thing planned to get some guy away from his girlfriend or some such thing. Cathy didn't know whether to feel sorry for Pam or forewarned.

"Almost?" Cathy asked.

A smile curled up Pam's face. "Next is the great job for Jamie, the big house for us, and living happily ever after, of course."

"Of course," Cathy said. Uneasiness churned in the pit of her stomach. She wondered just how she fit into this tidy little plan. "This has been fun, Pam. Thanks for the cocktail hour, but I really need to get some sleep now."

"Nighty night," Pam said, lifting her drink.

Cathy walked to her bedroom, more exhausted than she'd felt in a long time. Memory lane was not a place she wanted to walk down any longer.

Chapter Fifteen

Cathy's bedroom door flew open, jolting her awake. Amber ran in, jumped up on the bed, and crawled up next to Cathy's face. Her blonde curls were everywhere, and she had on the cutest Winnie the Pooh nightgown.

"Auntie, are we going rowing today? You promised."

Yawning, Cathy remembered the big plan for the day. Amber burrowed under the covers next to her and rested her head on Cathy's shoulder. Her hair smelled like baby shampoo.

"Amber, did you wake up Cathy?" Pam stood at the door, hands on her hips.

Cathy waved her away. "It's okay. I was awake."

Pam scowled and stayed in place.

Amber giggled, and Cathy joined her. They pulled the blanket over their heads for a private meeting. "Shall we plan everything we're going to do today?" Cathy asked.

Her eyes wide, Amber nodded her head up and down.

"Well, first let's plan—"

"What's all this laughing going on here?" Jamie said in his Papa Bear imitation. "And where's Amber?"

They giggled harder. Amber popped out of the blanket. "I'm here, Daddy!"

He took her into his arms and swung her around.

Cathy sat up to watch. She noticed Jamie's gaze flash over her body clad only in a skimpy nightshirt and pulled up the covers.

Jamie brought Amber in for a landing into Pam's open arms.

"Is everyone ready to go to the river today?" Cathy asked.

"Yes, yes," Amber said clapping her hands. "Can we, Mommy, can we?"

Pam looked to Jamie. "It can be an early Father's Day picnic. Let's go change into our swimsuits and pack some snacks."

She put Amber down, and the three of them raced toward their bedrooms.

Father's Day was tomorrow. Cathy hadn't even remembered. It was not a holiday with sweet memories in her heart. She really should do something for Jamie. Perhaps she could bring home dinner tomorrow night and give him a break.

Cathy took a quick shower and scarfed down an apple. She pulled on a one-piece bathing suit and packed some Coppertone and towels in a beach bag.

Outside, Jamie carried two striped backrests off her deck, and Pam had the lunch basket. Amber, in pink flip-flops and a bathing suit to match, was ready to go.

It was a gorgeous day already: warm, nearing eighty, not a cloud in the bright blue sky. Amber hummed as they walked down the trail to the river. The tall cedar trees provided shade, and a light breeze moved through the oaks. When they hit the sand, everyone tossed off their sandals and ran to pick a place. Warm sand oozed between Cathy's toes as she waited for Jamie to smooth out the blanket for them to sit on.

"Let's go in the water," Amber said, tugging at her mom.

"In a minute, Amber, we just got here." Pam started covering herself in suntan lotion.

"Pleeease, Daddy," Amber continued. Jamie gave in, and they ran into the water. The sun reflected off their hair and shoulders. Cathy had one of those rare "everything feels perfect" moments.

Pam spread out her towel and sat down. She took off her T-shirt and pulled the shoulder straps down on her avocado and turquoise bikini. She hummed as she coated her pale skin with suntan lotion. A recipe for a bad sunburn, Cathy mused.

Cathy propped up a beach chair and sat down next to her.

Pam lay back on the towel with a sigh. "It's so nice to have a minute alone to hear myself think."

Cathy was surprised, but only for a moment. Pam had been with Amber twenty-four hours a day, seven days a week, while Jamie and Cathy worked.

"I'm happy to watch Amber anytime you want a break," Cathy said.

Pam opened her eyes. "Cathy, do you mean it? I don't want to impose, but Jamie and I haven't had much time together since we got here."

"No problem," Cathy said. "You and Jamie should go out for dinner. I can cook too, remember?"

Pam stared out toward the water. "Those two sure have fun together. I sometimes wish there was more time for just Jamie and me. Don't get me wrong, I love being a mom."

"I can see that. And you're a good one. Even moms deserve some time off, an escape."

Pam leaned back and took a deep breath. "It would feel so good to just mellow out. I'll ask Jamie, see if he wants to go."

"Why wouldn't he?" Cathy asked. "Everything seems great between you two."

Pam's face dropped. "You really think so?"

"If anything, he might be a bit tired from me working him so hard."

"Really?" Pam said.

"Of course, he's obviously crazy about you two."

Pam looked back out at her family splashing in the river. "Yes, us two."

Cathy watched Jamie and Amber run and splash in the water. "They're so cute together," she said.

Pam started to cry.

"What is it?" Cathy asked. "Is everything alright?"

Pam wiped her tears on her arm and tried composing herself. Jamie and Amber ran back, kicking sand on the way. It was obvious Pam needed a longer break. Cathy took Pam's hand and pulled her up. "Come on, let's take a walk."

Dad and daughter wrapped themselves in towels as the two women walked away. Cathy led Pam down the bank of the river. Pam's face was red, and her breath was a little ragged. As they walked along the green, flowing water, Cathy waited for Pam to talk. A radio from a group of sunbathers blasted Boz Scaggs's "The Lido Shuffle" while kids ran and played along the muddy bank.

"Please don't think I don't love my life. I do," Pam finally said. "I know I have everything any woman could want."

Cathy stayed silent but couldn't help thinking: Yes, you do.

Pam walked over to a large log near the shore and sat down. Cathy joined her. The sun baked on their bare shoulders as they watched a family going down the river on inner tubes. They were obviously digging it.

"I worry about losing Jamie," Pam whispered. She kicked sand with her toes and stared out at the river. "I know he loves Amber."

It was unsettling to see Pam's perky, positive attitude crack. "Pam, you don't have anything to worry about."

"Do you really think so? It's just …"

Cathy held her breath, waiting for Pam to finish. Some kids splashed in the water with their exuberant black lab.

"I was pregnant. Before we were married."

Cathy turned toward her friend. Pam's face drained of color.

In a lowered voice, she continued, "Jamie proposed after he found out."

"He probably planned to anyway." Cathy tried to sound convincing.

Pam shook her head. "I don't think so. Actually, he'd been pulling away."

The look on Pam's face was heartbreaking. "Cut it out, Pam. I'm sure the pregnancy just got him over his fear of commitment. You know men."

Pam didn't respond. Cathy felt like a shark who'd been circulating in Pam's choppy waters.

"We're so different," Pam said. "It was his idea to move up here to the country. You know me; I'm a city girl. All Jamie was focused on was raising Amber in a good place."

Cathy gave her a sympathetic look. She could see the dilemma. Pam and Jamie wanted different things. Pam's dreams were front and center. Jamie deserved to pursue his dreams too. Amber seemed to be the glue that held them together.

"He's just not very ambitious. Caroline offered to get Jamie an interview at a fancy restaurant in Santa Barbara, and he still wanted to come up here."

"Maybe he's just trying to find his way professionally. It's hard on him dealing with these rejections."

"And hard on his wife too," Pam said. "He doesn't seem interested anymore. Not even in bed."

Cathy squirmed. "You're both under a lot of stress, and tired."

Pam stretched. "Yeah, you're right. Maybe I could distract him from his worries if I got a new outfit. Something sexy. We could go out and have some fun like we used to before Amber was born."

"That can be arranged," Cathy said "Let's plan a girls' day out and do some shopping soon."

Pam threw her arms around Cathy. "What a great idea."

Cathy rose and brushed sand off the back of her legs. "Now let's go back there before you get any more sunburned. You can go have some fun with your wonderful family."

Pam's happy mood was back and so was her smile. "Okay, let's go have lunch," she said. "I'm starved."

By the time they returned to the blanket, Pam was as perky as ever.

"About time you made it back," Jamie said. "We were just going to have lunch without you."

He opened the basket and pulled out thick chicken sandwiches on homemade wheat bread and a container of potato salad. Cathy couldn't wait to taste Jamie's version.

Everyone piled their plates with food and ate ravenously.

"So, Jamie, what do you put in your potato salad?" Cathy asked.

He finished chewing and thought for a moment. "Besides the usual, I add a pinch of mustard, diced green pepper, and use half mayonnaise and half plain yogurt."

Cathy continued eating. "It's very creamy."

Pam wiped Amber's face with a napkin. "Slow down, kid, you won't have room for dessert."

"What is it, what is it?" Amber demanded.

Jamie reached in the basket and brought out a plate of chocolate brownies. Everyone swooned. The plastic wrap was soon torn off and discarded, and the brownies were history.

Amber lay down and rubbed her tummy. "I'm so full."

Cathy knew the feeling and joined her flat on her back. The afternoon was warm and the river calm. Cathy flipped on her side to face Pam. "Why don't you and Jamie take the rowboat out while we nap?"

Pam looked over at Jamie. "Are you up to it so soon after lunch?"

He jumped to his feet. "I'm always ready."

Of course Cathy's mind went to other things when he said that. What kind of friend was she? One minute she comforted Pam, and the next she thought about Jamie's prowess. Her feelings for Jamie were clouding her mind.

Perhaps it was time to call David. Or head back to Sebastian's. Maybe Chuck would be there again. She needed to get out on a date and stop focusing on what she couldn't have.

They watched them hop into the boat and paddle downstream.

Amber piped up, "I want to row too."

Pam must be happy now. Cathy closed her eyes and let the sun soak into her body. Amber fidgeted next to her. Cathy put her hand over Amber's. "You okay?"

Amber scooted close and laid her head on Cathy's shoulder. This must be how it felt to have a child. Cathy's little girl would be nine years old, if she'd lived.

"I like it here," Amber said. "I hope my daddy finds a job soon."

"He will," Cathy said, opening her eyes.

Amber sighed and propped herself up with one arm. "Mommy says we might have to move far away."

"Not if I can help it," Cathy said. "Now let's close our eyes and get to work on our tans."

Cathy willed herself not to think as she drifted off. The next thing she knew, cold water splashed her skin and shocked her awake. Jamie stood over them, his cutoff jeans dripping wet. Water beads glistened over his brawny chest and shoulders. Cathy tried not to let her gaze wander to the wet cutoff jeans clinging to his thighs.

"It's your turn, sleepyheads. Let's go!"

Pam wrapped herself in a towel. "The water felt wonderful!" she said with a dreamy smile. She took her spot on the blanket, put on a hat and sunglasses, and picked up a *Woman's Day* magazine.

"You all have fun," she said, waving as they walked toward the river.

While Jamie balanced the boat, Cathy and Amber took a seat in the back. Jamie hopped in, sat on the narrower bench up front, and put the oars in the water. His muscles flexed with each stroke. It was hard for Cathy not to think about running her fingers over his smooth, golden brown chest. They moved downriver toward the ocean, flowing along with the current. The trees along the bank cast shadows on the water and wild irises bloomed everywhere. Suddenly, Jamie stood up in the boat, oars in hand, and started singing an Italian song. It took Cathy a minute to realize he was mimicking a gondolier from Italy.

His rich voice rang out, "Bene, bene verde river and bella donnas in the boaté, that's amore."

Amber giggled, and Cathy was loving it. His voice was melodic, and his mock accent was hysterical yet very charming.

Now he sang straight to Cathy as he waved his hands in the air, "Ciao, Catalina, with rosso hair and grande rowboat! Grazie, grazie and arrivederci!" He almost dropped the oars but caught them midair. His lopsided grin captured her heart.

For that moment, there was no one else in the world but the three of them floating down the Russian River. They joined him singing made-up love songs. He maneuvered the boat over to shore, next to a gnarly, uprooted Bay Laurel tree, and they got out to look around.

Jamie lifted Amber up into the large tree roots.

"Princess of the Trees!" Amber giggled.

They mock bowed. "Princess Amber."

"And you two can be the king and queen," Amber said.

Jamie glanced at Cathy. It was not hard to imagine being at his side. She jumped off the tree branch and walked to the water's edge.

Jamie and Amber followed her over to the water. Jamie picked up a small stick and sat down on the wet sand with Amber beside him. "Let's draw," he said.

Cathy watched him trace a heart and point to Amber. "I love you, little one."

Amber took the stick and drew a round face with a big smile.

Now it was Jamie's turn again. He added a figure eight over the heart.

"What's that, Daddy?"

"It's the infinity symbol. It means forever, little one. That I will love you forever."

Amber threw her arms around her daddy. "Love you infinity," she said before running down to splash in the shallow water's edge.

Cathy tried to embed the perfect moment in her memory. Jamie stood up beside her. They watched Amber play.

"Do you believe love transcends death?" Cathy asked Jamie.

He turned to her. "Absolutely. Why?"

"When you drew that infinity symbol, it reminded me of an experience with my father."

"Really?" he said. "Tell me about it."

Cathy shivered. "It was in the middle of the night several hours after my father died. I woke suddenly and felt a freezing whisk of air go through my room. My father, bright and slightly translucent, stood at the foot of my bed, radiating love to me like I'd never felt before."

"He came to say goodbye," Jamie said.

A wave of emotion racked through Cathy's body, sending goose bumps down her arms and legs. She hoped the vision was her father's way of saying, "I'm sorry."

"I believe love never dies," Jamie said, his blue eyes boring into hers. "People you love are always with you, even when they pass."

Cathy started to cry, and Amber came running up to give her a hug. "What's the matter, Auntie Cathy?"

"Nothing, nothing," she said, leaning down and giving Amber a tight hug back. "Sometimes grown-ups just need a good cry."

The sun moved behind the trees, and Cathy realized they'd been gone a while. She looked up at Jamie.

"I think we'd better get back," she said with regret.

They scrambled into the boat, and Jamie rowed them back to the picnic site. The oars pierced the water in a smooth even pattern. They were going upstream now, against the current. In many ways that was how Cathy had been living her life, fighting the flow of love.

Jamie pulled the boat ashore, and Amber ran to tell her mother about their adventure while the adults followed behind. Pam's head was still buried in her book, so Cathy felt some relief that they hadn't been gone too long. Just as she was about to sit down and join her friends, Cathy heard her name being called.

"Cathy, is that you?" A dark-haired man waved at her from up the beach, and she recognized David. That was timing. She waved back.

His tanned, olive skin, tall muscular body in red swim trunks, and black wavy hair turned women's heads as he walked over to join them. He was a good-looking man; she would give him that. His dazzling smile seemed to work its magic on Pam as Cathy introduced everyone.

"David, why don't you sit down and join us?" Pam said.

Cathy watched David check out Pam's body. "I wish I could," he said, "but I'm here with my buddies, and we were just about to leave."

Pam looked truly disappointed. "What a shame. Got any dinner plans?"

"Nope," he said.

Cathy could see where this is going. It would probably be better if she and David went out alone. Before she could say anything, Pam blurted out, "Oh good, my husband, Jamie, is an amazing chef. Why don't you join us tonight?"

David looked over at Jamie. "I wouldn't want to be a bother."

Jamie hesitated before answering. "No problem. I was planning on making pasta primavera for tonight. If you'd rather come another night, we could barbecue something."

"Spaghetti is cool, man," David said. "What time?"

"You'll have to ask the lady of the house," Jamie said, looking at Cathy.

Cathy groaned inwardly. This was not a great match of characters. "See you at seven."

"Check you later," David said turning to go. "I'll bring the beer."

When he was out of earshot, Pam leaned over and raised an eyebrow to Cathy. "He's a hunk."

Cathy shrugged. On the outside, there was no doubt. But her eyes strayed to Jamie as he packed everything and tossed Amber up on his shoulders. But some men had it all.

Chapter Sixteen

Cathy pulled out her makeup and applied mascara and lip gloss. She might as well look good for David. She didn't need the blush after the glorious day in the sun. Her turquoise tank top matched perfectly with her colorful peasant skirt, and her red Diwali sandals were her favorite. Cathy took one last look in the full-length mirror. She wondered what Jamie, not David, would think of her outfit. She could smell the garlic scent from the pasta sauce wafting under her door. Italian love songs flowed through her head as Cathy twirled in the skirt.

The doorbell rang; David was here. The songs stopped.

David entered the house like it was his own, his thumb and third finger looped through a six-pack of Budweiser. Not Cathy's favorite. He hugged her with one arm.

"Lookin' good," he said.

His white gauze shirt set off his tan with its low-dipping neckline. Pam, wearing a backless, hot-pink dress with lipstick to match, greeted him like a long-lost love and thanked him for coming. She put the beer in the fridge, then opened two, one for him and for herself, and joined him at the table where he waited to be served.

Jamie, in his classic T-shirt and jeans, popped the cork on a bottle of Merlot and pulled out wine glasses.

"Never had wine with spaghetti," David said, looking skeptical.

"A light-to-medium-bodied red wine pairs well with pasta, Jamie said. "The fruit flavors of the wine go well with tomato sauce." He poured Amber some juice then held up the bottle of Merlot. "Who wants wine?"

Cathy raised her glass then made a toast. "To friends."

David raised his beer can and clinked her wine glass. Women swooned over this guy. She had too when she first met him, but now his veneer wore thin.

Cathy watched Jamie pour the steaming sauce mixed with sautéed vegetables into a large serving bowl filled with pasta. The pungent smells of garlic, basil, and tomato were ecstasy.

"Dinner coming to the table," Jamie said, sprinkling the top with grated Parmesan cheese. He brought the food in and began serving.

David held up his plate.

"Ladies first," Jamie said with a grin. He took his time making David wait as long as possible. Cathy watched, amused by the dynamic between the two men. It was obvious Jamie was not too fond of her date.

David sipped his beer. At least he had the sense not to take a bite off her plate. His fingers pounded the table as he waited for his serving. Cathy suppressed the urge to laugh. Was Jamie jealous? Or perhaps he just didn't like David.

Amber stuffed a huge portion in her mouth, and warm strings of cheese dripped from her chin. Jamie placed a plate before Cathy and then served himself and David. He took a seat and held up his glass for a toast. "To fine dining."

Cathy's mouth was in sensual heaven. "Grazie, grazie," she said to Jamie.

He grinned as he twirled spaghetti with his fork.

Pam leaned over and asked David about his work. He basked in the attention and was more than happy to talk her ear off.

"You built that big home in only three months?" Pam asked.

David laughed. "Well, I did have some help, but I was the head contractor."

"It seems the area is really growing," Jamie said. "Your business must be doing well."

David nodded, stuffing another bite into his mouth. "Yeah, if you ever need a carpentry job on the side, let me know."

"We probably won't," Pam said. "But thank you for thinking of us."

Her stomach threatened nausea, but Cathy wouldn't let it spoil this fabulous meal. David had gotten Pam another beer and they were actually giggling together like teenagers. Cathy glanced over to see how Jamie was reacting. His brow was tense. Was Pam just so enamored with David that she didn't realize her husband was there too, or was she intentionally trying to make Jamie jealous? Cathy never knew just how innocent Pam really was or just how clever. She cleared her throat rather loudly. David looked up like he just remembered the rest of them were here. He gave her a weird look and then turned to Jamie. "So, what do you do for work?"

Cathy hated when things went quiet, and she really wanted to say something to stand up for Jamie.

"Actually," Jamie said, sounding very sophisticated, "I just graduated from culinary school in San Francisco, and I'm interviewing for executive chef positions here in Sonoma County."

"Pretty cool. You're not just a fast food cook then," he said, laughing at his own joke. "Ah, come on. I dig it. The spaghetti's great, man."

Cathy wanted to slap David. She realized she'd never taken a good look at who this guy really was. Their time together always ended in bed, which had been fine for both of them. Isn't that what she wanted? Even looking at him now, the physical attraction was there. His jet-black hair fell across a perfectly carved face, his spectacular hazel eyes sparkled under thick lashes, and his sleek swimmer's body was tanned and smooth. There was chemistry, but it didn't go more than skin deep.

Cathy took a long sip of wine. "Wonderful dinner, Jamie. But tomorrow, on Father's Day, there will be no cooking for you. It will be your day off. Mama Luca's makes the best pizza in town, and I'll bring home an extra large pie."

"Sounds good."

Amber perked up. "Me and Mommy are making Daddy a special breakfast too. Aren't we, Mommy?"

"Yes we are," Pam said as she cleaned Amber's face and hands with a napkin. "Shall we all go in the living room now?"

"Let's leave the dishes for now," Cathy said. "I'll get them later." She noticed David didn't offer to help.

Jamie took Amber by the hand and everyone followed him into the living room.

Cathy opened another bottle of wine and brought it with her to the couch. She usually didn't drink this much. David, another beer in hand, sat down next to her. His arm slipped around her shoulder, and he stroked her neck with his fingers.

Cathy's body reacted to his touch. The wine numbed the surfacing thoughts that tried to tell her she was finished with him. No, she told herself, this was the kind of safe relationship she'd wanted. Safe.

Libby jumped into David's lap. He sneezed and pushed her off. Cathy always wondered about guys allergic to cats. For some reason, it seemed to signify an allergy to women as well.

The conversation circled around summer activities coming up on the river, music festivals, parades, and the Fourth of July picnic. Pam pulled up the rocker nearer to the couch. More than once, Cathy caught her staring at David. She couldn't totally blame Pam for enjoying the attention. It had probably been a while since a single man flirted with her like this.

"It's getting late." Jamie ruffled Amber's hair. "I think I'll put this little one to bed now."

"Mommy, come too. Sing me a lullaby."

With a sigh, Pam rose and headed toward the bedroom, leaving Cathy and David alone.

David kissed Cathy's neck and reached a hand for her breast. "Let's go to the bedroom," he whispered in her ear.

She pushed his hand away. "Not here, with all the company."

"Let's go to my place then," he said, taking Cathy's hand and pulling her up from the couch. His lips moved to hers and his probing kiss ignited her senses. Perhaps it would be a good idea to sleep with him, relieve the sexual tension that had been building inside her.

Pam walked out and saw them getting ready to leave. Disappointment mirrored back briefly, then resolve. "Are you leaving?"

"We thought we'd just go to David's place for the night. I'll be back early in the morning." Cathy reached for her purse.

David took her arm. "No sense taking two cars, Cathy. I'll drive and drop you back in the morning when I leave for the jobsite."

That made sense.

Pam gave Cathy a knowing smile. "Have a good time. Jamie and I will take care of everything here."

At the sound of Jamie's name, Cathy almost changed her mind. Which was exactly why she turned on her heels and left.

His house was immaculate as always, which struck Cathy as odd for a bachelor. But David wanted everything in its place. There was never a dirty dish left in the sink for even a second. He opened another beer and offered her one.

"Do you have any wine?" she asked.

"No, hon, only beer."

He knew she preferred wine, but he never had any in the house. Cathy remembered something about wine and beer mixed and being sick and said no. But the buzz was wearing off from dinner, and she was unhappy she'd come. He pulled off his shirt and tossed it on a chair, then forcefully drew her into his arms. His beer breath deadened a few nerve endings. His hands were under her shirt, unhooking her bra, and his mouth pressed on her lips, demanding entry.

Cathy's body started to respond as he pulled her down on the couch. His hand moved up her thigh, taunting her. Then nothing. Cathy opened her eyes and saw David standing up.

"Want a snack before bed?" he said.

She just gawked at him. David shrugged, turned around and walked into the kitchen. He opened a cabinet, pulled out a bag of chips, and started crunching. The mood, what there was left of it, was gone for her. His looks faded and all she could see was a man she really didn't like. They had both used each other. The emptiness choked her. How far she'd run from her heart's longings. Cathy re-hooked her bra and straightened her skirt.

"I want to go home, David," she said, standing up and getting her purse.

He dropped the bag of chips on the counter; some were stuck to his lip.

"Why, babe?" he said, walking unsteadily toward her. He grabbed her arm and tried to kiss her.

"No, I mean it," she said, pushing him away.

David thrust her against the wall and shoved his tongue in her mouth. He forced up her tank top and started groping her. "You know you like this," he slurred.

Fear seared up her spine. He was strong, and the more she shoved him away the harder he jammed into her. Cathy finally screamed and he backed off, looking at her like she was crazy.

Then she remembered she didn't have her car. It was over five miles to her house in the dark, but she didn't care. She slid under his arm and yanked at the door to run. His hand held the door from opening. Then he burst out laughing.

"Come on, Cathy, what's with all the drama? Just stay the night and I'll take you home in the morning."

"I want to go now."

His bloodshot eyes narrowed as he sneered at her. "Then walk or get one of your friends to drive you. I'm going to bed."

The phone was on his kitchen counter. She inched her way around David and grabbed it. Praying Pam was still awake, Cathy dialed her home number. One ring, two, three …

"Hello," a sleepy voice said.

"Pam, it's Cathy. I need a ride home, now!"

"What?"

"Pam, is Jamie awake?"

"Yes. Are you okay?"

"Get him, please."

She put Jamie on the line. Cathy gave him directions, and without hesitation, he said he'd be right there. David watched the call with amusement. She still didn't trust him and stepped outside to wait on the porch.

"Suit yourself," he said, turning the porch light on and following her out. He stood there leering at her.

She wiped tears away with the back of her hand.

"Prince Charming in his chef hat coming to rescue you?" David said.

Cathy wrapped her arms around herself to ward off the evening chill. She counted the minutes, praying Jamie would hurry.

Headlights hit the drive and she couldn't run fast enough to the car. Jamie jumped out, took one look at her tear-stained face, and headed for the front door.

"No, Jamie," Cathy pleaded, taking his arm. "Please, just take me home."

He glared at David and then back at Cathy. "All right," he said, putting his arm protectively around her and walking her to the car.

David yelled after them. "Oh, so that's how it is. Real nice, Cathy, your friend's husband."

The minute Cathy got inside the car, she started trembling. Hot tears ran down her cheeks. Jamie gunned the engine and sped down the road for a few miles before veering over under some trees. He shut off the engine, slid across the seat, and took Cathy in his arms.

Gently, he stroked her hair as she cried into his shoulder. "You deserve better, Cat. You care so much for others but not enough for yourself."

Cathy cried harder. Jamie lifted her chin and wiped away her tears with his fingertips. She wanted to look into his caring eyes forever. Their lips met in a soft, lingering kiss. The tenderness washed over her and melted her. She looked up to Jamie.

Shock registered on his face. "I am so sorry. And after what you just went through."

Cathy touched his lips with her finger to shush him. "Don't be sorry. I'm the one who should be sorry involving you in my messes. You've been nothing but kind to me, Jamie."

His name resonated in the air. She'd never even looked at a married man before and did not want to cross that line now. He was the first man that had seen her, really seen her. Her feelings for him crossed every boundary, blocked out every rational thought, and claimed her soul.

They sat looking at each other, taking in what had just happened. Conflicted emotions traced across his face. She wanted to hold him, but he slid back into the driver's side, started the car. He gazed straight ahead as he drove them home. Cathy looked out the passenger window and watched the dark shadows from the trees loom over the road. She thought she was immune to this heart pain. She knew now she wasn't.

Lyrics from "Sometimes When We Touch" drifted from the car radio in the background. Cathy caught the words "touching" and "honesty." She reached over and turned it off.

Pam was in bed when they got home.

"Everything all right, Cathy?" she called

Cathy leaned her head in Pam's doorway and assured her she was fine. Gratefully, she crawled into bed and pulled the covers over her head. She prayed she would not hear them moaning from down the hall tonight, and she hated herself a little more.

There was silence except for the hoot of a lone owl.

Chapter Seventeen

*J*amie filled the Mr. Coffee with water and pushed the button to start. He needed coffee now. The early morning sun behind Cathy's house spilled into the rolling hills, setting them aglow. Libby rubbed up against his leg, and he bent down to pet her.

"Good girl," he said, scratching behind her ears. "It's just you and me up early this morning."

A ceramic mug of steaming coffee in his hand, Jamie took a seat in the rocker that faced the picture windows in the living room. The sky was clear except for a few marshmallow clouds. Pines and redwoods stood tall in the yard, and a blue jay swept in landing on a bough. It was so different from the cement-covered, noise-laden area they left in Oakland. He could breathe here, literally smell the roses. Silently he prayed again that a job would become available. He could thrive in this abundant fresh air, with sprawling hills and vineyards. They all would.

But would his wife be happy here? He knew Amber would. He'd worried about Pam's happiness for years. When they'd first met, she was a sweet, pretty, lost girl. He'd reached out to her, and she held on tight. When he was honest with himself, he remembered that rescuing someone was not grounds for a good marriage. He was ready to gently break up with Pam when she announced she was pregnant with Amber.

The announcement changed everything. Pam had been abandoned by her own father when she was four. She would be devastated. Jamie could never be the kind of man who left his child behind. And so, he married her. But now, sitting here in Cathy's house, he finally realized that he'd fooled himself into thinking he loved Pam.

Until he met Cathy, he never knew what love was. His decision last night to bring her home from David's was not done out of obligation. He'd made the choice totally from his heart. And he knew Cathy would have done the same for him.

With Pam it was always about doing the right thing. Did doing the right thing for the wrong reasons really help anyone? His mind raced: Cathy's face, her lips, her touch. Being with her felt so right. Was he betraying Pam in his mind and heart? Was it fair to continue with Pam when he knew beyond any doubt he loved someone else?

Amber: She was the light of his soul. He would never leave her. What was the honorable thing to do? Give up what his heart longed for. Put another before himself? It seemed it was.

He took his last sip of coffee and brought it to the sink to wash out the cup. It was Father's Day, and the girls would be up soon to make breakfast. Time to act like nothing happened last night. Put on a bright smile like Pam always did and push his pain down where no one could see.

Chapter Eighteen

It was Sunday morning, usually Cathy's day to sleep in. The clock said 8 a.m. Her internal alarm had reset itself to get up for work. She turned over and pulled up the covers, blocking the sun from her eyes. Memories hit like fists in her stomach. Jamie's kiss. She needed to get out of there today, away from them, away from him. Especially on Father's Day. Her heart beat in her ears. Where could she go? Jill's house? She was always up early. Perhaps Cathy could take them out to breakfast for the holiday. She dialed.

The phone rang once, twice. Come on, Jill, answer.

"Hello," a child's voice answered.

"Is your mom there?" Cathy said, keeping her voice low.

"I think she's resting. I'll go see."

Cathy felt the morning breeze move through the open window into her room. She stared at the lush colors in the Maxwell Parrish picture on the wall, of a girl swinging over water. She waited.

More silence and footsteps on a wood floor.

"Hello?"

"Jill, it's Cathy."

"Something wrong? What are you doing up so early on a Sunday?"

"Thinking of you." Even Cathy could tell she sounded ridiculous. "Can I take you all out for breakfast?"

"It's Father's Day," Jill said. "Dan insisted on making waffles. Why don't you come over and join us?"

"If you're sure it's all right."

"Come hungry. When you get here, I want to know what's going on."

"I'll be right there."

Cathy put on some jean shorts over a pink leotard. Deodorant would be enough today. A quick tooth brushing and a comb through her hair and she'd be out of there.

She peeked out her bedroom door. The coast was clear. She dashed for the bathroom. Her expression in the mirror made her want to laugh. She was hiding in the bathroom. Hysterical if it wasn't so pathetic. She finished getting ready and made her move to leave.

"Good morning," Pam said from the couch as Cathy headed toward the front door. "Where you going?"

Avoiding eye contact, Cathy turned. "I forgot to tell you yesterday, having breakfast with Jill and her family. Have a good day." Cathy remembered she'd promised to bring home pizza for tonight. "I'll still bring dinner back."

"I'm sure Jamie will appreciate that. He works so hard cooking at your café all day."

Cathy gritted her teeth. "Yes, some of us have to work." Cathy noticed Amber sleeping on Pam's lap like a little angel.

"We're letting Jamie sleep in while Amber and I make breakfast and then spend the day baking a special cake for her daddy."

Inwardly Cathy groaned at the probable mess she would come home to in her kitchen. "That's nice. You have fun." Cathy was out the door and into her car before she said anything she would regret. She suppressed the urge to laugh, then cry, and put her foot on the gas.

She could leave the house but not the memory of last night. How had she gotten herself in that position with David? Her body trembled. Why did she gravitate toward men like him? Like her father? They were safe in that she'd never fall in love with that type of man. Is that all she really wanted? David distracted her from her deep loneliness and was happy with their arrangement. She thought she was too, until she met Jamie.

Toys and bikes scattered the yard of Jill's sprawling, brick-red farmhouse. Kids screamed and ran to the door to greet her. The dog barked, and Jill was yelling to Dan that the waffles were burning. Cathy almost turned around and ran.

Jill walked over, looking so much better than the last time Cathy saw her. Her coloring was back, and she'd swapped bedclothes for a batik sundress.

"Girls, let Cathy alone. Come sit down." Jill's eyes searched Cathy's before she could even let go of the doorknob. "You too," she said, pointing at a chair. "Have a seat."

"Green eggs and waffles," Dan said, decked out in an apron reading, "Best Dad."

"Ewww," said her twin girls, but Tom, her four-year-old, seemed delighted with the green-tinted eggs. They made Cathy want to throw up, especially after drinking too much last night. She hoped they didn't expect her to eat them.

"Coffee," Jill offered. Cathy wanted to kiss her.

Eggs were dished out and waffles piled with strawberries and powdered sugar. It looked like Christmas on plates.

The girls, looking cute in their matching braids and barrettes, mashed the waffles with their forks. Strawberry juice ran down Jill's son's chin. She took a napkin to his face, and Dan observed in mock dismay. Even her older daughter was polite and helpful. This was a family, a happy, normal family. In Cathy's childhood, Father's Day was silent and on edge. Cathy and her mother prayed her father would not seize the day to start drinking even earlier. At Jill's table, everyone laughed, and somehow breakfast was finished. Some landed on the floor, and the dog looked quite satisfied about that.

"Go wash up, girls," Jill said, scooting them toward the bathroom.

Dan cleared off the table and offered to do the dishes so they could go out and talk on the deck.

"It's Father's Day. Perhaps I should go," Cathy said. "You must have plans."

Jill was not going for it. She opened the French doors to the deck Dan built last summer, overlooking the river, and waved her through. They sat side by side in canvas recliners. Yellowthroats sang, and the light scent of cedar floated in the air. Blue jays screamed, taunting the squirrels. The day was right out of a Disney movie.

"Give," Jill said.

No wonder they were such good friends. There was no pretense between them. But this time, how could Cathy tell her everything?

"David and I are finished." Cathy said.

"No surprise there," Jill said, looking at her like an interrogator. "And?"

"And we had a horrible scene last night. Jamie had to drive me home."

Silence. Jill liked to process, as she called it. Cathy let her muscles relax as the morning sun lingered on her body. She could lie there all day.

Jill huffed. "What a jerk. I know he's hot, but there are things to look for if you want another relationship one day."

"When did I say I wanted another relationship?"

"Touchy today, aren't we? You think that invisible armor of yours fools me?"

Transparency was not something Cathy was known for. A relationship? Jill had no idea how close she was to Cathy's real problem. Perhaps she shouldn't have come here today, but going home was certainly not an option. She didn't feel like being alone.

One of the twins, dressed head-to-toe like the other, ran outside, whining about her sister taking her toy. Cathy couldn't tell them apart.

"Back in the house," Jill stated firmly. "Your dad will take care of it."

No messing around there. Jill had backbone, and no one doubted it.

"Mind if I stay here a while?" Cathy tried to sound casual.

"You're kidding, right? You barely ever make an hour here before you're running out the door."

"That's not true," Cathy said, although her words rang false.

Jill sat up and put her legs over the edge of the chair facing Cathy. She lifted her sunglasses. "Why don't you want to go home?"

What could she say? I'm falling in love with a friend's husband and I can't bear to look either of them in the face? Jill would not take lightly that kind of confession.

"It's nothing, Jill, I just wanted some time away." Cathy looked around, trying to think of a way to change the subject. "I love your deck. I really should have one built at my house."

Jill laid back and flipped her glasses back down. "Fine, stay as long as you want."

Cathy closed her eyes and tried to relax. Her body twitched. She could not get comfortable in her chair or her own skin. She looked at her watch; 1:30. She really couldn't stay here all day. It was not fair to Jill or their family on this special day.

"I think I'd better be off now," Cathy said standing up. "Brian's at the shop alone. The weekend guests in the attic suite will be checking out, and the room needs cleaning."

Jill waved but did not get up. Did she know? Did she hate her now?

"Thanks for the breakfast." Cathy headed back into the house and out the front door.

Brian was playing the flute behind the counter when Cathy entered the shop. Their agreement was that he could play if he kept the music soft and there were no customers upfront. And, that awkward detail--he had to be dressed! At home he played in the nude, but not here. She could hardly call him covered today, though, in his skimpy tie-dyed armless T-shirt and rolled up denim shorts.

"Hi, boss lady," he said.

"Great tan. Your trip to Montana must have gone well."

He lowered the flute under the counter.

"Mostly good, when my mom wasn't freaking out over the bugs or something."

A customer entered, and he turned to help them. Cathy headed upstairs.

The guests had left their room a mess. Wine glasses, open bottles, and empty chocolate wrappers littered the nightstand and table. The bed looked like a hurricane hit it, and there were wet towels everywhere. How many showers did they take?

She started stripping the bed, making piles of laundry in the corner, and dumping the trash. It felt good to scrub the sink and tub until they shined. Before long, the room was in pristine condition, and Cathy felt better too. She opened the window to air it out for the next guests, arriving later in the week. Both rooms were booked for the Fourth of July weekend, but midweek was still slow. She scanned the room. Nothing was out of place; everything was back to the way it should be. She wished her life was the same.

Downstairs in the back room, she plugged in her adding machine and attacked the bookkeeping. She ran a tape and caught up on the bills and invoices. An inventory was completed next and a list of what she needed to order for the shop and café. Cathy posted it on the bulletin board for Tim to see on Monday. She was back in the routine. Everything was under control, and it was not even five o'clock. Jill seemed a lot better, and she would probably be back to work soon. Everything would return to normal.

Cathy waved at Tim as she stepped out the front door for some air. He must have had some catching up to do, as he wasn't scheduled to work today. The sun was still warm, and tourists lingered around the shops downtown. The scent of garlic from Mama Luca's Pizza reminded her she had not eaten since breakfast and that she'd promised to bring an extra-large pie home with her. On the way over to Mama's, she saw that the toy shop was still open. When she spotted cute kids' books in the window, Cathy decided to buy some for Amber. She scanned the shelves and found *The Runaway Bunny* and one of her favorites, *Charlotte's Web*.

With her bag of books in hand, Cathy entered the pizza parlor and ordered a super garlic, basil, and cheese pizza to go, then sat down to wait. She wondered how Father's Day had gone back at her house. She couldn't have faced it. The clerk finally handed her the heavy box of pie. The scent made her salivate and long to rip open the box and eat a slice. Instead, she carried it back toward her car. She stepped in through the back door of the café and dialed home. Cathy twisted the orange phone cord around her finger and waited.

Pam answered, sounding her perky self. "Hello. Cathy's house."

Cathy could hear kids' music playing in the background. It sounded like a party.

"Pam?" Cathy said, raising her voice. "I just wanted to remind you I'm bringing home pizza for dinner."

"Awesome," Pam said. "Hey guys," she yelled, "Cathy's bringing pizza home."

"See you soon, then," Cathy said.

"What?" Pam yelled.

"I'll be home soon," she shouted back and hung up the phone.

Cathy turned out of the parking lot and took a quick right to get to River Road. It sounded like they didn't miss her. Perhaps they were glad to have some time alone. She couldn't remember one day like that as a child with her own family. Maybe she could have if her dad had stopped drinking, if she and Todd had stayed married, if her child had survived.

If, if, if.

The music still blasted on the tape player when she walked in, and Pam hurried to lower it. Cathy froze. Stretched to the limit around Pam's waist was Cathy's favorite silk wraparound skirt from India.

"Hope you don't mind, Cathy. I borrowed some of your clothes. Remember? Like we used to. I couldn't resist this glittery skirt."

Cathy wanted to pull it right off her. But Pam looked so happy in it. "It's fine this time, but please be sure to cover it when we're eating pizza."

Amber joined Cathy at the door. "Can I carry it?"

"You can carry half and I'll carry half," Cathy said, lowering the box for Amber to reach. Together they carried it to the table that was already set with plates and glasses of pink lemonade.

"Thanks for bringing dinner," Jamie said as he took the pizza out of the box.

He was so close she could catch the faint smell of his spicy aftershave.

Cathy looked down at the table and mumbled, "I'm glad to do it. Happy Father's Day."

He cut each slice, oozing with cheese, and handed a plateful to each of them. The yeasty dough smothered in chopped garlic and mozzarella melted in Cathy's mouth. She stole a glance at him. His hair swept across his eyes and rested on the collar of his pale green button-down shirt.

"Guess where we went today?" Amber said.

"Where?" Cathy said, grateful to have somewhere to look. Amber looked so cute in her miniature peasant blouse with Ric Rac trim and full sleeves.

"We went to the movies and saw *Winnie the Pooh*!"

"You did? How fun. Tell me all about it."

"We ate popcorn and drank big cokes," Amber said before shoving a huge bite of pizza into her mouth, leaving red tomato sauce trailing around her lips.

"I'm sorry I missed it," Cathy said. "But I have a surprise for you too."

Her big blue eyes lit up. "What, what?"

Cathy took a few bites and let the anticipation build. "I bought you two new books."

Amber started to get up and look for them, but Pam told her to sit down and finish dinner. Amber pouted.

"Auntie Cathy, will you read me one after dinner?"

Cathy looked to Pam for approval.

"We were going to play a board game after dinner, remember?" Pam said.

Amber looked torn.

"No problem," Cathy said. "I'll read you the books tomorrow as soon as I get back from work."

Amber seemed content.

Cathy's plate was empty. She took her dishes to the sink and started cleaning up the kitchen. Pam cleared the rest of the table and joined Cathy.

"You didn't have to buy Amber anything."

"I wanted to," Cathy said. "Do you mind?"

"Of course not," Pam said a little too quickly. "I just didn't want you to feel like you had to."

"It's only a couple of books. It's my pleasure." Cathy put the dishes in the drain to dry and started for her room.

Amber yelled after her, "Aren't you going to play games with us?"

Cathy thought there were enough games going on already. "Not tonight, Amber. You all have fun, I'm going to take a bath and head to bed."

Jamie looked straight at her with a concerned expression. She wished he could take her in his arms and hold her.

"Here, let's play Candyland," Pam said, opening the box and spreading it out on the table.

Cathy turned quickly and snatched a towel from the linen closet. A hot soak in the claw-foot tub sounded perfect. She turned on the warm water, added lavender bath salts for calming, undressed, and stepped in. The water caressed her skin as she sank into the silky warmth. Laughter from the dining room crept under the door. She plugged her ears but could still hear it. She held her breath and let her head slip under the water. Drowning crossed her mind as a sensible way to stop the noise and longing of her body for his.

Chapter Nineteen

A familiar silence permeated Cathy's house. Everyone had left early. Pam had taken Amber to visit her grandma for the day and make sure her mom got to her doctor's appointment. Oakland was a long drive and the traffic was terrible, but Pam's mother's Alzheimer's seemed to be progressing. Every visit could be the last time her mother would remember them. Cathy speculated on the possibility that some people's lives were so hard to cope with that they had to lose their memory to survive.

Jamie had volunteered to take Cathy's car and go in early to do inventory, so Cathy could enjoy a quiet morning. The plan also ensured Cathy and Jamie were not alone in the house together again.

Cathy did a little dance in her living room. Alone, alone, finally alone. Today she would get a grip on herself; all this little girl crush stuff was not like her. She peered in the fridge and pulled out yogurt and ripe strawberries. No white flour, sugar, and butter-drenched breakfast for her. Fragrant, peppermint tea brewed and she had two luxurious hours to herself until Jamie picked her up at ten. She took her tea and yogurt and moved to the rocker on the porch. The cats joined her, and they watched the sun play in the redwoods and basked in its warm rays. Cathy shoveled the tart yogurt and fruit mix into her mouth and let the flavors blend like a cocktail. The birds were in rare form this morning, so happy to greet another day.

Snowy circled her feet and purred like a crazy boy. Libby leapt on her lap and rubbed her head against her. Love, or a plea for yogurt? Cathy dipped her finger into the white creamy blend and let the cat's coarse tongue lick off every drop.

Putting the carton down, Cathy rocked and let the peace fill her senses and hopefully put her broken pieces back together. She could hear the inner doors of her mind closing and the padlocks snapping back in place around her heart.

She lingered on the porch, letting the warmth lull her. No clanking dishes or child's squeals. Perhaps she could change the locks, and they would never come back. Huge locks that said, "Keep away."

She needed to wake up. Life was not a fairytale. Not hers anyway.

Jamie and Cathy had kept their distance from each other since the night at David's. She knew she should say something, she wanted to, but what? The phone rang, breaking her solitude. She didn't want to answer it, but the possibility it was important forced her up. It was Jamie. He could pick her up in an hour. He rattled off what they needed: goat milk, apple cider, and strawberries. Cathy's mind floated away. He knew his stuff. With him there in the café, she was not even needed.

She went inside and took a long, leisurely shower. No one was home to turn on another water tap, so she never got a cold spray. Yes, it felt good to have some space.

Who was she kidding? She already missed them. Amber's giggle warmed a house that had not seen much laughter.

Cathy walked around naked, then slipped into jean shorts and a red embroidered peasant blouse over a tank top. She felt girly today, so she added lip-gloss and some rose scent. She checked her full-length mirror; her tan set off the blouse nicely. Maybe she would go dancing tonight. She could always drag Tim to the Pink Elephant downriver.

The sound of Jamie pulling up the drive startled her. Wild eyes looked back from the mirror. Cathy watched her tight-fitting armor crack from the pounding of her heart. For a moment she considered hiding in the closet. She couldn't tell if she was laughing or crying as she heard the front door open.

"Cathy, you ready?" Jamie called.

She closed her bedroom door and leaned her back against it.

"In a minute," she yelled back. Breathe, breathe. Her nervous laughter started again. This was ridiculous. She opened the door and walked out. Jamie was waiting in the living room. He looked up with those clear blue eyes and was completely innocent of the high drama that had just played out in her bedroom.

"What are you laughing at?" he asked.

"Nothing," she said, gathering her things and biting her lip. She didn't want him to think she was completely crazy.

"Pretty funny nothing." He was smiling now.

"Let's just go." She followed him out the front door.

Cathy hopped in the car, anticipating another day in the kitchen together.

"Awesome day," he said. "Makes me want to hit the beach and enjoy it to the max." His tanned fingers gripped the wheel.

How she would love to just take off with him, forget the shop, forget everything. Maybe just for a few hours. "Thank you for taking the inventory this morning," she said. "It was a nice break."

"Happy to help," he said.

"Jamie, I want to thank you for the other night."

"There's no need, Cathy."

She touched his bare arm. "I mean it."

He pulled into the parking lot, killed the engine, and turned to her. She felt tears creeping up from some ancient burial ground. His warm fingers took her hand in his. Cathy felt naked under his stare, like her clothes had fallen away, and her skin.

"It's so hard to be around you and not tell you how I feel." He paused. "I know it's hard on you too."

She wanted to ask, "What do you mean?" His eyes lingered on her lips and she felt them part, wishing his mouth would cover them. He drew his fingers through her hair and pulled her close.

"Cat, Cat," he whispered. "What are we to do?"

It was too real now. Her limbs went numb.

"I don't know," she said, afraid to look at him.

The backdoor flew open and Tim stepped out looking like he had just got up off the ironing board and appeared at work. His outfit was pristine, a perfectly ironed button-down shirt with rolled sleeves and very low-waisted, very tight, very bell-bottom white jeans, but his expression was frantic.

"Brian is late. The place is mega packed. Thank god you two are here. I'm good, but not that good."

Jamie grinned, displaying his dazzling smile and adorable dimple. He leaned his head out the window. "I'm not so sure about that, Tim!"

They got out of the car, and Jamie held the back door open for her as they entered the café. Jamie marinated the soft tofu in tamari and garlic while Cathy grated beets, carrots, and zucchini to top off the tostada. This special would be popular today with the tahini and lemon dressing.

Cathy heard the back doorbell ring and a familiar male voice yell, "Delivery."

Mr. Taylor, in his faded overalls, walked in carrying a large ice chest filled with fresh goat milk and cheese from his local farm. It was the best in the county.

"I brought some Gravenstein apple cider today too," he said. "Still frozen from last year, but we'll have fresh pressed starting in July. I'll set them in the back refrigerator if that's okay with you."

"Sure thing. Thanks," Cathy said.

After a few minutes Brian slid in.

"Sorry, dudes. My ride was late."

Cathy scoffed. "It's a hot one, so start making lemonade."

He tied an apron around his waist and started cutting lemons.

"We could offer strawberry lemonade too," Jamie said, "with a sprig of mint."

As the place filled up, Cathy went out front to take orders and quickly relay them back to the kitchen. "One tofu tostada, one curried chicken salad in papaya, and two lemonades."

"Can't you move any faster?" Jamie asked with mock disapproval.

Cathy threw an apple at him, just missing his head.

He held his head and moaned. "Do you have workman's comp around here?"

x

Cathy attempted to glare at him. "Just get to work or out with you."

"What would you do without me?"

She couldn't even imagine that anymore. His T-shirt clung to his back. She loved the way he moved in the kitchen. It was like watching a graceful dancer. Beads of sweat moistened the soft place above his top lip. Cathy imagined tasting them with her tongue.

He hurried by and brushed against her. She didn't know how much longer she could take this proximity and not reach out and grab him. Instead she seized a large chopping knife and took it out on some fresh mint leaves.

Jamie leaned over her shoulder. "They don't need to be pulverized," he said. Cathy held up the knife. "But you do!"

Jamie took a step back. "Okay, I see the heat is getting to you," he said.

She lowered her head and the knife. "You're getting to me."

He stepped behind her. "Do you want me to leave?"

Cathy looked out at the full dining area. Tim was swamped up front. It would be hard to handle the rush without him. But they could. However, she did not want him to leave her side. "Just get to work," she said.

"Yes, boss," he said.

The knife no longer held its appeal for her and the mint was close to mush.

"Order in," Brian yelled.

"Got it," Jamie said.

Brian hustled around clearing tables and washing dishes while Cathy and Jamie kept the food and cold drinks coming.

After an hour's rush of customers, the place was dead. Brian turned the fans on in the shop, but it was still stuffy.

Everyone was probably out swimming at the river or having a cold beer.

Jamie and Cathy sat at the counter and picked at a grated salad. It was too hot to eat and having him sit so close did nothing to cool Cathy down. She watched Jamie pick at his food then drop the fork on the plate.

"I can't keep pretending forever," he said.

"Sitting on the job, I see."

Cathy jumped in her seat. She then turned around and found Jill standing behind them. How much had she heard?

Cathy hopped off the stool and hugged her. "How are you feeling?"

"It's been long enough. I'm fine, but bored and ready to work."

Jamie put his hand out to shake Jill's. "Nice to finally meet you."

Jill looked him up and down before shaking his hand. "I've heard some pretty good things about your cooking."

Jamie beamed. "And I've heard the same about yours."

Jill waved him away but not without a smile. She walked behind the counter and put on an apron. "It's a gorgeous day out. You two have been working too hard. Go play hooky, everyone else is. Tim's got the front handled and Brian and I can handle it from here."

"Did the doctor give his approval?" Cathy asked.

"Yes. He approved a few hours a day to start. I'm fine."

Jamie and Cathy exchanged glances. She was not sure it was a great idea to spend more time alone with him, but the offer was too tempting to turn down. She threw off her apron.

"Why not?" she said and kissed Jill on the cheek. "Are you sure you can handle it?"

"Of course. This will help me get back into my routine. Now you two get out of here and go cool off somewhere."

"Ready when you are," Jamie said, tossing his apron behind the counter.

Was he really? Cathy thought. Was she? Cathy took out her keys and they waved goodbye.

Chapter Twenty

*J*amie got into the car and immediately rolled down his window. Not that there was a hint of a breeze today. "Where do you want to go?" Cathy asked him as she started the car.

"Somewhere cool would be good." He wondered if there was such a place on this blazing hot day. With the back of his hand, he wiped his brow.

Cathy pulled the car onto the street and started up River Road toward Forestville. "Even the river will be warm today," she said. "And we don't have time to go to the ocean and back."

Just as they made the curve past Rio Nido, the old brick tower at the Korbel Winery came into view.

"I've got an idea where we can cool off and taste ice cold champagne as well." Cathy turned into a tree-lined parking lot.

"What a great idea," Jamie said. "The wine cellars will be cool, and I can finally sample some of the *méthode champenoise* California Champagne I've heard so much about."

Cathy led the way up the brick steps. Jamie admired the historic tan building with the flags on top. Ivy crept around the big letters that read: KORBEL WINERY est. 1882. They proceeded into the quaint two-story brick building to start the tour.

"Welcome," the tour guide said. "Today we'll chill down in the wine cellars while I tell you about our vineyard's history."

The small crowd laughed and followed him downstairs. Cathy and Jamie listened carefully as he spoke about the two-thousand-acre estate that produced award-winning, internationally recognized California Champagne.

When they reached the cellars, the guide pointed out the antiques, historical artifacts of the trade, and old photos of the family on the walls. "And every brick of this building was made by hand by the Korbel brothers," the guide said.

Jamie whispered to Cat, "That must have been a labor-intensive job!"

She kept walking, admiring the photos. "Look how wild the land was in the old pictures." Cathy motioned to a faded black and white picture behind the winery of miles and miles of untouched forest.

He stood behind her, not too close, and read the caption. "I would have liked to have seen those dense redwoods lining the hills when the brothers arrived in 1850."

The crowd moved in behind them, forcing him next to her. Her hair had a faint smell of mint and he wanted to bury his face in it. Instead he turned away, looking for something to distract himself.

"Look at this," Jamie said, pointing to an old sign on the wall for the train station that used to run there around the turn of the century. "Can you believe it? Guerneville to San Francisco by train for $1.75."

Cathy joined him for a look. "The old days," she said.

The guide continued talking about the politics, innovations, and scandals behind the scenes and the crowd moved on.

"This must have been quite a place back then," Jamie said.

They followed along, proceeded through the rooms like any normal couple on vacation, hitting the local tourist areas. He could almost pretend this was just a regular day with Cathy. Almost.

The guide opened a large door and waved them in. "I'll leave you here now in the competent hands of Mark, who will be pouring three different tastings for you today."

Cathy walked over to the bar. Jamie followed. He wanted to reach out, put his arm around her.

"Today we'll be serving the famous Korbel Brut that was formulated in 1956 as a lighter, dryer champagne for the American taste."

Mark placed glasses before them and filled them with champagne. Jamie sipped the cool, crisp liquid. "Excellent," he said.

The next glass was Blanc de Blancs, made from 100% chardonnay grapes, followed by Blanc de Noirs.

Jamie finished the last sip and set his glass on the wood bar. "Delicious. I would carry this in my own restaurant."

"High praise coming from you," Cathy said, sipping the bubbly champagne. "Which one did you like best?"

Jamie thought for a moment. "The Blanc de Noirs is quite dry. It was my favorite."

Cathy ordered a bottle of the Blanc de Noirs to take with them. "When you get the perfect job, we will open this and all celebrate together?"

Jamie wished he had as much confidence about finding a job as Cathy seemed to have in him. The look in her eyes motivated him to keep trying. "Thank you," he said. "I hope we'll pop that cork soon."

As he spoke, the whole picture of what getting a job meant unfolded before him. It meant moving out of Cathy's house and probably out of her life as well. A dull headache started at the back of his neck. It was probably the champagne and the heat.

The tour guide reappeared and reminded everyone to walk through the rose gardens before leaving the grounds.

Jamie looked over to Cathy and held open the door. "Care for a walk?"

"Sounds lovely," she said. "I hope it's cooled off some."

They walked down the dirt paths bordered on both sides by rose bushes of every color and size mixed in with native plants and other varietals. The old homestead was off in the distance, with miles of vineyards stretching behind it.

"What a truly beautiful place," Cathy said.

"You have great gardens too," Jamie said.

Cathy smiled. "Nothing like this. Maybe someday."

Someday. Jamie wondered when his someday would come. "I'd love to have my own vegetable garden sprawled behind my own home."

Cathy touched his arm. "You'll have that. Soon."

He placed his hand over hers. "How can I stay in my usual funk when you say things like that?"

Her laugh was musical and light. He closed his eyes and let it move through him. Desire welled up. He wanted this woman. To be with her. Not just today, but always.

She turned and wandered back toward the main building. He followed close behind, hoping she would not head back to the car.

Cathy stopped and fanned her face. "Let's sit down here for a while," she said.

Jamie joined her on the shady bench under a massive redwood tree. He rested his arm around her shoulders. For several minutes, they sat quietly and people watched. It felt like the most natural thing to be side-by-side, enjoying the day. Cathy nestled her head against him. He wanted to hold her forever, let all his responsibilities disappear and walk off together into these lush woods. A few sips of champagne and his thinking was crazed. But he knew the alcohol wasn't what muddled his thinking; it was Cathy.

Jamie caressed her arm with his fingertips. Her bronze skin was electric under his touch.

Cathy sighed and looked up into his eyes. His lips brushed hers and he was lost. He pulled her into his arms and let this kiss linger.

She pulled back, breathing hard.

"Cat, I don't know what to say."

"We're in an impossible situation. What can we say?" she said, looking up at him.

Jamie hated seeing her sad. He kissed her forehead. "You have it all together on the outside, Cathy, but I see the pain in your eyes. I don't want to cause you any more."

"The pain would be not seeing you," she said. "But the guilt …"

Jamie clenched his teeth. "It haunts me too."

"We must stay away from each other then," Cathy said.

"It's too late for that," Jamie said. "I care too much about you."

A tear rolled down Cathy's cheek. "What kind of person am I, falling in love with my friend's husband?"

"You're the kind of person who needs love. Just like the rest of us. I'm the one who is not being fair."

"Good people do bad things sometimes," she said. "I don't know how long I can keep doing this."

Neither did he. Just how long before someone got hurt? Or was it already too late?

A breeze off the river hinted at a cooler evening to come. People walked by them, voices trailed off.

"Don't think I haven't thought about leaving. Even before I met you," Jamie said. "If I got a divorce, there is not a court in this state that would award me custody of Amber. Pam would take her away and I couldn't live with that."

Cathy squeezed his hand. "Amber comes first. We both know it. And Pam."

Jamie sighed and pulled his feelings in check. The names of his wife and daughter brought him to reality. The warm buzz from the champagne dissipated, and he dropped his arm from Cathy's shoulder.

"You're right," he said. He stood and stretched his legs. "We better get back." They walked toward the car in silence, followed by the sweet scent of roses on the breeze.

Chapter Twenty-One

It felt like there was a forest fire in the kitchen today, with flames racing down Cathy's neck. The café at Health & Hearth never felt so much like a hearth before. The heat was supposed to break tomorrow. Her three houseguests were out swimming somewhere, laughing and having fun. Cathy felt left behind. At least lunch was slow enough to handle and now, with Brian showing up, she could go home.

"Help is here," Brian, said clearing the last table.

"And not a moment too soon." Cathy threw off her apron.

"Everything copacetic?" he said.

"Fine. I'm just tired." The kind of tired that sleep would not fix, she thought.

"Bummer," Brian said before turning to wash dishes.

Bummer was not the word for it.

Cathy wondered where to go now. It was darn depressing being in the house alone. The bills called to her from her office, but that was the last thing she felt like doing on a hot sunny day.

She pulled into her driveway and headed inside. She might as well go down to the river and work on her tan, and her skimpy, black bikini would help with that. She packed a large beach towel, thermos of iced tea, and Coppertone, then hunted for a junky book to keep her mind occupied. *Oliver's Story*, the sequel to *Love Story*, was on her nightstand. It was probably a tearjerker. Perfect. She slid her beach-back chair under her arm, pushed down her sunglasses, and headed out. Cathy's flip-flops snapped her heels as she walked down the dirt path to the road where she could cross.

She tried not to think about where Jamie and his family went and what they were doing, but without much success. Cathy was the one who told them to go to the beach, so she had no right to be upset at being left behind. She kicked a pebble out of the way and entered the sandy area. A mob scene awaited. Some good-looking guys with great bods were playing volleyball on the sand. Cathy staked her towel close enough to watch. Men in shorts, no shirts, and in motion were always a good distraction.

The suntan oil glistened on her skin. She hoped no one kicked sand or tried to put the move on her. She dove into the book and threw it down after a few pages. Oliver's best friend was telling him he looked ill and what did he recommend? That Oliver marry again. The guy's wife, his soul mate, recently died and he should get married again? Like that would cure anything.

It was hard to concentrate. The smell of Coppertone permeated the air, and kids were screaming as they ran in and out of the river. Shouts came from the volleyball game, and Cathy turned her attention there. Bodies jumping, sliding in the sand, pounding the heck out of the ball—it was fairly entertaining.

"Hey, man, out of my way," some big guy yelled as he lunged for the ball.

A tall, dark-haired guy in yellow trunks gave Cathy a side-glance and a mega smile that must have worked like a charm on most women. She picked up her book and buried her face back in it. After a minute, she peeked over the cover to see if he got the hint and saw the volleyball heading right at her. It landed right by her towel, scattering sand all over her smooth, oiled legs. Mr. Good-Looking was heading her way to retrieve it. Peeved, she held the ball up to him. He grabbed her hands and pulled her up with it.

His eyes scanned her sparsely clad body. "Come on and join us. You sure look in good enough shape to play."

His grin was contagious. Maybe she would. Hitting something might feel really good about now. She followed him onto the court and took her stance in the warm sand.

"Name's Jeff," he said, watching for the ball.

"Cathy."

He made a grand dive and saved the ball from hitting the ground as he set it up for her. She pounded it over the net with great satisfaction.

"Good shot," he said as his hot, moist skin brushed against hers. "Live around here?"

"Nope." It was none of his business.

They won the serve and Jeff easily sent it over the net. It felt good to work off some of her tension running around in the sand and pounding something. The afternoon breeze moved through her hair and cooled her sweaty body. After a few games, the players dispersed and Jeff followed Cathy back to her towel.

He pointed up the beach a bit. "Want a beer? I've got some over at my cooler."

"I don't like beer."

His eyes roamed her body. A month ago she would have been more than tempted.

"How about we clean up then and I'll take you out for a glass of wine and dinner?"

Much better offer. She weighed her options: eating alone at home wondering about Jamie or having Jeff take her out.

"Sounds fine," she said, "but I'll meet you there."

His smile showed triumph. Don't get too excited there, boy, it's only dinner, she thought.

"I'm renting a place for the week downriver a little," Jeff said. "I don't know my way around yet. You choose. Where should we meet?"

He seemed like he could afford a good dinner and nothing nearby was particularly interesting. "The Village Inn it is then," Cathy said. "They have great food, and it's only a few miles down River Road in Monte Rio."

Jeff stood up and brushed sand off his rear. Cathy took in his tanned, muscular legs.

He flashed a smile. "See you there at seven?"

"Why not?" She could think of quite a few reasons, but caution and reason had left her when Jamie and his family walked out the door that morning.

After showering, blow-drying her hair, and painting her nails, Cathy chose a revealing red sundress and low-heeled sandals. Why am I doing this? she thought. Wearing red like *The Scarlet Letter*. I'm not interested in seeing Jeff's bedroom, and this dress will send the wrong signals. Too damn bad, I feel like wearing it.

A Stephen Stills song came on the radio and she hummed along until she realized the words were talking about if you can't be with the person you love, you might as well love the one you're actually with.

She parked in front of the quaint Village Inn, nestled in the giant redwoods. Years ago, the inn was used as the filming location for the movie *Holiday Inn*. She could imagine Bing Crosby singing in the bar and Fred Astaire dancing on the outdoor patio. It didn't look much different now. Painted window boxes filled with red geraniums set off the yellow paint and white trim exterior.

Inside, the place buzzed with tourists. Jeff was easy to spot in the waiting area with his deep tan against a white linen shirt that set off his good looks. He waved Cathy over and she took a seat in a cane-backed chair. Over in the bar, she could see people drinking margaritas. At one table they were working on a puzzle. The mom and son team that owned the place kept it real friendly. It had a casual but elegant atmosphere with cloth table coverings, fresh flowers, candles on every table, and great food with an Italian flair. Not to mention their famed homemade desserts.

"You look gorgeous," Jeff said, rolling out the last syllable.

"Thanks. You look great yourself."

Before Cathy could get comfortable, the hostess, dressed in a full-length silk caftan, led them to a table in the back. Cathy loved these seats by the window that faced the river.

Jeff helped her into her seat and then took his across from her. She perused the superb wine list and freshly printed daily menu. The smell of garlic and fresh fish made her mouth water as she considered her options.

"Shall we order a bottle of champagne first?" he asked.

"That would be nice." Cathy wondered if he thought this was a special occasion.

"Schramsberg Vineyards is superb."

She nodded. Expensive taste.

"Then we'll order that," he said, closing the menu.

The waiter approached their table and went over the evening specials, including the vegetarian chef's special cheese soufflé.

Cathy ordered the shrimp and linguine fra diavolo and a butter lettuce salad, and Jeff ordered the pork lasagna and minestrone soup. Already she questioned why she'd come. She couldn't think of a thing to say and she would rather be home weeding her garden. Her impulse to join him was just like her old self, only looking for the next good time. She also really needed a good distraction.

"Do you come here often?" he said.

"Once in a while, when I'm in town," Cathy said.

"Where do you live when you're not vacationing on the River?"

"Around." She shrugged, trying to convey a look of mystery.

He winked then rambled about his new job—"Right out of law school! At a top San Francisco firm, Pillsbury and something. We take the most high-profile cases."

Cathy nodded and tried not to look at her watch too often. He didn't ask her one more question about herself. However, he did manage to ask how her shrimp was and ask for a bite. She was rather possessive over her food and was not thrilled to give him one.

After the dinner dishes were cleared away, Jeff reached across the table and took her hand. "Would you like to have dessert at my place? I have a suite right over the river. We could soak in the hot tub and then …"

By now the two glasses of champagne had loosened her inhibitions, and he was one gorgeous specimen. But she was no longer the same woman looking for a heart-numbing good time. Her mind drifted to Jamie. "I'm pretty tired and I have to work tomorrow. Not all of us are on vacation."

He looked disappointed but not deterred. He didn't even wonder why she was working if she was supposedly here on vacation. Or perhaps he had already figured out Cathy's game.

"Then how about you come down to San Francisco next weekend? I can show you the town and my place on the Embarcadero."

She was about to say, "No, never, I'm leaving," when she saw Jamie, Pam, and Amber enter the restaurant. Cathy wanted to shrink under the seat, but they saw her and walked over.

"Cathy, what a surprise to see you here," Pam said. "And who is this?" she said. Pam looked at Jeff as though he were an entrée.

"Jeff Chandler," he said, standing and shaking her hand, then Jamie's.

Pam smiled away at Jeff, but Jamie looked right at Cathy and then at the plunging neckline of her red dress. Her stomach dropped. She didn't want him to think … what? That she was with another man?

"Can we sit with them?" Amber asked.

Pam looked ready to say yes, but Jamie shook his head no. "Let's give them their privacy," he said, motioning the hostess to another table across the room.

His back was to Cathy now. She could see Pam chattering, but Jamie looked rigid. Cathy looked over at Jeff and then back again, and knew without a doubt there was no one else she wanted to be with but Jamie.

The waiter brought the check and Jeff glanced over the bill. Cathy pulled out a twenty-dollar bill and dropped it on the tray. "I'm sorry, Jeff, I shouldn't have come. I gotta go."

He looked dumbfounded, then stood and took her arm.

"Let go," she said, making sure he knew she meant it. Released, she walked straight out the door, past Jamie's table, feeling his eyes burn through her back. She sped out of the parking lot and up the road, trying to get away, but tears followed her all the way home.

Chapter Twenty-Two

Could Cathy have created a worse hell than spending day after day working with Jamie in this little kitchen? She should have asked Brian to come, but he was probably zonked out somewhere. Jill had something to do with the kids and then a doctor's appointment to get a permanent back-to-work release, so Cathy was stuck. If Jamie did one more helpful thing, she would kill him. Not a word about last night, not even a look. She erased the menu board that he had carefully written out for the day. "It's too hot for soup," she said.

He raised an eyebrow before returning to his expertly chopped, matched carrot slices. Perfect and kind, how did he expect her to …? She realized he did not expect her to do anything.

Cathy scribbled the menu again. Chinese chicken salad, veggie burgers with guacamole, cold cucumber soup, and sautéed chard with tofu. He glanced over and nodded.

What was he doing now? She leaned over his shoulder and watched him chop, chop, chop. Such perfect knife cuts. Now he mashed avocados with his hands, gooey green slithering through his long fingers. "Don't forget to add garlic," she snapped.

"Yes, ma'am."

"And don't make it too spicy."

His glare was not friendly. More like a dog's warning look before it bites. "I know how to cook," he said.

Why was she mad? Jamie had been out with his family. She was the one on a date. What did she want from him? What could he give? What could she?

He stopped mashing and looked her squarely in the eye. "Is something wrong, Cat?"

Wrong? she thought. What could be wrong? All she could think of was Jamie. "Please call me Cathy. No one calls me Cat."

Another raised eyebrow. "Okay, Cathy. If I'm crowding you, I'll just clean up and head out."

How had he managed to make her feel even worse? He washed his hands and took off his apron. She felt desperate for him to stay. She knew she hurt his feelings, but she couldn't stop herself.

"Take the car. You or Pam can pick me up at four."

She threw him the keys and choked on her words. She watched him close the door.

Guacamole was the perfect place to vent her frustration. She saw Tim wandering over and hoped he had the sense to remain silent.

"Looks like you're pulverizing those avocados."

Cathy gave him a fierce look.

He stepped back. "I'm sure they'll taste divine."

Tim knew her moods. She sometimes wondered if gay men made the best friends and the rest of the male sex should be avoided altogether. Sweat ran down the back of her shirt as she rushed to prepare the lunch by herself. It was her own fault. Jamie probably went home and told Pam how difficult she was. Of course he wouldn't do that. He was too much of a gentleman.

"Sorry, Tim. Could you call Brian and find out if he can come in today?"

"Sure thing." Tim made a quick exit.

She pounded her fist into the veggie burger mix and pretended it was Jamie's head. How dare he walk out of the kitchen? Tears threatened, shutting down her throat. She grabbed a towel and wiped off her hands and stomped out the back door before anyone could see her. Outside, a slight breeze brought reprieve, but the tears came anyway. Cathy recognized the pain pouring down her cheeks. Her ex-husband, Todd, flashed across her mind—his face when she told him she was pregnant, the same sinking feeling of hopelessness. She leaned against the wall. Jamie, his face … that hurt look. If she didn't chase him away or run the other way herself, there would be more pain.

Tim stuck his head out the door, took one look at Cathy, and closed it back up. All men were basically the same when they saw a hysterical woman. This made her laugh. She dragged herself up and wiped the tears. There was work to do.

Inside, the seats at the counter and a few tables were filling. Why was everyone eating here today for lunch? Tim did what he could to help in the back and cover the front register too.

"It will be a minute" became Cathy's mantra.

When she was ready to yell for everyone to leave, Brian rushed in and threw an apron around his waist. He took one look at Cathy's face and moved even quicker.

"I'm all over it," he said as he filled the ticket orders.

Cathy didn't even have time to thank him. She was too buried in avocado and cold soup for two hours. Her head pounded. Everyone eat and leave, she prayed. When the last person paid his bill, she phoned Jill.

"Has the doctor given the approval for you to come back to work?" Cathy asked, trying not to sound desperate. Mercifully, Jill said yes she'd be in tomorrow. Jill was approved to come back to work without restriction. It was a good thing, because Cathy needed a break.

They needed to plan the menu for the Fourth of July picnic too.

And she owed Jamie an apology.

The fog had rolled in from the ocean and cooled the temperature. Even so, Cathy couldn't wait to get home and take a nap. Curling up with the cats in her comfy bed sounded perfect. But when she walked in the door, Amber pounced.

"Auntie Cathy, will you read me a story now? This one, this one." She held up Cathy's old worn copy of *The Velveteen Rabbit* she'd shown her the other night.

Cathy was tired, but those innocent blue eyes tugged at her heartstrings. "Sure, let me just get cleaned up a bit and we can sit down and read together."

Amber jumped up and down in place. Pam leaned over Jamie's shoulder and whispered something in his ear. From the look on her face, Cathy guessed she wanted to use this reprieve from mothering for some time alone with Jamie. His shoulders stiffened, or had Cathy imagined that? He looked like he could use a nap, too.

Cathy could cover for him for the night. It was the least she could do after giving Jamie such a hard time today. "You two go ahead and go out if you'd like," Cathy said. "Amber and I are fine here."

Pam looked to Jamie. Her eyes pleaded.

"Le Bistro called, and I have that interview tomorrow," he said. "I really should take some time to prepare."

"Wonderful! You'll do great. Just be yourself," Pam said. "Now we have to celebrate. Let's go out for a glass of wine. Okay?"

His smile was not ecstatic, but he agreed.

"What about dinner for you two?" Jamie said, looking directly at Cathy.

Cathy winked at Amber. "Perhaps mac and cheese with ice cream for dessert?"

A smile curled up her rosy cheeks. "Yes," Amber whispered back, eyeing her parents in case of disapproval.

"Done," Cathy said.

"Well, thanks," Jamie said.

"No thanks necessary. Sorry about today."

"No sorry necessary," he said.

Silence hung in the room. "Can we go now?" Pam asked. She took his hand and led Jamie to the door.

Jamie turned back to Cathy. "Are you sure this is going to work for you?"

"I'm looking forward to it. Now, you two get going." She couldn't believe how much she was looking forward to an evening alone with a four-year-old.

Cathy and Amber watched them leave from the porch.

Amber waved madly. "Bye, Mommy. Bye, Daddy."

They watched them take off down the dusty road from their perch on the porch swing. Amber's warm little body curled up next to her, and she rested her head on Cathy's chest.

Amber opened the shiny cover of *The Velveteen Rabbit* and placed it over their laps. The swing creaked as they rocked gently back and forth.

"I love this story. It's still one of my favorites," Cathy said. "You know it was written a long, long time ago."

Amber ran her tiny finger over the illustration of the fluffy rabbit on the cover page. "I want my own bunny."

"You'll have to ask your parents about that."

Cathy imagined that the last thing her parents wanted about now was a bunny hopping around. The cats might find it amusing, but the bunny would not. A cool breeze moved across the porch as they settled in to read.

There was once a Velveteen Rabbit and in the beginning he was really splendid.

Cathy's mind reeled. She'd been really splendid once too, before Todd.

She continued reading about the boy receiving the bunny for Christmas and how it was his favorite toy. Then after a while, the boy put the rabbit on the shelf, forgotten.

Familiar. This was not the story of her marriage, she reminded herself.

Rabbit was made to feel himself very insignificant and commonplace, and the only person who was kind to him at all was the Skin Horse. He told the rabbit that someday he might become real.

Had Cathy ever had a Skin Horse? Someone who was kind to her?

"What is real?" asked the Rabbit one day.

"Real isn't how you are made," said the Skin Horse. "When a child loves you for a long, long time, not just to play with, but REALLY loves you, then you become Real."

Cathy put the book down in her lap. Tears stung her eyes. She never cried and now she was doing a lot of it.

"Why are you crying, Auntie Cathy?" Amber asked.

She sniffed and wiped away her tears with her bare arm, frantically looking for a tissue. "No reason, just the story makes me sad sometimes."

"Am I Real?" Amber asked.

"Your mom and dad love you very, very much and you were made Real a long time ago."

Amber smiled, her face glowing.

Cathy thought she was Real once … a long time ago before her father started drinking. She remembered being loved. She pushed down the feelings and kept reading.

Once you are Real you can't be ugly, except to people who don't understand.

"What does that mean?" Amber said.

"It means when someone loves you, they always think you're beautiful. Those who don't see your beauty can't really see you at all."

"Oh," she said thoughtfully. "Read some more, please."

The story went on to reveal how the Rabbit once again became the boy's favorite toy. One day the boy couldn't sleep until Nana found the Rabbit.

"You must have that old Bunny!" she said. "Fancy all that fuss for a toy!"

The boy sat up in bed and stretched out his hands.

"Give me my Bunny!" he said. "You mustn't say that. He isn't a toy. He's REAL!"

With a sigh, Cathy wondered what it would be like to be loved like that. Amber was loved like that, Pam was loved like that, Jamie was loved like that, Cathy was … not. Not by a person who would stay at her side. Not in a way that could be real.

The story saddened when the boy got sick with scarlet fever and his rabbit, now riddled with germs, was taken from him and tossed outside, and left all alone to be burned. Amber looked panicked, so Cathy held her close.

And while the Boy was asleep, dreaming of the seaside, the little Rabbit lay among the old picture books in the corner behind the fowl-house, and he felt very lonely … What use was it to be loved and lose one's beauty and become Real if it all ended like this?

Cathy wondered this herself. Amber was looking at her with wide, panicked eyes and she knew she needed to get to the happy ending before Amber started crying.

And a tear, a real tear, trickled down his little shabby velvet nose and fell to the ground … Where the tear had fallen, a flower grew out of the ground … And presently the blossom opened, and out of it stepped a fairy.

"Ahhhhhhh," Amber sighed. "A real fairy?"

Cathy shook her head yes and continued.

"I am the nursery magic Fairy," she said. "I take care of all the playthings that the children have loved. When they are old and worn out … then I come and take them away with me and turn them into Real … You were Real to the Boy," the Fairy said, "because he loved you. Now you shall be Real to everyone."

Amber looked dreamy. Cathy remembered when she was young and still believed in happy endings. How much love did it take to become real again? Hope glimmered in the distance.

Amber gave Cathy a big hug. "I love that book. Will you read it again soon?"

"Sure," Cathy said, thinking, No, never. Crying over a children's book, what was next? "Let's go make dinner. Mac and cheese coming up!"

Amber jumped off the chair and they raced into the kitchen to fix a comforting meal. After dinner, Cathy tucked the sweet girl into her bed and sang the only lullaby she could remember.

"Hush little baby, don't say word, Mama's going to buy you a mockingbird."

She couldn't remember the lyrics, so Cathy made up a few verses about Mama buying French fries and a Coke. Cathy could get used to this: having a little girl to read to, sing to, kiss goodnight. Someone she could love into real.

Chapter Twenty-Three

"Jamie is out on his interview, so it's time to have a girl's day out," Cathy declared. The three girls jumped into the car, looking forward to some fun. Pam and Cathy sang along to "Love is in the Air" blasting on the radio as they sped down the freeway to the Coddingtown Mall in Santa Rosa.

"This feels like the old days," Pam said, striking a harmony with Cathy on the chorus.

They did have fun, Cathy thought. Just the two of them sometimes. And along with Caroline in high school. So many boys and parties and Friday night football games. Cathy watched from the stands, but Pam was a cheerleader and everybody's sweetheart. It was an easy friendship based on one thing … having a good time. Perhaps for Pam it was the closest thing to having a real family. For Cathy, it was somewhere she fit in. Two friends who focused mostly on themselves, never asked many questions.

Amber joined in singing with her little-girl voice; they were a trio now heading out for some heavy shopping and eating.

The Coddingtown Mall was packed because there was an event for kids going on in the central area. Waiting in line, they saw a nearby clown making balloon animals in all shapes and colors. Many other parents had kids in tow. One baby with a tiny pink bow in its singular black curl was screaming loud enough to hear outside. Part of Cathy wanted to run into the nearest shop or ice cream store and escape. Another part was considering, is this what I'm missing not having my own child? A longing she suppressed for many years had resurfaced. She imagined a little blonde cutie like Amber calling her Mommy and jumping into her arms. And a husband …

It was finally their turn. Pam shepherded Amber to the clown.

"I want a kitty just like Snowy."

"And what kind of kitty is that?" asked the clown.

Amber scrunched up her face. "A white one."

He laughed and started twisting white and black balloons into a body and head with ears. The squeaking of the balloons sent goose bumps up Cathy's arms, but the long wait was worth it when he handed over the cat. Amber giggled and hugged it to her heart.

"Are you girls hungry for lunch?" Pam said.

"Sounds good to me," Cathy said as Amber flew her cat in the air, ignoring the question.

"Amber?"

"I want McDonald's," she said.

They decided junk food just this once was acceptable, and the thought of a creamy chocolate shake sealed the deal.

After lunch, they hit the shops in earnest, starting with a stylish women's clothing store. Pam eyed the small sizes longingly. "I remember when I used to fit in these cute little dresses."

Cathy nodded sympathetically.

Pam chose some jean shorts and a skimpy white knit top to try, while Cathy picked out a flowery skirt and a sea green tank top to match. Amber sat on the floor in the dressing room, waiting for her fashion show.

"What do you think?" asked Pam, assessing herself in the full-length mirror at the end of the room.

"It looks cute," Cathy said. "Flattering."

Pam looked expectantly at Amber. "And what do you think?"

Amber made a face. "It doesn't look like mommy clothes."

Amber was probably right, Cathy thought. The outfit, with its low cut, tight-fitting top, and hip-hugger waistline, did look a bit sexier than most of her other clothes.

Pam raised an eyebrow and looked at herself again in the mirror. She looked at the price tag and gasped.

"Hey, moms deserve some fun too," Cathy said.

"Should I buy it?" Pam said, guilt written all over her face. She never could say no to pretty things.

"Jamie will love it," Cathy said, wishing she could swallow the words.

Pam's flirty expression left no doubt why she wanted the outfit.

Cathy turned to look at herself in the big mirror to see all angles. The colors were perfect on her and the skirt seemed flattering.

"You look great," Pam said. "Like a forest nymph."

Amber ran her fingers along Cathy's flowery skirt.

"What's a nymph?" she said, looking up at her mom.

"Kind of like a princess who lives in the woods."

"I like your skirt, Auntie Cathy."

"Thanks, Amber," Cathy said. "I think I'll buy it then. And your mom said we're going to go buy you something next."

She clapped her hands. "Yes! And something for Daddy too."

They paid for their purchases and exited back out to the mall. Cathy led the way to PlayTime Kids store. Amber ran ahead, telling the others to hurry up. By now, Pam was carrying the balloon cat and lagging behind.

"How about a new doll or a book?" Cathy suggested as they roamed the aisles.

Amber ran over and started playing with a tin stove. "I want to cook like Daddy."

The kitchen set was expensive. Cathy knew Pam couldn't afford it right now, so she offered to buy it as an early birthday present for Amber.

"You're doing enough for us already," Pam frowned. "Amber doesn't need such an expensive toy."

Amber teared up. It broke Cathy's heart. No one ever *needed* a toy, but sometimes they sure felt good.

"I would like to buy it and keep it at my house for whenever Amber visits."

"Well, I can't keep you from buying your own toys, can I?" Pam said. Besides, if Jamie gets a job in the city, Amber won't be playing with it much anyway.

Cathy was taken aback. She did not want Pam to feel bad, but she had the money for the kitchen set and keeping it at her house was a good compromise.

Amber continued to play with the plastic pots and pans.

Cathy pulled Pam aside. "Are we cool on this?"

"You always had to show me up, even back in high school with your new car and perfect everything."

Cathy froze. "I'm really sorry if my offer came across that way. It makes me happy giving Amber gifts."

"Well it isn't always about making you happy, Cathy."

"Fine," Cathy said, "I won't buy the kitchen set."

Pam looked over at Amber, obviously completely enthralled with the kitchen set. "Well ... I know Jamie would love Amber to have it."

"If you're sure it's okay with you then?"

Pam smiled. "Whatever." She walked over to Amber. "You love this kitchen, don't you?"

Amber's eyes were wide. She nodded.

"Let's get it then! And we must get daddy a present too."

Cathy purchased the cooking set, but the carefree feeling of the day was lost.

After they managed to get out of the toy store and promise to pick up the box at loading in an hour, they hunted to get Jamie a present. Pam and Amber laughed over items he might enjoy in the men's department at JC Penney's.

Cathy wanted to go to the kitchen store and get him something she knew he'd really love, but she didn't want to interrupt or cause another rift. She also couldn't very well go off and buy him a present now too, or Pam would have a cow.

Cathy could imagine Jamie opening a box from her with a coveted chef's knife inside.

"Oh, Cathy," he would say adoringly.

In her dreams maybe. Her guilty conflicted dreams.

They decided on a nice shirt for his interviews. A practical choice. Pam's mind was on getting him a rock star chef job where he would be famous, make lots of money, and she would bask in the glory as his wife. High school never left some people. Perhaps Cathy was being a bit high school herself, thinking something so snippy.

Pam spotted a pay phone. She decided to call the house to see if Jamie was there yet. Amber and Cathy window-shopped while they waited.

"No more shopping. It's time to go home. Daddy is waiting." Cathy turned and Pam was right behind them, looking smug.

"How did the interview go?" Cathy asked.

"They loved him. With any luck, you'll have the house to yourself again next week."

Cathy forced a smile and headed for the exit. Now they needed to find the loading zone and pick up the kitchen set for Amber.

After the oversized box was loaded into the car, Cathy was happy to finally leave the mall. There was no singing in the car on the way home. Amber slept in the backseat as Pam gazed out the window. Who knew where Pam's mind was? Somewhere in the past? Or planning their bright future?

Cathy pulled into the driveway and parked. She was exhausted from the day.

"I'll have Jamie carry that thing in." Pam opened her door and let Amber out.

Amber ran up the deck stairs and into Jamie's waiting arms. "Daddy, Auntie Cathy bought me my own kitchen. Now I can cook like you."

Jamie's eyes flashed to Cathy, then to Pam.

Pam pecked him on the cheek on her way into the house. "It's in the back of the car if you want to bring it in."

Jamie walked over to Cathy. "Thank you, that was very kind. But please don't feel like you have to do this."

"I wanted to encourage the next budding chef in the family," Cathy said. "It makes me happy to make Amber happy."

He smiled. "I understand."

Jamie headed toward the car. Amber galloped behind him.

Cathy entered the house and tried to avoid Pam, but she was standing right in the living room with her arms folded across her chest.

"Where do you want him to put it?" Pam asked.

Pam followed her into the kitchen, and Cathy pointed out a corner where it would fit well. "This will work."

"Yeah, I guess," Pam said. "You know, Cathy, she's *my* daughter, no matter what you buy her."

Cathy's breath caught. Pam's expression was ugly, but before she could say what she was really thinking, Cathy forced herself to rest a beat. Pam knew the baby Cathy miscarried had been a girl. Why was it so hard for her to let Cathy enjoy Amber a little?

Before Cathy could respond, Jamie swept into the kitchen with the big box in his arms.

"Amber's kitchen arrives!"

Cathy pointed. "Put it right here for our new little chef."

"Jamie, can I talk to you in the bedroom for a minute? Now," Pam said.

Jamie looked at Cathy with a puzzled expression. She shrugged as she watched in dismay as they walked away.

After a few minutes Jamie returned to the kitchen.

"I'm sorry if I caused a problem," Cathy said softly.

Jamie looked at her with tired eyes. "I know you meant well," he said, glancing over at his daughter. "Shall we set up your kitchen now?"

"Please, please, Daddy," Amber chimed.

Jamie unloaded the toy stove and placed a child-sized tin pot on top of the little burners painted just the same size.

"I made pasta for dinner. Would you like to help me stir the sauce on your stove, Amber?"

"Yes!"

Cathy watched Jamie pour a little of the cold sauce in Amber's pan, then heat up the rest on the grown-up stove. The aroma of fresh tomato, basil, and garlic made her mouth water. Especially after the fast food at lunch.

Amber stirred briskly.

"Good job," Cathy said.

"I'm cooking, just like Daddy."

"She loves it," Jamie said.

"She does. I hope Pam understands."

Jamie sighed. "She never had nice toys like this growing up. This brought back memories, but she's feeling better now."

Cathy remembered when they were teenagers. She'd always needed to be careful about sharing with Pam when her parents bought her new things. She didn't want Pam to feel bad because her mother couldn't always buy her nice things. And Pam loved nice things. As a cheerleader, Pam was the happiest Cathy had ever seen her. Pam thrived as the center of attention. Cathy preferred watching from the sidelines. Cathy's father said Pam needed to be treated special. He was the perfect dad when Pam was around, but not to his own daughter. She didn't want to think about that.

"Earth to Cathy," Jamie said.

She looked up and smiled. The table was set and Amber helped her dad dish out the spaghetti.

"Pam," he yelled toward the bedroom. "Dinner is on the table."

Pam came out all dressed up in her new outfit, with bright pink lipstick and blush to match. She had obviously spent some time fixing up her hair as well.

"You look pretty, Mommy."

"Yes, you do," Jamie said. "Really pretty." He pulled out a chair for her and Cathy sat down in one by Amber.

Cathy helped Amber cut up her sketti into small pieces. Pam would not make eye contact with her. Cathy secretly hoped Pam would spill spaghetti sauce on her new outfit. She smiled, tried to eat, and not lose her appetite while she watched Pam bat her eyes at Jamie.

Cathy felt like an intruder. She needed to back away no matter what her feelings were for Jamie. After clearing the table, she retreated to her room with the cats for peace, quiet, and time to get her head straight.

Snowy, Libby, and Cathy curled up in the bed under the patchwork quilt. She glanced at the novels piled up at her bedside. There was *How to Save Your Own Life* by Erica Jong, but she was not in the mood to figure that out. Cathy chose an old Mary Stewart book she had not read, *The Crystal Cave.* She loved Arthurian legends and she'd heard this rendition was one of the best.

It was dark by the time she surfaced from Camelot. The cats were stretched out sleeping, and she thought she would do the same. But first a quick trip for a glass of water. It was quiet when she opened her door. Everyone must have gone to bed early. As she entered the hall, she saw Pam closing her bedroom door behind her.

"Be right back, Jamie," she said, blowing kisses. Pam's eyes met Cathy's. The flush on Pam's face was evident. Small red blushes mingled with moist beads of sweat. Afterglow? Cathy's stomach contents gagged in her throat at the mental image of Pam and Jamie intertwined.

Strategically, Cathy pushed past her and entered the bathroom, locked the door and headed to the toilet. Hunched over, she choked up what was left of the spaghetti dinner into the pale gray toilet water, colored by old pipes. The smell of fresh-washed bath towels and the garlic from dinner made her head spin as she puddled to the floor. Memories surfaced of lying on the same cold floor years ago after the miscarriage: endless blood, tormenting pain, and a broken heart.

They were still having sex. Of course, why wouldn't they? They were married! Her stomach felt like it was being fed through the ringer of an old-fashioned washer.

A rap on the door made her groan.

"Cathy, are you all right?" Pam asked in her sing-song voice.

All right? When was the last time Cathy was all right? Before they showed up? Before Todd had deserted her? Before her dad died and left them nothing but debts?

Her persistent knock made Cathy want to open the door and wring Pam's not-so-dainty neck. Instead, she fanned her sweaty face and tried to stand. "Fine!"

Go away, Cathy prayed. Go away.

Chapter Twenty-Four

*J*amie left the girls at the house fixing dinner and went for a walk by the river to clear his pounding head. Days had stretched to weeks with his job hunt, and nothing had come to fruition yet. He knew Pam was restless and not as pleased as he was with the beautiful country living Sonoma County offered. Pam always seemed to want more, and usually it was something big and fancy. He also knew he was in dangerous waters staying much longer with Cathy. He'd let his feelings for her color every thought. He'd always been the good guy everyone could count on. But now, what had he become? Pam was the mother of his child, and in his own way, he loved her too.

He walked along the shore and admired the glistening sun skidding across the water. Tall pines cast shadows across the sand as he walked downriver and let his mind drift.

When they'd first met at the café in Santa Barbara, Jamie had been drawn to the sweet, pretty girl who needed rescuing. He'd wanted to help Pam, to show her happiness. She needed constant reassuring and he'd given it to her. Pam thought Jamie was her prince who had arrived to take her off to a castle, like her friend Caroline's husband. But castles were not Jamie's goal. He wanted a home in the country with a big garden and a swing set in the yard

It didn't take long for Jamie to realize they were not compatible for the long term. The last thing he wanted was to cause Pam any more pain. She'd already grown up in a broken home with little money or security. But he couldn't be everything to her. Her childlike attitude demanded a high price, and Jamie had dreams too.

He stopped and stared out at the green water. He remembered the day Pam had pulled him into the back room at work and broke down in tears. He'd held her close, told her that everything would be all right, if she'd just tell him what was wrong.

She was pregnant. The child was his.

Jamie's world had imploded. His father saved lives with his physician's hands. His mother was always busy with charity work. Jamie was left with nannies. The message was loud and clear … others' needs came first.

There was only one right thing to do. He'd done it. Everything would be all right. They would get married and the three of them live happily ever. He committed. He gave. He tried. His parents had not been happy with his choice of a bride or a career. But they agreed he was doing the right thing under the circumstances. They'd barely seen them after the wedding.

Pam encouraged him to go to culinary school and build his résumé. But lately her relentless pushing for him to have a bigger career made him wonder what would finally be enough for her.

He sat down on a washed-up tree trunk and watched the river currents move briskly toward the town of Jenner and then out to sea. Cathy had taken him there for the interview. She'd shown him around and he had fallen in love.

In love with the area? Yes. In love with the woman too?

Guilt seized his insides. Were his feelings for Cathy screwing up everyone's lives? Cathy had been through some hard times too. But it was different with her. She'd grown stronger, self-sufficient, and had so much to give. She made him feel stronger, and understood that pursuing what he loved mattered.

He rose and stared up at the sky. Red-tailed hawks circled as sunlight reflected off their wings. That bird of prey always reminded him of his grandmother. An avid birdwatcher, she'd been very attuned to nature. Jamie had loved their long walks through the hills and forests of Marin County. Once they had rescued an injured owl and had taken it to a wildlife animal sanctuary. Life, people, and love were sacred to her. To Jamie as well.

Was life meant to be lived without the person you love? Was it best for Amber to have two parents even if the love was gone? Was it fair to anyone to go on this way? What in the hell was he supposed to do when there was no right answer?

Chapter Twenty-Five

Another busy Wednesday at the café followed by a satisfying but exhausting day at Head Start with Jamie, and Cathy was happy they had some fun plans for the evening ahead. Barb had revealed today the very confidential information that Annie was being taken into the foster program. Her mom was in rehab and there wasn't any family that could take Annie in. Cathy wondered if she could qualify as a foster mom. Was this really something she could take on? She definitely would look into it. Annie deserved love. Even Jamie said he would mention it to Pam. Cathy didn't think that avenue would go anywhere, but Annie deserved a loving and safe home, so it was worth a try.

With all the stress building in the house, everyone was ready for a change of scenery. Lucky for them, Brian rented a cabin off the river in Summerhome Park, where he got cheap rent because he froze in the winter from absolutely no sun. He had the coldest toilet seat Cathy had ever felt. But in the summer months, it was wonderful. The tiny one-bedroom log house came furnished with everything, including silverware, and had a covered deck facing the river. The park had a recreation center with a snack bar and arcade, a private sandy beach accessible only by a footbridge or canoe, and an outdoor movie theater. Brian invited them all over for the Saturday night movie.

Back to her cheerful self, Pam folded up some light blankets while Jamie packed popcorn and other snacks in a bag.

"What movie is showing again?" Pam asked.

"It's called *The Point*."

Jamie took Amber's hand and they headed toward the car. "Isn't that the animated movie narrated by Ringo Star?"

"Right," Cathy said as she climbed into her Honda. Pam sat up front with her.

"What's 'animated' mean?" Amber asked as Jamie snapped her seat belt in place in the backseat.

"That means it's a cartoon," Jamie said.

As she drove, Cathy hummed the theme song from the movie, "Me and My Arrow." "It's a cute movie. I think you all will like it."

The setting sun threw shades of orange across the river as they drove down the narrow road leading into the park and located the outdoor seating area. Brian waved as they pulled in. He'd saved them seats in the second row. Pam and Amber scooted in on the bench next to Brian.

"How about I get us some popcorn before the movie starts?" Jamie asked.

Pam nodded. "Make it a large."

"Will do," Jamie said.

Pam held her hand up to stop him from going. "And a coke. Oh, and some juice for Amber."

"I'll come along and help carry," Cathy said, following Jamie to the snack bar. The grounds were very crowded tonight and there was a wait to get snacks. A couple of teenage boys pushed to get ahead of them in line. Cathy ended up pressed against Jamie. She let her head linger against his chest. His musky smell reminded her of their kiss.

"Boys," Jamie said, rolling his eyes.

She felt his fingers slip into hers, squeeze, and release.

When they got to the counter, Jamie ordered and Cathy offered to pay. He pushed her money back to her. "My treat."

The outside lights lowered and the pre-movie cartoon began as they made their way back to the seats with two large bags of popcorn and drinks for everyone.

Jamie moved in next to Amber, and Cathy was left sitting on the aisle. They were right on time. The movie began and Ringo's distinctive voice told them about a village where everyone and everything had to have a point, literally and figuratively. They all even had pointed heads.

Amber giggled.

In this place, Ringo continued, one poor little boy, Oblio, was sadly born with a round head. Even though everybody else liked him, the town bully wanted him gone. He was different. Period. No action was too devious for the villain to achieve his goal.

Cathy remembered how most of her so-called friends in high school had disappeared after Todd had banished her. She could relate.

They watched little Oblio and his faithful, pointy-headed dog, Arrow, begin their journey alone, hoping to figure things out. Up and down, over and through they went, all accompanied by Harry Nilsson's sweet songs.

While everyone's eyes were glued to the screen, Cathy peeked at Jamie's profile. It was glowing in the reflected light from the screen. His lips were slightly open, his hair lazily framing his face. She longed to put her head on his shoulder and nestle against him.

A cool breeze picked up and Pam passed out blankets for their laps. Jamie's leg brushed Cathy's as they all squeezed together to share the covers. It was enough to distract her from the movie again.

But Oblio was in trouble now as giant bees swarmed him. His dog ran for cover. Upsetting for sure. But not to Oblio. He believed everything had a point no matter how confusing or hard to find. Good attitude there, Cathy thought.

The blue dog, Arrow, cracked Cathy up as he tagged right along. With his pointed head and ears, he mugged at the camera with expressions that said, "Can you believe this?"

A happy ending came when Oblio finally returned home with his newfound wisdom: It was not necessary to have a pointed head, to have a point in life. The whole town rejoiced and the villain was overcome.

Amber sang along to the song, "Me and My Arrow," as the credits rolled.

Jamie chimed in and so did Cathy. "Everywhere we go, it's me and my Arrow."

"Daddy," Amber said. "I want a dog just like Arrow."

Jamie smiled. "As soon as we get a house, we'll get you a puppy too."

"A blue one?" she asked.

Pam chuckled. "Maybe a gold one like Cathy used to have. A retriever."

"Buddy was his name," Cathy said.

"I'd like a gold dog," Amber said, grinning ear to ear.

Buddy had been a great dog. He followed Cathy everywhere. Pam had a way of bringing up the memories she'd buried. It was Christmas, her senior year of high school. The fragrant pine tree her dad brought home was decorated and stood tall in their living room. Doris Day sang "Silver Bells" on the cassette player. Buddy warmed his old arthritic bones up by the fire that sparked and glowed. Dad was right next to him, holding his hands toward the flames. Mom offered sweet hot chocolate. Fluffy marshmallows floated like clouds on its surface. Dad had not had a drink all day.

Dad's booming voice asked, "Who wants to open presents?"

Cathy's mom slipped her arm around her and the light scent of gardenia was subtle on her clothing. "Cathy first," she said.

The sweet memory lingered in her heart.

By the following May, both Buddy and her father were dead. By July, Cathy was married to Todd and her mother was forced to sell their family home and move to their summer house on the Russian River.

A golden dog, a golden dad, a golden moment. Lost now in time.

In the movie, even when lost in the forest, little Oblio didn't blame anyone. He was excited about what was ahead and did not look back. What lay ahead for her? More of the infinite emptiness that she tried to fill with work and denial? And what was the point of feeling this way about a married man who would soon be gone?

Everything had a point; Cathy just had to figure it out.

Chapter Twenty-Six

Another Sunday. Days of the calendar were flying by as they set a new routine. It was hard to remember Jamie hadn't always been there. From the minute Cathy met him, she recognized him from some other place and time. She'd never believed in soul mates before. But how else could she explain this feeling of finding her other half, the person that made her whole?

Cathy floated through the days, happier than she'd been in a long time. Health & Hearth was humming along through the summer, making a bigger profit than last year. Tourists filled the Guerneville shops and cafés, families poured into the resorts along the River, and gays with great tans hung out at fine restaurants and nude beaches.

The ringing of her phone startled her. She pounced to quiet the noise so as not to wake Amber from her afternoon nap. Some man she'd dated in the spring was on the line asking if she wanted to go out for a drink later. Code language for get drunk and jump into bed, she supposed. It certainly wasn't a date. Who were these men she'd been choosing to hang out with? Placeholders until the real thing came along? Temporary distractions while life passed by? Now she could see these relationships were not safe, they were damaging. Another reinforcement that she did not deserve love. And now, she had love. But at what cost?

No sooner did she say "no thank you" to him—even though he was pretty cute—and hang up then it rang again. This time it was for Jamie. He took it on the phone in his room. Pam followed him down the hall.

When they didn't come out after several minutes, Cathy made her way down the hall towards the bathroom. She heard Pam and Jamie arguing and stopped at their bedroom door to listen. It was her house after all. He must not have gotten the job. How awful he must feel.

"What am I suppose to do, invent a job out of thin air?" Jamie's voice was strained. Cathy couldn't hear Pam's reply. "I can't just wait and hope, Pam. I need to work."

Cathy hoped Amber was in a deep sleep and could not hear them. She covered her ears and moved quickly away. Pictures of her marriage to Todd floated back, along with the ugly scenes that followed only months after their wedding day. She hurried back to the living room and took a seat in the rocker. This was not her business.

When they walked out again, the look on Jamie's face was so painful Cathy pretended not to see it. Her heart dropped as she turned away.

He stood before her. "The Inn at Napa said no. It just wasn't a good fit. They emphasized it was not my fault," he mumbled. He avoided eye contact and walked toward the kitchen. Jamie held up the bottle of Chablis. "Who wants a glass?"

Pam nodded. Cathy rose to join them. "A small one for me," she said.

Jamie poured the wine and slouched down into a dining room chair. "Our options are looking pretty limited. Perhaps we should start looking back in the Bay Area?" he asked Pam.

Cathy gulped down the wine.

Jamie's eyes stared at the wood grains of the table. Pam, a vision in a lemon-yellow empire dress, stood behind him and rubbed his shoulders. Her fingers alternately caressed his cheek and tussled his hair. Something Cathy could not do. Pam was the wife. Judging Pam's wardrobe or anything else was beneath Cathy. She still had her dignity and did not need to resort to petty thoughts to ease her own guilt.

"Whatever. It'll work out," Pam said. "This is our dream. We can't give up now."

For once Pam's smile looked wilted. Cathy wondered just what dream Pam was referring to. Jamie certainly loved Sonoma County. Pam loved the city. But she had a way of making everything seem right out of a Disney movie. Even back after Todd had walked out on Cathy, Pam had said, "He'll be back. Just wait."

Of course, Todd never even called to check on her pregnancy, much less returned. Pam lived in a fantasy world all her own. Cathy didn't know whether to pity Pam or wish she could live there too.

Fleetingly, Jamie's red-rimmed eyes met hers. Cathy's heart propelled her forward to comfort him, but she locked her legs in place and tried to breathe.

He stood and leaned on the chair to face Pam. "I only have one more interview, and if that doesn't work out, that's it."

"Don't say that," Pam said. "The one next week will be it; you'll see. Or we'll go somewhere else. Then we can start looking for our own house." The two of them paused, frozen in time.

Cathy forced herself to breathe. She could hear Amber singing "The Eensy Weensy Spider" in her bedroom. At least one of them had a father who loved them. And no matter what, Amber deserved that.

Cathy rose from the chair. "You guys can stay here as long as you like. You know that."

Pam threw her arms around Cathy. "Of course we do. You have been wonderful, Cathy, we don't know what we would have done without you."

Over Pam's shoulder, Cathy saw Jamie watching. He looked so discouraged. She wanted to shake him, tell him how wonderful he was.

Pam finally stepped back. Cathy continued to look past her to where her heart called. Words poured out of her mouth. "Jamie, I've been thinking … we could expand the dining area at my café by taking over the upstairs rooms and start serving high-end dinners."

Jamie blinked like waking from a dream. He tilted his head and looked at her.

Cathy was improvising, but she didn't care. She wanted Jamie's dream to come true. "It wouldn't take much and the only other fine dining in the immediate area is at the hotel, with no charm, no healthy options."

He just stared. Pam glanced back and forth between their faces. "What do you think?" she asked him.

"You don't have to do that for us, Cat," he said.

"It would be for me too. I've been wanting to expand, and when could I ever get a chef like you up here?"

His color was returning.

"What about Jill?" he said.

"Well, of course you will need a fantastic sous chef. And she primarily does lunch anyway."

His blue eyes stared into hers for what seemed like forever. She prayed he couldn't read her mind. What was happening to her? Was this the right thing to do? Perhaps it would be best if they left. Soon.

"Only if you're sure," Jamie said.

"Let's just see what happens next week." Cathy tried to sound casual as she picked up her wine glass and retreated to her office to give them some privacy. She could hear them whispering behind her as she walked away. From the hall, Cathy heard a sweet little voice yell, "Out came the sun and it dried up all the rain!"

She closed the office door and sat down at her desk. Heart racing, she fanned her face and neck with her hand and took a deep breath.

Would it work? She had about $8,000 in the bank and could probably get a loan for the rest. The guest rooms didn't fill every weekend, especially in the winter, when they just sat there. An intimate, fine dining area upstairs would draw tourists and locals. Getting into debt, a business partner, a higher overhead—there went her peaceful life. But it would be exciting. She punched some numbers into her new desktop calculator.

It could work. Cathy called Jill to fill her in on the idea and get her opinion. Mostly Cathy talked and it was silent on Jill's end.

"Why don't you come over tomorrow night at seven and we can all have a meeting about this at my house?" Cathy asked.

Jill was still silent 'except for the sound of her measured breathing.

"It is a bit sudden," Jill finally said. "That will give me time to think about the repercussions from this."

"Not really, I've thought about it before," Cathy said. "Jamie's cooking will draw in extra business and it would benefit all of us. You could manage the downstairs and he could manage the upstairs café."

"It might work. See you tomorrow, Cathy."

The Upstairs Café. Cathy liked the sound of it. Once money started coming in, Jamie, Amber, and Pam would move out of her house. But they would live close and she would see Jamie almost every day. And Amber.

What about Pam? She had been a friendly face once, when friendly faces were scarce. Of course she meant Pam too. They would all be close friends. Cathy could see all of them smiling like a big family.

At seven on the dot the next night, Jill knocked on the front door.

"Thanks for coming over," Cathy said.

Jill entered and made her way into the house. "No problem. It's Dan's spaghetti night, so I'm off the hook for dinner."

Jamie was at the table. Pam sat next to him drinking a Tab. Whoever formulated that disgusting diet cola had no taste buds! Amber was absorbed in the coloring books and crayons spread in front of her. Cathy took a deep breath and then walked over and joined them. Eyes glowing, Jamie pulled out the plans he'd drawn for remodeling the upstairs rooms into a fine-dining loft. At first glance they looked brilliant. Perhaps this would work after all.

Jill leaned over the plans. "I like the way you created a small waiting room on the landing. How many will the dining rooms seat?"

Jamie pointed to what was now the small attic bedroom. "If we work it right, we should be able to seat about twelve to fourteen in here and even more guests in the bigger room. Each dining area could have a name and theme."

Pam tilted her head. "Are you going to have to go downstairs for everything?"

"I took care of that some too," Jamie said brightly. "The larger bathroom between the guest rooms will be made into a waitress station with all the drinks, wine, coffee, refrigerated items, a limited pantry, and more."

"Looks like you've thought of everything we'll need," Cathy said. In her head she added up the costs for all of this and tried to keep breathing.

"My husband is pretty handy with carpentry work," Jill said, seeming to be on board now, "and remember, Susan from our book group has a remodeling business. I'm sure she'd give us a good price."

As Jamie spoke about tableware, seating options, and menu printing, Cathy felt panic set in.

"Let's get real," Jill said, staring at Cathy. "The more we all pitch in, the less the cost, but whatever way you look at this, you're looking at some big bucks."

Pam was staring at Cathy as if she were going to wave a magic wand and say, "Jamie, your wish is my command." Actually, that was probably not far from the truth.

Jamie stared down at the plans.

"We'll make this work," Cathy said, "and it will be a big success."

There was a moment of silence at the table before Jamie opened another folder and showed them a basic list of food and wine that would need to be ordered for the first week. They'd need a liquor license too. How long would that take?

"We're looking at a minimum of three thousand in remodeling costs, about that for supplies and furnishings, and another thousand plus to stock up the kitchen," Jamie continued. "Then we have the wine, menus to print, advertising, and staff to consider."

Cathy heard Jill exhale beside her. "You would need at least six months of costs behind you as well," Jill said. "Especially because, if you decide to move ahead, the restaurant won't open until after the summer rush."

"That's true," Cathy said, staring down at the massive lists of costs. "We need to think about our profit margin and when we might start making money." She looked over to Jamie.

"I'll work on a profit loss statement and have it to you in a few days," he said. "We can probably start a little smaller and build up."

Jill glanced over the sheets on the table. "Have you considered writing up a partnership agreement?"

What could Cathy say? They hadn't even discussed it. She felt foolish. "We will," she said, avoiding Jill's probing glare. She stood and walked toward the kitchen. "Anyone for iced tea?"

"Me, I do!" Amber waved her hand in the air.

Heads nodded. While she poured the sun tea over glistening ice in frosted glasses, she could hear Pam rattling on and almost dropped the pitcher.

"You know," Pam said, "we could always ask Caroline and Bentley to invest. They have the money."

Clever girl, that Pam. But Cathy thought she would rather die than ask them. She pounded down a glass of iced tea in front of Pam and smiled sweetly through gritted teeth. "Let's not go there yet, Pam. I have some money of my own."

She shrugged. "They are very successful and—"

Jamie held up his hand. "We can discuss financing later. Right now we're just throwing ideas around."

Jill continued to bring up practical questions. Concern was written all over her face, but Cathy knew Jill would be totally onboard when the decision was made.

Pam put her hand over Jamie's. "These are great ideas, sweetie. I'll do whatever I can to help."

He looked like an excited little boy who just got his first bike for Christmas.

In that moment, Cathy realized his happiness was her happiness. "Are we all in then?" Cathy asked.

Jill lifted her glass of iced tea as if making a toast. "To success."

Chapter Twenty-Seven

Cathy sank into a chair in the back room of the cafe. It had been a long week. Jamie walked in, took one look at her, and began rubbing her tight shoulders and kneading out the knots.

"Too much thinking. Relax," he said.

Her muscles melted into his hands. She closed her eyes and let the warm feeling sink in. She imagined ripping open his shirt and kissing his smooth chest, then running her tongue over the rest of his skin.

"I appreciate everything you're doing, but I hope you aren't opening this new café out of sympathy," he said.

Cathy stood, her body inches from his. Heat rushed up her body, burning a trail to her lips. Did he see her need? His eyes caressed her lips.

She let herself smile. "And here I thought I was being selfish keeping you as my chef."

"Cat," he whispered, pulling her into his arms. His warm breath penetrated her hair.

Her heart skipped a beat. "Jamie."

Their lips met, gently as first, then with urgency, blocking out anything but each other.

He held her close. "Thank you," he whispered.

"For what? The kiss?"

He gazed into her. "For caring, for offering to share this business that means so much to you."

Words wouldn't come. She knew what she wanted to say, but how could she say I love you? It was so wrong. "Jamie, what are we doing?"

His face went white. "Do you want to cancel the restaurant plans?"

"That's not what I mean."

Jamie stared at the floor. More than anything she wanted to reach out and say all was fine. But it was not, no matter how much she wanted it to be.

Obviously pulling together his feelings, he stood tall and sighed. "I'll go and let you think things out. Let me know what you decide."

"Jamie," she said. "I haven't changed my mind, and I won't."

Emotions crossed his face but he held his composure and turned to go.

She walked out into the dining room and crumbled into a booth. It was almost closing time and Tim was straightening up the shelves. Perhaps a good cry followed by several glasses of wine would help her feel better.

"Hey, Tim," she yelled. "Want to go get a glass of wine somewhere?"

Tim walked over and gave her his all-knowing look. What was it about gay guys? They seemed to pick up on everything. And in Tim's case, wear impeccable threads. His jeans still looked ironed after a full shift, and his tight T-shirt showed off the results of his weight lifting routine. He sat down next to her and shot her a look that said, "Oh you're sad, come cry on my shoulder."

She so wanted to. She was dying to tell someone, and Tim didn't tell … or judge.

"Cathy," he'd say, "I've done it all and more. We're just human, ya know."

Predictably, Cathy's head landed on his shoulder and Tim took her hand in his.

"You've got it bad, girl."

Her exhale came out as a sigh. "Bad."

He ruffled up her hair and started singing the song about everybody needing somebody to love.

Cathy slapped his shoulder and they both laughed.

"So tell me, what does this one have that all the other pretty boys parading through here drooling over you don't have—other than that little detail about him being unavailable?" Tim said.

She shot him a look. With all the cute men coming through the café either checking out Tim or Cathy, it was a loaded question.

"Jamie's not my type, girl, not enough muscles. Not like Peter. Now there was a specimen."

She saw the pain in his eyes at the mention of Peter's name. The breakup last year had just about killed Tim. Cathy and Tim had been on the same relationship course for a while: Keep it light, safe, skin deep, heart shut tight. Now Tim was sighing. She saw that faraway look in his eyes when he remembered Peter. The supposedly straight men, often married, who fought their attraction to Tim, were his deadly magnets and his downfall.

Tim kissed her forehead. "You were there for me, girl, during my high-drama heartbreak. Darling, I am right here for you now."

For the first time in what seemed like weeks, Cathy took a deep breath. "I love him," she whispered, hardly believing the words herself.

Tim nodded, understanding emanating from his eyes.

"I don't need your sympathy, I can work this out," she said, skirting out of the vinyl booth.

He took her arm. "Are you sure?"

Cathy's defenses cracked and she plopped down into the seat. Pain oozed from her pores like a breaking fever. "What am I going to do?"

He scooted Cathy out of the booth, pushing her to her feet. "Up with you," he said. "Go wash that pretty face and put on some makeup. We'll go drown our sorrows at Fife's."

It was the most popular gay resort on the river, packed with men vacationing from the Bay Area. "Well, I'll certainly be safe from temptation there," she said.

"Go," he said, pointing to the back room. "And come back looking gorgeous."

Gorgeous was the last thing she felt as she ran a brush through her thick hair that hadn't been washed that day. Cathy applied some blush to her cheeks to perk up her fading tan and raspberry lipgloss to her full lips. She removed her over-shirt and revealed the low cut leotard she was wearing under her hip-hugger jeans. Finally, she made her entrance.

Tim clapped. "Much better. Girlfriend, let's go have some fun."

Behind the tall front fence that blocked the entry of Fife's on the river in Guerneville, it was a whole new world. The upstairs bar was crowded even at 5 p.m. on a weeknight. It was summer, after all. Music was blasting from the large speakers and Cathy recognized Stevie Nicks' mind-blowing voice singing "I Put a Spell on You." She bet that happened here quite a bit.

They took seats at the bar that offered a good view of the beautifully landscaped grounds. Rolling green lawns dotted with tall pines meandered down toward the Russian River.

Out by the Olympic-size pool, naked men were parading around or draped across plastic chairs. She could smell the Coppertone from here. Tim and Cathy admired the sleek, tan bodies posing and glistening in the sun.

"What a hunk," Tim said watching a raven-haired man stretch in front of the window.

"Nice abs," Cathy said.

"And a very nice butt," Tim finished.

"I admit, I'm a bit jealous of their all-over tans."

Tim's eyes wandered over the scantily clothed men lounging on chairs all around them. "They probably spend a lot of time at Wohler Beach," he said. "I used to love it there before the police cracked down on the place. Now you have to sneak in."

"Too much of a good thing, maybe. I guess all those guys coming up from San Francisco made quite a scene," Cathy said.

Tim's smile broadened. "They sure did," he said with a wink.

The bartender came up and put some paper coasters down on the wooden bar. Tim flashed a dazzling smile and ordered two margaritas.

The bartender, dressed in a skimpy apron over tight shorts and no shirt, barely looked old enough to serve drinks. His strawberry blond curls circled his broad shoulders and his skin looked like polished bronze. An Adonis.

"Coming right up," he said with a smile that could melt a glacier.

Cathy nudged Tim. "He looks interested."

Tim beamed then frowned. "I'm sure he gets plenty of action at this place."

"You're not just action, you're wonderful and talented … and you live here all year."

Tim was pretty hot himself with his jet-black curls shaping his Jim Morrison face and his steel-grey eyes. He once toured with one of the NY stage productions of the musical *Hair* and he had a great tenor voice.

"Thanks," he said, squeezing her hand. "Ditto."

Other than one other woman, Cathy was in the minority here. She hoped Tim was not going to suggest a nude volleyball game outside next. Tim couldn't take his eyes off the bartender, so Cathy scanned the room. Interesting pictures lined the wood-paneled walls. The place had quite a history. It was even rumored a murder happened here several years ago.

Adonis placed their icy margaritas in front of them and brushed Tim's hand as he did.

"See, he can't resist your charms."

"Toast," Tim said, raising his glass. "To men!"

Cathy clinked her glass. There were certainly enough of them in this place. Kissing in the corners, flirting, eyeing each other.

She leaned over and raised her voice to be heard over the raucous laughs and conversations. "What am I doing here anyway?"

Tim cocked his head. "Getting drunk with your best friend, forgetting about your married lover for five minutes, and most especially, letting your hair down."

"Right, thanks for reminding me." She finished her first drink. "In that case, I'll have another."

"Whoa, hold on. How about we order a little food first?"

The room spun a little, and food seemed like an excellent choice. Tim looked over a bar menu then waved over the waiter. "We'll have Fife's special salad and some chunky fries." He turned to Cathy. "Their salads are made from produce grown in their own garden out back."

"Yum," she said. "Good greasy comfort food along with healthy greens, perfect."

Evening was setting in and the lights dimmed. The place was really rocking now. It looked like a fashion show from *Gentleman's Quarterly*. The alcohol had done its job and Cathy was pleasantly numb and happy. The Bay City Rollers were singing, "I Only Want to Be with You" over the speakers, and she tried not to think about Jamie.

He was not some high school crush and, yeah, she needed to get over this. It was so much more than a crush. Just watching him was enough some days. The way he moved in the kitchen, his fingers caressing the food, gripping the knife and cutting with precision. When they were together, the moments were magic. He saw right through her, to her very soul, and reflected unconditional acceptance. No one made her feel this way before.

Cathy ordered another drink, a double. She'd only finished half of her salad, but what the heck, she was supposed to be letting loose. The song changed swiftly to Marvin Gaye's "Let's Get It on." In the candlelit room, she saw men dancing with each other. It was getting uncomfortable being the only obviously straight woman here. Cathy noticed a few men making eye contact with her. Just what she needed next was to date a switch hitter. No drama there.

Tim's eyes roamed the room, making contact, assessing prospects.

"How about I just go home and leave you unencumbered in this paradise?" Cathy said.

Just as she finished her sentence, a devastatingly handsome man in tight black swim trunks, with dark hair glistening in a thin pattern down his bronze chest, pushed his way between them. He put one arm around Cathy and one around Tim.

"I'm Gary. May I join the two most attractive people in the room?" His smile was taunting and his black eyes sparkled with mischief.

Tim moved a seat down and patted the bar stool between them for their guest to join them.

Gary slid in between. "Now don't go moving too far," he said, grinning. "Let's just stay nice and cozy."

Tim's tongue was almost hanging out as he stared at Gary. Cathy could see the fascination. He was very androgynous-looking, with a tall swimmer's body and charisma rising off him like steam from a boiling pot.

"The night is young," he said, staring deeply into Cathy's eyes. "How about we head over to The Woods and dance the night away?"

Tim looked at Cathy as she considered the offer. It was a fantastic place to dance, and the company was certainly distracting her from her problems.

"I'm in. Let's go," she said. She gulped the rest of her drink and was ready to go.

Tim rose. "Let's boogie then."

Gary pulled on a skin-tight slinky top he retrieved from his bag. "Cool, lead the way," he said.

They were up and out the door and in Tim's sparkling new yellow Volkswagen Beetle convertible. After having a couple drinks, Cathy was glad Tim was driving, even though it was just down Armstrong Woods Road a few miles. They pulled over behind a long line of cars parked on the shoulder of the road. The place was so popular they had to walk a few blocks just to get in. All those San Francisco gays coming up for a wild weekend on the River really boosted tourism.

The main building was awesome. Once a conservatory of music, it was built completely of wood and almost three stories tall. They entered through the open hexagon-shaped dance area with its mega acoustics resonating music at top volume. The smell of sweat and Brut aftershave turned Cathy's stomach, but the array of shirtless men vibrating to "You Make Me Feel Like Dancing" completely sidetracked her.

Tim took Gary's hand and pulled him seductively toward the dance floor. Gary gave Cathy sad eyes for abandoning her and blew her a kiss.

Cathy found a seat at the bar and ordered a drink.

An obviously drunk, half-naked man was swaying in front of her. "Like, hey, pretty lady, how's about a dance?"

Dream on, she thought. The music was so loud she had to yell, "Not right now."

"Perhaps you'd prefer a trip to the hot tub?" He winked as he swayed. "Can you dig it?"

Cathy had heard enough about that notorious, secluded hot tub in the woods to stay away forever.

"No thank you."

He leaned his face in close, and his smelly beer breath was nauseating. "Why not? Ah, c'mon."

He grabbed her arm and tried to pull her to the floor.

"Not so fast, buddy." Tim spun the guy around and pushed him back to the dance floor. He turned back to Cathy. "Hope he didn't bother you," Tim said.

"I'm fine. You go have fun with the hottie."

Tim waved Gary away. "Catch up with you in a sec, G-boy."

Tim hopped onto the bar seat next to Cathy. Sweat rolled down his naked chest.

"New crush?" she asked, watching Gary swagger back to the dance floor.

Tim raised a brow and smiled. "I hope so."

"Go on after him, Tim. I'm fine."

"You sure?"

"You're a sweetheart. I'm fine, go."

When the band started to play "The Hustle," Cathy gulped down the rest of her third margarita. She still had barely eaten, but so what. This was a must-dance-to song. She jumped up to join the groups forming to line dance. All of sudden, giant fans blew wildly and misters sprayed water into their faces. She'd heard of this hurricane theme night, but had never danced in the storm. Everyone screamed out the lyrics, walking, turning, and clapping in unison. The mirror ball threw rainbows over the floor, walls, and people's faces. Cathy thought she saw Jamie's face again and again.

Bodies bumped into her, arms waved in the air as the frenzy built in the room and the temperature skyrocketed. Her shirt was soaked from the mist, but sweat still dripped down her back. The room started to spin along with the flashing rainbows, and the crowd seemed to close in on her. This, combined with too much alcohol, made everything seem surreal. The Doors' song "People Are Strange" blasted over the speakers next. The words about people being ugly rang in her head. Faces contorted around Cathy and raucous laughter rang in her ears. She tore for the exit, hoping for air, and threw herself through the metal doors into the night.

The club's exterior wall braced her as she leant into it.

"You okay?"

A skinny guy with a ponytail trailing down his back stood a few feet away smoking pot. The smell turned her stomach, but she nodded.

"Cool, man," he said, puffing away. "Didn't I see you here last week when Sylvester was playing?"

"Not me, no."

Her stomach was rebelling and she wanted to go home. But she did not want to go back inside to ask Tim to drive. Armstrong Woods Road went on for several miles and was black dark, and too far to walk. Balanced precariously against the wall, she tried to walk to Tim's car. The trees were spinning and her knees gave out and she hit the pavement just as Tim walked out looking for her.

"Cathy!" He scooped her up and managed with the help of the ponytail guy to get her off the ground.

"I want to go home." She didn't even recognize her own voice.

"I'll have you home in a jiff," Tim said.

Cathy was drifting off, hardly aware they were walking now. Tim helped her into the backseat of his car, where she promptly passed out.

Chapter Twenty-Eight

Cathy's head was splitting and she vowed never to drink that much again. In the kitchen, every knife chop and cupboard door slamming pounded in her brain. Even the clock was blurry. If Brian didn't come in soon, she was going to fire that stoner. Jamie continued to avoid eye contact as he had in the car all the way to work that morning. Right now, Cathy just didn't care. She was done letting her life fall apart over some man. A married one at that.

She walked over to the dairy case in the store area and rummaged around looking for soft tofu for the tostadas. Jamie was right behind her.

"Where were you last night?" he said. "Did you ever think I might be worried?"

"Dancing. Tim took me dancing."

His expression was strained.

What was she supposed to say? You don't own me? You have a wife, and I can do anything I damn well please?

His heart was in his eyes.

"Sorry," she said. And she meant it.

Satisfied, he turned back into the kitchen and started chopping something.

Cathy took a breath, turned, and found Tim stocking vitamins right behind her. He had obviously heard everything.

"Sorry I ruined your night too," Cathy said.

Tim winked. "Not your finest hour, princess."

She rolled her eyes. The smell of cream of garlic soup was intolerable. "I'm going out for air," Cathy said. She walked out the back door. Brian was chaining up his bike in the parking lot.

"Mornin', boss. What's up?"

He was overly cheery and his eyes looked a bit glazed.

"You're late. Again."

He gave her the smile, the one that must have charmed girls out of their panties. His words were like butter. "I was jamming with some friends and we lost track of time. We're playing a show next weekend at the Inn of the Beginning. You gotta come."

He had charisma; she'd give him that.

"Maybe I will. But right now I'd like you to go help Jamie in the kitchen. I'm not feeling well."

"Sure thing," he said, opening the door to go inside. "You do look a little zapped."

He closed the door behind him and finally she had a moment of peace. Cathy dropped onto the wooden bench bordering the entrance, closed her bloodshot eyes, and let the sun warm her face. Before she could take a deep breath, Cathy heard the back door open. She swung around and snapped, "What now?"

Jamie flinched. "Brian told me you weren't feeling well. I just wanted to see if you need anything."

"Sorry. My head is pounding, and I don't think I'll ever want to eat again."

He sat down beside her. "Let go," he said. "It's all right."

Cathy closed her eyes and let the tension drain into his adept hands as they caressed her temples and ran though her hair. She leaned into his chest and heard the racing of his heart.

"What's going on, Cathy?" he asked.

She wanted to tell him she loved him and that nothing else mattered.. Her eyes opened and there, standing at the back door with hands on her hips, was Jill.

Jamie froze for a second.

There was no escaping Jill's knowing look. Cathy thought about playing stupid, but that was one thing she was not, no matter what her ex-husband had said.

Jamie held his ground. "Cathy has a bad headache." He looked down at her. "Go ahead home if you want. Brian and I can handle it today." With that, he returned to the café.

Jill sat down next to Cathy. "Do you want me to take you home?"

She shook her head.

"How about a walk then?"

They strolled along Main Street without saying a word. The usually bustling Rainbow bar was quiet as they passed; it wouldn't be that night. She followed Jill to the other side of the street. They passed Rosemary's Garden as they headed to the back street toward the historic bridge that spanned the river.

As they crossed the footpath, cars passed, probably heading for the Pee Wee Golf Course. Cathy needed to remember to suggest they bring Amber this summer. Jill stopped and stared over the cement barrier to the waters below. Sunlight sparkled on the green river as it curved past Johnson's Beach and moved slowly toward the Pacific. A blue heron skimmed across the water.

Finally Jill looked up at Cathy.

"What can I say?" Cathy fumbled. "I know how to deal with men who are jerks, but put a truly kind man in front of me and I'm clueless."

Jill's eyes were steel. "I wouldn't say 'clueless' is the right word for what you are doing. I would say reckless."

The word rang in Cathy's ears. Reckless. A total disregard for the consequences to everyone. She wanted to yell at Jill that she was in love and deserved happiness finally, but how could she? At whose expense? She imagined Jill's husband leaving her and the kids for some "reckless" woman and Cathy wanted to crawl under the bridge and hide.

"You're right," Cathy said. "But you don't always get to choose who you fall in love with. It isn't always tied neatly in a pretty box with a big, satin bow. Sometimes love just grabs your heart and yanks it out of your chest and you have no choice but to follow."

Cathy felt naked under Jill's penetrating stare.

"You always have a choice, Cathy."

She glared back at Jill. "Hormones are one thing, the heart another. You think I would have chosen to fall in love with a friend's husband?"

"Do you know what love is?" Jill asked her.

"I do now. I didn't before I met Jamie."

Jill released her breath and uncrossed her tightly-woven arms from around her chest. "What about with your ex-husband?"

"That is a low blow, Jill. You know that story."

She reached out and took Cathy's hand. "I'm sorry. I just keep thinking about one of my friends falling for Dan. It's just not right."

Fate? Right? Wrong? Did the heart understand those words? Did Cathy? It felt like she would die if she had to let him go. How dramatic; she hated women who said things like that, and now she was one of them.

Families on inner tubes floated by on the river below. Their carefree laughter floated up to her ears. Would she ever be part of that?

"You're right. I'll let him go."

Jill faced Cathy. "I hope for both of your sakes that you can."

Jill left Cathy at the river to contemplate her fate. Cathy thought about the possibility of telling Jamie the expansion was off. She'd promised him she wouldn't change her mind. Perhaps he could run the upstairs and she would only come in once a week. Would that work? They would move out and everything would go back to normal. But nothing could ever be normal again after loving Jamie. She would have to tell him tonight.

Cathy started back toward the shop and passed the Five and Dime. In the window sat a big stuffed Velveteen Rabbit. It was the perfect birthday present for Amber. She stopped in and bought it. All they had to do now was get through the Fourth of July picnic, and then they could plan a big party for Amber on the twentieth. Cathy imagined baking a cake in the shape of a rabbit with chocolate frosting and a marshmallow tail. The eyes could be gumdrops and the whiskers made of licorice.

She put the bag with the fluffy rabbit in the car and went back inside the café. Brian and Jamie were cleaning up the last of the lunch dishes.

"Thanks for covering for me, guys."

"That's cool," Brian said. "We're just about done."

Tim came over and gave Cathy the once over. "You're looking better."

"I am."

He handed her a hand-printed list. "While you were out having your afternoon stroll, we three boys put together our menu for the Fourth of July picnic."

Grilled veggie burgers with all the trimmings, red, white, and blue homemade shortcake, and strawberry lemonade. "Good work, boys. I'll put the order in for supplies tomorrow and we can prep over the weekend."

They all looked relieved. And to be honest, so was she. Her head had not been into planning this event.

Jamie finished drying some pots and laid the dishtowel down on the tile counter. "Ready to head out?" he asked her.

She followed him toward the door. "Everyone, thanks again for covering for me. See you tomorrow."

On the way home, Cathy tried to figure out how to tell Jamie their dream restaurant plans were over. It wasn't fair to offer him this opportunity and then take it back. There had to be another way. She couldn't add to this man's grief. Perhaps if she kept her distance, they could both win. She turned her attention to the tall redwoods whizzing by the window. The lush ferns created a fairy-like glen up the hills under the trees.

"What's in the bag?" he asked.

She showed Jamie the Velveteen Rabbit. "For Amber's birthday."

His face lit up. "She's going to love that, Cathy."

"We'll have to start planning soon. We can do a big outdoor party at my house, invite Jill's kids, and maybe get a clown."

Jamie made the last curve and turned up the driveway. "Let's sit down right after dinner and make those plans."

"Sounds good to me."

He smiled at her and that was all that mattered. Right or wrong, Cathy knew she could not call off the café expansion. She would have to find another way to still her heart.

Chapter Twenty-Nine

Jamie looked around for his wife and daughter, but they were not in the house when he and Cathy got home from work. A note scribbled on colored paper was propped up on the kitchen counter. "Gone swimming," it said. Amber had drawn a picture of a green wavy river and a big yellow sun.

Cathy put the bag with the stuffed bunny on the counter and leaned over him to read the note. "How cute," she said. "You're lucky to have such an adorable daughter."

"Do you want children someday?" he asked. The pained look on Cathy's face made him sorry he'd asked the question.

"I did once." Cathy picked up the gift and started for her bedroom. "I guess I better hide Mr. Rabbit before Amber gets home."

Jamie followed Cathy and stood in the door of her bedroom, watching her decide the best hiding place. "Want me to put it up high in the closet?" he asked.

"Great idea." She handed him the bag and pointed. "Up there behind the shoe box."

Jamie tucked the package securely on the top shelf, well out of sight. When he turned, Cathy was sitting on the edge of her bed rubbing the back of her neck. She looked exhausted and a bit forlorn. "You look like you could use a nap," he said.

Cathy looked up and held him with her eyes. Jamie knew he should leave her room, knew he shouldn't sit down on the bed and touch her soft skin. But only for a moment he told himself as he moved in beside her. He slipped the gauze shirt off her shoulders revealing the pale pink leotard against her tanned skin. His fingers moved up between her shoulder blades and down her smooth arms.

She moaned and his pulse raced.

He kissed away the knots in her neck, breathed in her salty scent, and felt his body quiver. "Cathy," he whispered into her hair.

She rolled over to face him, a tear glistening down her cheek.

Jamie kissed it away and let his mouth linger along her jawline. Cathy's lips parted as she whispered his name. How he loved the way her top lip curled at the sides. He wove his hands in her silky hair and pulled her to him, pressing his mouth to hers. Fireworks exploded in his head and he was floating. Floating in colors and sensations with Cathy to a place he never wanted to return from.

He dragged himself back with a sigh and sat up, putting some distance between them. Reluctantly he slid Cathy's shirt back over her shoulders. He searched his mind for something to say. Something that would make it right. But there were no such words.

Chapter Thirty

On the Fourth of July weekend, the whole town was always jumping with tourists. The café was no exception. Cathy could barely hear the radio playing in the background with all the chatter in the store. She'd drunk too much coffee that morning trying to make up for being late. It's back to green tea only starting tomorrow, she promised herself. Grease and sweat coated her hair, and she felt grimy. Why, of all days, would Caroline and her husband decide to appear in her café?

It was probably a surprise attack to assess whether to invest in the remodel. Pam must have told them all about it, even after Cathy had said she wasn't interested in their money. She thought about hiding in the office, but it was too busy to leave Jamie alone out there. Jill was at her doctor's appointment, and Brian was off playing his flute at the Lotus Sutra today.

Caroline sauntered in, wearing a white linen jumpsuit with a plunging neckline. She walked arm in arm with Bentley, who was dressed totally in Armani. Their eyes took in the surroundings. Cathy watched them whisper to each other. Caroline broke out in her high-pitched laugh, the oh-look-at-me one Cathy had so hated in high school. All the bad memories of having to stand behind Miss Perfect in gym class made Cathy want to gag. Some of them had nicknamed her "Shallow Carol" and used to mimic her airs. Pam, of course, adored Caroline, and she reminded everyone that "Caroline" was pronounced with a hard "i," like "wine." It fit perfectly. Everything about Caroline was hard.

They slid into one of the few open booths. It had to be the one with the crack in the vinyl seat leaking stuffing. The table was piled with plates and needed cleaning. That left only Cathy to do it. She cringed at the thought of bussing dishes in front of the royal couple. Oh damn it, she didn't care. Cathy kept her head low, hoping they wouldn't make eye contact with the lowly help. But Caroline's fake drawl was loud enough for the whole place to hear.

"Cathy, is that you?" she said, her voice rising at the end of the sentence.

Cathy smiled with her lips, no teeth. Her eyes could kill. "Yes. Is that you, Caroline?"

"Honey," Caroline said, placing her left hand over Mr. Perfect's, making sure Cathy saw her knuckle-to-knuckle diamond engagement ring on her finger. "You remember Cathy from the wedding. Remember, we were in high school together? She's the one we came to see."

"Good to see you again," Bentley said, extending his hand. "Weren't you married to Todd, that quarterback, for a while? He was quite the football player at your alma mater."

How did he manage to have cold hands on a day like this?

"Yes, I was," Cathy said, sharing no details.

She handed them two menus, hoping to escape.

"It's been a while," Caroline said. "Can you believe it?"

Cathy wanted to grab the big Gucci purse from Caroline's lap and hit her over the head with it.

"So, honey, don't you have a waitress here?"

Cathy bared her teeth. "Yes, Caroline. But, as the owner, I sometimes waitress too."

Caroline looked around, a slight frown on her face. "Oh, right, of course. We do what we have to do." She fanned herself. "It's a bit hot in here, but I guess that's part of the country charm."

Brian chose that moment to rush by and apologize to Cathy for being late as he sprinted for the kitchen. He looked like he'd slept in his tie-dyed T-shirt and his cutoffs were ready for the trash.

Caroline's eyebrow shot toward the ceiling. "Lots of hippie types out here on the River. Does he work for you?"

"Yes, he does," Cathy shot back. "He's a prep cook and helps us out when we're busy."

Caroline rolled her eyes at her husband. "Bentley and I came up to meet with you. Pam thought we might help you all out with this little venture. And …"

Another one of Pam's plans, Cathy thought. I wish she would not include me in them.

"We were coming up this direction anyway to scout for a vacation home." When Caroline smiled at Bentley, all Cathy could see in her eyes were dollar signs. From the look of them, they must be millionaires by now.

"You might want to consider Mendocino," Cathy said, hoping to distract them from considering anywhere in Sonoma County.

"We've heard it's divine up there. More sophisticated."

"I'll leave you two to decide what you want to order." Cathy left the lovebirds and stomped behind the counter. Jamie gave her a "what's up?" look.

"Please," Cathy said, "can you take their order and serve them? They're the potential investors Pam invited up."

"I didn't know," he said. "Pam mentioned a surprise would be arriving soon, but I had no idea she did this, Cathy."

"It's fine. Just go."

Jamie picked up an order pad. "I thought I recognized Caroline and her husband. I'll take care of them."

Cathy kept herself busy smashing avocados and garlic cloves. Jill arrived a few minutes later. "Can I help?" she asked.

Cathy nodded toward Brian. "Can you see what he needs? Thanks, Jill."

Cathy watched Jamie bring out his lunch and join them at their booth. She could imagine how they were grilling him. Customers kept pouring in and Cathy was running in every direction to fill orders. Finally, Caroline and Bentley got up to leave after lingering over the meal and making sure Cathy saw how well they all were getting along. Bentley headed up front to pay the bill, but Caroline couldn't resist coming to the counter to say goodbye.

"Cathy, it's so good to see you and your quaint little place. We'll discuss our options and get back to you two soon."

"Thanks for stopping by," Cathy said. She wanted to yell, "Have a happy life," but Cathy held back. She also did not say, "Lunch is on me." Let Mr. Moneybags pay for it.

Cathy turned her back and retreated into the back office, before anyone saw her blow.

Jamie followed close on her heels. Cathy brushed past him and slammed the office door behind her.

"Cat," he said cautiously with a light knock on the door. "Can I come in?"

"No." She really didn't want him to see her like this.

"Are you sure?" he said, sticking his head in the door anyway.

He walked in, took the chair next to Cathy, and waited One look into his eyes and all she could think was, Please hold me.

"What is her thing, anyway? I hate that woman," Cathy said, daring him to contradict her.

He grinned and leaned forward on the metal chair. "The one with the sparkler on her hand big enough to light the city of San Francisco?"

Reluctantly Cathy laughed and felt a bit better.

Jamie wrapped his arms around her. "I'm sorry," he said, kissing her forehead. "They're gone now."

"She's always been a bitch. I'd rather go bankrupt than take a dime from her. And I am working on some other plans so we won't need anyone like her."

His light, warm kisses roamed over the top of Cathy's head, soothing her frayed nerves. She knew Tim had seen them over the last week touching hands, staring into each other's eyes. But she didn't care. She was tired. Tired of doing everything alone, being strong, holding on.

"Pam said you all were good friends once," Jamie said.

"Are you kidding? I think Pam had a crush on Caroline. The three of us hung out at one time. Caroline lived in the Oakland Hills, drove a fancy new car her parents bought her, and was a

Queen Bee. Worker bees circled her and she took full advantage. By senior year she'd become my favorite person to avoid."

Jamie frowned. "She doesn't sound like much of a friend."

"She actually gloated over my divorce from Todd. She, like every other girl in the school, had a crush on Todd herself. When Todd left and took his friends with him, he counted Caroline as one of them."

"Is that all?" he said, suppressing a smile. "Pam mentioned Todd a little. Sounded like it ended pretty badly. I'm sorry about that, Cat."

"Pam came by when I was packed and ready to leave for Forestville. I was never sure if it was to comfort me or out of curiosity. But she was there. No one knew how bad it was and no one asked." Cathy turned toward the metal desk, brushed away some order forms, and rested an elbow.

Jamie paused. "I'm here. Go ahead and dump it all out."

Cathy's breath was shallow. She swung around in the desk chair and faced Jamie. "I'm sure Pam told you about my marriage just out of high school to Todd."

"Truthfully, Pam has told me very little."

"Todd had perfection down to an art. I didn't like him when we first met, I just saw a spoiled golden boy. Money, looks, and captain of the football team, not my type."

Cathy closed her eyes and remembered being sixteen and popular. Pam was her buddy and they hung out at school.

She felt Jamie's hand on hers. "What happened?"

"The other girls doted on him. Maybe that's why he set his radar on me. The more I ignored him, the more he pursued. Flowers, poetry, gifts, you name it. He even used a sky message to ask me to the prom during an outdoor assembly."

"The guy pulled out all the stops. You must have been swept off your feet."

"Off my feet was an accurate statement. I was tackled and never allowed to get up for air."

She stared out the small window to the parking lot and saw Brian hop on his bike and leave. His life seemed so simple.

The words poured out.

"During senior year, my dad died unexpectedly, leaving us with no choice but to sell the family home and move away. I faced graduation with no plans. My dad, always putting his family first," she said sarcastically, "had stopped paying on his life insurance because he didn't want to be worth more dead than alive."

His eyes never left hers. She wanted to tell him everything. It had been buried so long. Not even her mother knew the whole truth. Cathy's body shook until it felt like it would shatter if she did not get the words out. Jamie's eyes coaxed her on.

"I really did not love Todd. I was just so lost and he took advantage of it. The whirlwind courtship and his insistence he would take care of me. He won me over. What did I know of love? There was a huge void in my life. Todd was insisting I let him fill it. At graduation, he proposed on one knee with a two-carat diamond ring. It seemed like the sensible thing to say yes."

"You can't blame yourself, Cathy. You were so young."

She stared at Jamie. "Is youth an excuse for stupidity?"

He took her hand and squeezed it. "You're so hard on yourself and deserve so much more."

She pushed that word around in her brain. Deserve? "Some people wouldn't agree with you, Jamie."

"Some people are not worth your time," he said.

"The worst were Todd's parents," she continued. "They didn't think I deserved their darling son. They threatened to cut him off financially, but we were married anyway that August, with his mother mourning the union."

Cathy could still see his mother arriving in a somber brown dress with dark glasses. No words for Cathy, she just reached over and pulled a thread off Cathy's dress like she was not even there.

"Come here," Jamie said, pulling Cathy into his arms. "You don't have to tell me anymore if you don't want to."

She buried her head in his shoulder. She had to tell him or it would fester forever. She took a deep breath and continued.

"We played house for a few months. I thought I'd found my prince and my happily ever after. But then his parents really did cut him off financially. Todd had never worked a day in his life and refused to start. He pouted and spent money recklessly. He stopped coming home at night, pushed me away, and blamed me for everything."

Cathy needed to move. She stood up and paced the small room, avoiding eye contact with Jamie. What must he think of her? Every man she'd ever known before blamed her in the end.

"Cathy, come here."

His arms were wide. She went to him. He gently pulled her into his lap and stroked her hair. "I wish I could have been there for you. What kind of guy could treat you like that?"

That's easy, Cathy thought. A jerk.

Jamie ran his fingertips across her cheek then leaned in and brushed his lips to hers. His moist kisses trailed down her neck. He rested his face on her breasts and pulled her tight. "Cathy, I wish I could love your pain away."

Love. There was that word. An empty word when Todd spoke it. A word Cathy had avoided … until now.

"There's so much pain," she said. "It would take forever." She stood and walked toward the door. Jamie took her arm and spun her around.

"I'm not going anywhere Cathy."

Cathy tried to breathe. Would he be there forever? She remembered Jamie drawing the infinity symbol in the sand with Amber. Was anything forever?

"You might as well get it all out," he said tenderly.

Cathy counted the gray tiles on the floor. The room was getting warm with the door closed so she pushed up the window and stared out at the rolling hills. The cool breeze brushed against her flushed skin. "After six months of wedded hell," she said softly, "I found out I was pregnant."

Jamie said nothing. Cathy turned to face him. "Todd went berserk, accused me of planning it, and took off, leaving me and our debts behind. I had nowhere to go but back to my mother up here at our vacation house."

Jamie shook his head. "I'm glad someone was there for you and there was a place for you to go."

"Pam, who was on winter break from college, came to help me load the car and say goodbye. We've written on and off since, but except for Caroline's wedding, that was the last time I saw her until now."

The room fell dead silent. A faint sound of children playing drifted through the window. Cathy searched Jamie's face for disgust, hate, or judgment and saw none.

"The child?" he asked.

Cathy leaned against the wall, memories flooding her brain. The room, the blood, the cramps. "A few weeks later I miscarried. The baby and the marriage were over and so were my dreams of happily ever after."

Cathy trembled from head to toe. The dam was breaking. She feared the tears would drown them both. But Jamie rose and held her steady and let the tears run their course. He was her anchor as the storm reached its zenith and finally blew over. Her mind was clear now, her breath deep. She had forgotten how to breathe.

His beautiful face was pale and drawn. "I'm sorry," he said. "So much sorrow, I don't want to bring you any more."

She couldn't imagine this man ever intentionally causing pain.

"And don't worry about Caroline," he said. "We'll find another way to fund the expansion."

He whispered, "Cat, my Cat" as he stroked her hair. Cathy was aware of the beat of their hearts as they melted together. Pain melted away extinguished by love and acceptance.

"Jamie," Cathy whispered as their lips met.

She'd almost forgotten she shouldn't be in his arms. Cathy dared not let hope lift its fearsome head. She felt she would die from lack of oxygen without him. Asphyxiate. End of problem. How dark an aching heart can be.

Chapter Thirty-One

*J*amie sat out on the deck taking in the beauty of the view. Clouds drifted by, sending shadows across the grass. He watched Pam playing in the yard with Amber. His heart went out to her. It was like watching two children playing. Pam's life growing up had been rough and she wanted better for Amber. They both did. But to Pam, better meant big houses, fancy cars, and enough money to never feel afraid.

He had grown up that way and it had been just as empty as Pam's life, only in a different way. Money had brought with it fear: fear of losing it, fear of not having as much as the next guy, and fear of your children not carrying the torch so they too would be of the privileged set. But Pam longed for that life, and Jamie would do his best to give her what she desired and not compromise his own soul in the process.

Though the screen door, Jamie heard Cathy singing as she straightened up inside. He thought about what Cathy had told him about her past and felt sick over what she'd been through. He'd sensed her pain; now he knew why. She was a vibrant, intelligent, kindhearted woman. She gave to everyone but herself. How he wanted to be the one to truly love her.

He closed his eyes as the sun peeked through a cloud and beat down on his face. What if he'd met Cathy first? Then there wouldn't be Amber. Amber was growing up knowing she was loved by both parents. She'd been sheltered from the kind of life both Cathy and Pam had. And Jamie alone could keep her that way.

Two wounded women, one wounded man. Pam's real father had abandoned her when she was little. Cathy's father had abused his own family before abusing himself and leaving them with almost nothing. Could these women's pasts be patched up with enough love? Cathy was strong, that was one of the things he loved about her. She'd weathered her storms and put down roots that held her firm and sprouted branches that reached for the sky.

A hummingbird flickered loudly beside him, causing him to open his eyes. In the next second, it was gone. Jamie's father had been mostly gone. The hospital was his family, and his patients came first.

Now here he was thinking about something he never imagined he'd contemplate. Cathy. A life with her filled with shared passion, his dreams coming true. Her heart beat right with his. How could two people fit so well, make each other better, whole, and yet not be meant to be together?

Amber's squeal carried up from the yard. "Look, Daddy."

Jamie stood and peered over the railing as Amber attempted cartwheels. "Great job, honey. That's my girl."

Pam looked up and waved. His heart clenched. Pam needed him. He had rescued her and carried her off to his castle—however humble—and now she expected the happily ever after. What he'd never really considered was what he needed.

His precious Amber's needs were clear: to have a mother and father who loved her and were there for her. She was the most important thing in his life and she came first.

Yet his insistent heart continued to yearn for Cathy and was calmed only by her presence. Her laugh was like water flowing over pebbles. It played with the corners of his heart. Could hearts really break? When he thought of leaving Cathy, the pain cut through his chest and surged through his soul. His mind searched for a solution. Whatever he chose, he would always feel like a part of him was missing.

Chapter Thirty-Two

*P*am had been pouting all day. Probably because Cathy and Jamie weren't thrilled with her big surprise investor's visit.

"I wish you would have told me Caroline and Bentley were coming," Cathy said.

Pam sat next to Cathy on the couch. Her hair was disheveled and her T-shirt inside out. "What?" she said.

"Are you okay?" Cathy asked.

Pam looked at her with faraway eyes. "Dakota just called. My mother doesn't remember who she is anymore. She's sleeping a lot. We're going to go see her today and hope she recognizes us."

"I'm so sorry." What could Cathy say? Pam's mother had been sick for twenty-five years, and now it was almost over. Would it be a relief for Pam? "I'm happy to watch Amber if you think it would be too distressing for her."

"You're too busy with all your work plans. My daughter is coming with me."

"Whatever you want," Cathy said.

Pam stared at Cathy with the old pleading look she used in high school, the one that always got her whatever she wanted. A shadow crossed Pam's face, and her mouth tightened.

"You've always had everything, Cathy. I had nothing but a sick mother to care for, and now she's disappearing."

Cathy couldn't bear seeing her this desperate. She'd always been poor Pam—no dad, a sick mom, stuck living in a dingy apartment. Pam had covered it well, wearing hand me down clothes from Caroline and fluffing out her blonde curls. Her mom was her only relative, even if they weren't close. Cathy gave her a hug.

Pam pushed her away and looked at Cathy with accusatory eyes. "Even Todd wanted you. I was the cheerleader, but I was invisible to him."

Cathy shook her head in disbelief. "Did you ever think how lucky you were that Todd picked me?"

Pam rolled her eyes. "Maybe he would have really loved me." Her voice sounded five years old. Was she talking about Todd or her father? Jamie? Cathy's heart went out to her.

Pam tilted her head, smiling. Her eyes twinkled. She was in her own little dream world where rich boys like Todd rescued poor little girls like Pam.

Then she snapped. "Perhaps Todd left you for a damn good reason, Cathy."

Cathy was horrified and cut to the bone, but this wasn't a time to argue. She just wanted to placate Pam and help her face her mother's decline. And Amber would be back any minute and did not need to hear this.

"You have Jamie now," Cathy said, "and he loves you both very much."

"He does, doesn't he?" Her eyes begged Cathy to confirm.

"Yes, Pam. He does."

Pam's lips curled up in a doll-like smile. Cathy could see her brain clicking away. "Jamie's going to be a big chef someday. We'll have a nice house like yours and a place for Amber to play."

Cathy's mind raced to the shabby little apartment Pam lived in while growing up. Without Jamie, would that be Amber's fate, too? She could hear the happy little girl singing to herself from the other room. So innocent of all that was spinning around her.

"He is very talented," Pam said, putting her shoulders back. "That's why I'm not so sure about this Upstairs Café idea."

Cathy's breath caught in her throat. "Why?"

"What's really in this café for Jamie? For us? You haven't even written up an agreement yet. It could end up being we get forty percent of nothing. And then what? We would be wasting away here in Hippyville living with you forever."

"That's not fair. I'm taking a huge risk too. If that's how you feel, why have you been going along with the idea?"

"You think I don't know what you're doing, Cathy? You want a great chef to make your business better. It's always about what you want, but not this time. You couldn't keep your own husband and you can't have mine!"

Cathy felt punched in the stomach. What was worse, she realized Pam was right. She did want what Pam had. How life had reversed. "I don't know what to say," Cathy stammered. "If you want me to cancel the plans for the café, I will."

Pam glared at her. "And tell Jamie it's all my fault? No way. Just keep up with your precious plans and we'll see what happens."

A chill raced through Cathy's body. She needed to rethink everything. Now.

Amber skipped over, looking adorable in a bright flowered dress. "I'm ready to go see Grandma now."

Cathy looked to Pam. "Do you feel up to the drive?" She hated the thought of Pam driving all the way to Oakland this upset and with Amber in the car.

Pam rose. "Of course, why not?" she snapped.

"Let me know if I can do anything," Cathy said. "Just call."

"I will." Pam took Amber's hand and moved toward the door. "Tell Jamie we'll be back as soon as we can."

Jamie had gone to the shop for a few hours to help Brian and Jill with prep for the picnic. Cathy called to let him know that Pam and Amber got off safely for Oakland. He thanked her and mentioned he was leaving in a couple of minutes and would be home soon.

Emotionally exhausted, she lay down on the couch and rubbed her temples. Did Pam know? She closed her eyes and felt herself drifting. She was far, far from here. There was a sound in the distance …

Suddenly she felt herself fall back into her body with a familiar thud. The echo was clanging, clanging in her head. "Stop," she yelled over the sound of her pounding heart. She sat up on the couch and tried to breathe.

"Cathy, what's wrong"

Jamie's face, pale as chalk, looked down at her.

She pulled a pillow over her head and shrank lower. His warm body slipped in next to hers. He wrapped his wondrous arms around her.

"Everything's all right now," he said.

If only it could be, she thought.

Her heart slowed and her breath returned. In his embrace she felt safe, but she knew that dream was lurking behind her eyelids every time she lay down to sleep. Cathy peeked over the pillow and into his lake-blue eyes. It was like melting into a warm bath.

"Tell me what's wrong," he said.

"I had a bad dream. That's all."

"Not all," he said. "Tell me about it."

She inhaled deeply. She'd never told anyone else and she was not sure she could put it into words. "It haunts me and it's always the same."

"Tell me."

Cathy sat up on the couch and hugged the patchwork pillow to her chest. "My dad and I are on a swing set. We are swinging higher and higher, laughing in the sunlight. His swing starts to go so high I can't catch up. Soon I cannot see him at all. I'm falling back to earth screaming. A wrenching pain as I hit the ground wakes me with a jolt. All I can hear is the clunky echo of a swing going back and forth, back and forth."

She lowered her gaze.

"Cathy, look at me." He lifted her chin and brushed his lips across hers. "Swing to me," he said. "I am your echo now."

Chapter Thirty-Three

Overnight tourists could really trash a room, and speaking of trash, didn't anyone ever throw anything away? The River View Room was the worst. It looked like a bunch of rock stars had partied there all night. Thank goodness tomorrow was the Fourth and they would leave after that. Closing up these guest rooms could not come soon enough for Cathy. She'd gotten the loan and already written several checks to get things started.

She finally bagged the last of the wine bottles and chocolate wrappers and dragged the big plastic bag outside to the dumpster. Pretty soon they'd be moving the beds out and the oak dining tables in. Italian tablecloths were on order, along with new dishes to match. Later this week, she and Jamie were going to taste local wines from Napa and Sonoma and make their wine list for the Upstairs Café. Tough work. The healthy but classically prepared items on Jamie's menu would draw tourists all the way from San Francisco.

Jill and the crew were downstairs baking shortcake for the picnic and washing berries. Jamie stayed home this morning to comfort Pam after her difficult trip yesterday to see her mother. Cathy moved on to the attic room and made up the beds before heading downstairs to see how things were going.

It was nice to see Jill back at work and really taking charge again.

"So, do you guys need any help?" Cathy asked.

"Not really," Jill said, popping a ripe blueberry in her mouth.

Everything looked under control, so Cathy decided to head home and lock herself in her office and get some work done. She had so much paperwork to catch up on and figures to review. If things still looked as tight for the restaurant, she might have to consider getting a second mortgage on her home. The thought made her gut twist. But the new addition excited her more every day.

"Okay, I'll see everyone bright and early here tomorrow morning, ready to load up and head to Duncans Mills."

River Road was slow with all the cars heading to the coast due to the hot weather and the holiday weekend. Billy Joel's "I Love You Just the Way You Are" was playing and Cathy sang along. Her mind drifted immediately to Jamie, so she turned the dial to another station and caught some lyrics about needing someone and reaching out to touch them. She tried once more and got Dolly Parton singing about a man she couldn't resist whenever he came by. Off you go, radio.

With no music to distract her, thoughts demanded attention. Was she going out on a limb financially? Her best friend was questioning her integrity, and for good reason. The man she loved was unattainable. How could everything change so fast? Just a few short months ago, she took comfort in being alone, her own person, unreachable and safe. Sure, a handsome face and great body could turn her head, but her heart was out of reach. And now she was on shaky ground. Cathy hated this sinking feeling, the floating sensation that something bad was going to happen.

A red warning light flickered in her mind with each racing heartbeat. Signs that said stop jumped out before her like a crazy ride at Disneyland. Go back ... wrong way ... stop! She remembered Mr. Toad's Wild Ride from when she was a little girl and they'd gone to the Happiest Place on Earth. She sure thought it was. She'd loved the castle and the wishing well. But Mr. Toad had made the biggest impression. Just when you thought that you would crash and drive off the road forever, bam, the ride was over and you were out in the sunshine again.

How would this emotional ride end? Cathy didn't want it to ever end, but the bridge across the raging river was collapsing and a decision would have to be made soon.

Not today. Today she had numbers to deal with. She needed to get home and concentrate, figure out what orders to place for the new restaurant kitchen and how to pay for them. The costs were double what they'd planned. They needed at least nine months' backup in the bank, and even then, a bad month could close both businesses. She needed to write up a partnership agreement between herself and Jamie and Pam. Risky ventures were not usually her way of doing things.

Dark roads, dark thoughts, what's the matter with me today? she wondered. She turned down her street and took a deep breath. Wildflowers and ferns lined the road, and puffy white clouds drifted across a cornflower sky. She was home.

Everyone stared at her when she walked in the house. Pam was flushed, Jamie pale, and Amber looked confused. Oh no, Cathy thought, she hoped Pam's mother hadn't passed.

Pam walked over, her sharky little teeth pasted in a smile, her eyes triumphant. "We have good news!"

Cathy looked to Jamie and he looked down at the floor.

"We might move by the ocean," Amber said.

The room spun. Jenner maybe?

"Jamie has a solid interview in Santa Barbara. They booked him a ticket, for Tuesday," Pam said.

"When?" Cathy managed to get out. "But I thought …"

"Sorry, Cathy," she said, "but it was just too good an opportunity to pass up. Sous chef at the five-star Santa Barbara Inn!'"

Jamie looked up and met Cathy's eyes. "Pam arranged it all. I didn't know."

Cathy felt her limbs go numb. Did Pam's scheming ever stop? But what choice had they left Pam except to protect what was rightfully hers?

"Caroline pulled a few strings for us because Jamie deserves the best," Pam said, stepping between them.

Damn Caroline, Cathy wanted to scream. And "the best" meant lots of money and prestige for you, Pam. It was a strategic move that would make Jamie's career. Much better than what Cathy had to offer. But Santa Barbara was almost 700 miles south. That posh environment offered more opportunity, but would Jamie really fit there? Be happy?

"I'm sorry, Cat," he said. "I'll still be able to work the booth with you tomorrow for the community picnic."

"Don't be," Cathy said between clenched teeth. "What a great opportunity. You can't turn it down."

"I hate to leave you stranded. I'll come in early Tuesday and do all the prep before Pam drives me to the airport. Perhaps Jill can come in for lunch?"

Cathy nodded. Behind her back, knowing all the plans they'd made, Cathy had no idea Pam was so, so what …? Aware? Crafty? What would Cathy have done if she was his wife? The same and more, for sure. And Caroline? Cathy was sure she was only too glad to help.

"Thanks, Jamie," Cathy said in a fog. "I'll handle it." She retreated to her room before she said something she might be sorry for. Drawing up a partnership agreement was no longer necessary.

Chapter Thirty-Four

Fireworks were going off early in the café kitchen as the five of them finished last-minute prep and started to load up for the community picnic. The guest rooms upstairs were full for probably the last time before they began renovation for the new Upstairs Café. If there was still going to be one. She'd told Jill that Jamie might be leaving. They both decided to wait and see before making any decisions on the expansion.

If he stayed, there was so much they could do. Cathy pondered the idea of arranging a junior chef training at the café for the kids at Head start. That was if Jamie didn't get the job, or if Cathy still decided to go ahead without him. I can't think about that now, Cathy thought. Dressed in shorts and a halter top, she was up to her elbows in strawberries. Jamie was yelling for someone to come help peel avocados for the guacamole for the veggie burgers. She walked over to help.

Every fiber of her being longed to touch him. Finally he turned to her. "I don't want to leave you." He waved his hand around the café. "Or all of this."

"I know," Cathy said. "Let's talk about it later. Lots to do for now." She turned and walked away.

Tim looked depressed, probably another relationship gone bad, and Jill was searching for aspirin for a headache. Sparks flew as they rushed around trying to package everything into ice chests and coolers.

"Make room for the whipped cream, it needs to stay cold." Tim procured a large chest filled with ice and shoved the cans in. "I sure hope it doesn't get too hot out there today. It will melt the food and us alive."

Jill glared at him. "We have plenty of ice and the grocery store is just across the street there in Duncans Mills. So let's all chill."

Cathy stayed out of it, hummed a little to herself, and closed the Tupperware lids tight.

Tim's face matched his bright red shirt as he huffed and walked away. "I hate the Fourth of July. It's all noise and mess!"

Jamie chuckled. Cathy could barely look at him. The thought of him possibly leaving next week fanned her panic.

"Shhh," she said to Jamie, finger to her lips, trying not to laugh. All they needed right now was for Tim to have a full-out meltdown right before the event. Hundreds of people were expected to be there and they could use the money they'd make to order new tables, chairs, and kitchenware. Who was Cathy kidding? Jamie would probably be gone next week. Any ordering would be done by her. Alone.

"I'm taking a load to the van," Jamie said, carrying two stacked coolers. Brian, in his uniform of jeans and a rocker T-shirt, was right behind him with more.

With the block of ice in the coolers, they must be very heavy. Cathy ran to the back door and held it open for them. Jill's old VW van had plenty of space for everything.

Jamie loaded them inside and looked up at Cathy with a grin. "Hustle, girl. We've got a picnic to get to."

Cathy imagined pouring her red, white, and blue short-cake mix over his head. "I just have to load a few things, then you can come and get them."

Back inside she finished packing up the food and carefully sealed the lid on the chest.

She snapped her fingers at Jamie. "Boy, these are ready for loading."

His grin was so cute it was hard to be angry as he scooped everything up and carried them outside.

"Ten o'clock!" Jill yelled.

One more time: Shortcake stuff, check. Burgers and fixings, check. Lemonade, check. Cathy ran through it all, satisfied.

Jill walked over holding a tray of fresh-baked shortcakes. "Forget anything?"

"That's why I have you," Cathy said.

Tim had the charcoal and grill in the back of his pickup.

"Who has the condiments?" Cathy shouted in the park-ing lot. Her voice stopped everyone and they all looked at each other.

Brian shook his head.

Jamie held up a small blue cooler. "All packed and ready. The guac too."

She couldn't imagine Jamie leaving. He was whistling, "Happy Days Are Here Again." She wished they were. Perhaps everything would be fine after all.

Jamie rode in the pickup with Tim. Cathy followed in her plate-bowl-napkin-and plastic-silverware stuffed car. Sun glared in from the window, baking her bare legs until the redwoods finally shaded the highway and a cooler breeze whispered that they were closer to the ocean. Traffic slowed down as they approached Duncans Mills. It was certainly the destination that day. The town was a perfect setting for the picnic with its picturesque turn-of-the-century buildings, Old West style post office, and candy shop. The nostalgic North Pacific Coast RR train depot was still there even though the trains stopped running there in the late 1930s.

They pulled over and parked by the rodeo grounds. Red, white, and blue banners and flags dominated the scenery. People were scrambling to set up booths, get rides ready, and assemble music stages. Amber was going to love the little train ride. Cathy couldn't wait to see Amber's eyes when she saw the Clydesdale horses too. She hoped Pam got her here early. Kids definitely made holidays more fun. Cathy wondered if she was getting into this Auntie thing too much. What if they packed up and went away next week? She wouldn't let her mind go there. If they did, they did. She would deal with it then.

They all unloaded and carried things to the booth. Thank goodness Brian and Tim had set it up the day before. Cathy grabbed a load and followed. "Hey, it looks great," she said, admiring the hand-painted flag, sparklers, and large strawberries and veggies floating on the big wood sign. Tim must have painted them. What a talent.

"Cathy's Veggie Treats," good name. The Health & Hearth logo was on the sign as well.

Jill put up a small tent behind the booth so they had some shade and could store the coolers in there as well.

"Cat, should I start the grill now?" Jamie said, loading charcoal in. He looked very festive in his Hawaiian shirt that Amber had suggested he wear.

A crowd was milling around and it was almost eleven o'clock. "Sure, fire it up. Brian and I will handle the shortcake." Cathy began stacking bowls and opening Tupperware.

Jamie moved in so close she could feel his warm breath on her ear. "How about I'll grill the veggie patties and pass them to Jill and then to Tim to dress?" he said.

Tim thought this was hysterical. "How about a pink satin dress with red polka dots?"

Jill hit Tim in the shoulder but couldn't suppress her smile. "I'll dress *you* if you don't get to work."

"I think we're all getting a bit giddy from lack of sleep," Cathy said.

People were lining up as fast as they put the food out.

"Hi, Miss Cathy!" Rio and Annie from Head Start came running over to the booth, followed by Barb, the counselor.

"How about some strawberry shortcake piled high with whipped cream?" Cathy asked.

Barb caught Cathy's eye. "Maybe small ones."

"It's on the house," Cathy said. "We'll have them ready in a second." She piled the strawberries high and smothered the plates in puffy whipped cream. "Here you go."

"What do you say?" Barb said.

Annie licked the top of her treat. "Thank you!"

Rio was already gulping down bites. "Thank you," he said. His mouth was red from the berries as he smiled.

She waved them away. "Go have fun now," Cathy said.

Cathy watched Jamie in action. His tanned arms moved gracefully as he tossed burgers on the grill.

"Five more minutes for the best veggie burgers you've ever tasted," Jamie called to the line forming in front of the booth. Small beads of sweat ran down his forehead.

His eyes met Cathy's, steadfast, reassuring.

The local high school marching band went by blasting out an unrecognizable song. Cathy could barely hear the four hippie types, obviously stoned at the front of the line, ordering everything on the menu.

"Order up," Jamie said, holding a plate of burgers for Tim to retrieve.

Their assembly line worked well as the line lengthened and everything became a blur of faces for over an hour. Finally there was a lull. Cathy sent Brian out to play the pied piper with his flute and bring more people over. Her stomach growled so loud she knew she'd better take a quick minute to stuff-her-mouth break. "Jill, can you handle the shortcake while I take five?"

Jill fanned herself. "Sure thing, then I'm next for a break. My feet are killing me."

As Cathy sank down onto the grass floor of the tent and took her first gooey bite, a big golden dog pulled his owner, Paula, toward her.

"Sorry, Cathy. This big lug just had to come say hi."

"Come here Charlie," Cathy said. She laid the burger down and pulled his head to her face for a kiss. "What a handsome fellow you are."

The dog covered her in kisses. She'd missed seeing him these last few crazy weeks.

"How's he doing?" Cathy asked.

Paula kneeled down beside them and petted Charlie's back. "Just fine, thanks to you. And isn't that the man who helped with the rescue over there, cooking veggie burgers?"

"Yes, that's him."

"Do you think he'd mind if we went over there and thanked him too?"

Cathy smiled. "Go right ahead. He won't mind at all. Perhaps he can come up with a snack for Charlie too." She watched them walk over to the grill. Jamie's face lit up at the sight of them.

Just as Cathy started eating her veggie burger again, Amber came running in and landed at her feet.

"Bite, bite," she said, opening her mouth like a little bird. Amber took a good size chunk out of the sandwich and a green track of guacamole trailed down her chin.

Pam followed close behind, her face flushed. "I told you to wait for me. Don't ever run ahead again."

Amber swallowed her mouthful and stared back at her mom. "Dad is here, and Auntie Cathy."

"But I'm your mother, and I need to see where you are all the time."

"Okay," Amber said. "I'll run slower next time."

Pam sat down next to them and fanned herself with a flyer advertising hayrides.

"How about some lunch?" Cathy asked Pam, handing her last bite to Amber.

Pam shrugged. "Shortcake sounds good, with extra whipped cream."

"Me too," Amber said, following Cathy to the counter. "Can I shoot the whipped cream myself?"

Amber looked up at Cathy with eyes that no one could say no to. She looked particularly cute in her jean shorts and crop top.

"Of course."

Together they built a three-layer, slightly lopsided, whip-cream-smothered dessert. Three spoons in hand, they joined Pam on the blanket and dove in, oblivious to the frantic activity in the booth. The noise from the crowd was building and a line formed again. Jamie was now dripping with sweat, working over the hot grill. He could use a break to cool off and Cathy decided to relieve him soon.

"Mommy, let's go now. I want to ride the ponies."

Pam got up and took Amber by the hand.

"See you later. You girls have fun," Cathy said before heading back to work.

"Bye, Daddy," Amber yelled as she trailed off.

"Bye for now, honey," he said waving.

Cathy reached for the spatula. "Out of here, Jamie. Give me that and take a break before you melt."

He wiped his brow. "Not a minute too soon," he said, handing it to her. "Don't burn 'em."

His wicked grin prevented her from hitting him over the head with a large blunt object.

"Don't be mad, Cathy," he whispered. "Everything will be fine."

"And the interview," Cathy said, scraping veggie burgers off the grill.

"I'm sure it will be like all the others," he said.

She felt his hand on her shoulder and looked up.

"I'm not leaving you." He looked so sincere as he said it. Cathy wanted to believe him.

"Go." She waved him away. "Take your break so I can relieve Tim with the strawberry shortcake before he gives it all away!"

Standing over the grill, perspiration poured down her back. She felt Jamie watch her every move.

"Lightweight," he yelled.

Out of the corner of her eye, she saw Tim smothering the shortcake in whipped cream. "Hey, Tim, save a little for the next customer."

He lifted up a can and pointed it at her.

"Don't you dare!"

"Toss it to me," she heard Jamie say behind her. She turned to see Jamie catching the can in his hand. "Armed and dangerous," he said, moving in close.

"You wouldn't ..."

The cool whipped cream hit her cheek and she licked off its sweetness. The whole booth was laughing now.

"I could kiss it off," he said, soft enough for only Cathy to hear.

With great precision, Cathy lifted a half-raw veggie burger off the grill and mashed it in her hand. Before Jamie could register her intent, she rubbed it in his face.

He dropped the whipped cream can and seized her hands. "I give, I give."

Jill brought over a napkin and wiped both of their faces. "Back to work, children," she said, rolling her eyes.

Cathy poured herself some ice water to cool off.

Flute music filtered into the booth as Brian, dancing as he walked and flute in hand, led a few couples back to the booth. "Success," he said.

Pam and Amber skipped behind him into the booth.

"You have whipped cream in your hair, Cathy," Pam said, reaching over and flicking it off.

"Look what I won, Daddy. Look, Auntie." Amber, her face beaming, was holding a small stuffed teddy bear.

Jamie looked at Pam. "And how did you win that fine prize, little one?"

"I threw a ball and hit down pins. Mom helped me."

"Teamwork," Cathy said patting Amber on the back.

Jill yelled out some orders for veggie burgers.

"Back to work," Jamie said, returning to the grill. He flipped the burgers and chanted of their magical taste properties to the crowd.

Amber skipped over to Jamie. "Daddy, we're going to go on a hayride next. Wanna come?"

"I wish I could but I have to work," he said, looking disappointed. "You girls have all the fun. But I'll be done soon and then we will watch fireworks together!"

Amber giggled and dragged her mother toward the old farm horses attached to a red wagon piled high with hay. Cathy lost sight as they meandered off behind the wagon.

"I'll have three hundred shortcakes, but I don't want red, white, and blue, I want orange!"

Cathy turned briskly to see Jill's husband, Dan, and their kids. "Nice try," she said. "Are you guys having fun?"

"We went on a pony ride," one of the twins said.

Not to be outdone, her son held up a lopsided cotton candy. "And I got candy."

Jill wiped off her hands and stepped over to the counter. "Kids, come on back here and tell me all about it."

Cathy could hear their little voices going on about buttery corn on the cob, firemen in a big red truck, and gigantic horses with hair on their hoofs.

Dan laughed. "So, can I borrow my wife for a little while to go on the hayride?"

"Just as soon as Tim returns," Cathy said. "He took off with some shirtless hunk for his fifteen-minute break but should be back any minute."

They decided to wait.

Things had slowed down to a few stragglers coming up to order shortcake. Most everyone's attention was on the relay games now and sack races out on the fields. Tim, now shirtless, slid into the booth, a much-improved smile on his face.

"Good break?" Cathy asked.

He winked and then returned to his workstation.

"Okay, Jill, go ahead and join your family."

Jamie and Cathy manned the counter and people-watched. It was quite a crowd. The clothing ranged from tie-dyed dresses to short shorts and halter tops.

"It's not even dark yet," Jamie said. "I'm not sure Amber will stay awake long enough to watch the fireworks."

"She has to, that's the best part. Perhaps she can take a nap in the tent for a while?"

"Good idea," Jamie said. He slipped his fingers through Cathy's and she squeezed back. Gently he let go. He won't leave, she told herself. They'd both invested so much energy in the Upstairs Café.

"Our café is going to draw people all the way from Oregon," he said, reading Cathy's mind as he so often did.

"Next week we can start the wine orders and make up the menus for the first month," she said.

A few customers wandered over and walked away with piled-high shortcake Tim made to order. The gang was like one big happy family at the Fourth of July picnic, and she wanted it to last forever.

"When do you think we should shut the booth down?" Tim asked.

Cathy shrugged and leaned over the counter. The hayride passed near them. Jamie waved at his girls propped up on hay bales with big smiles. He turned to Cathy. "Sometimes I feel like a team of horses is pulling me in two different directions."

"We could close up early and you could go spend some time with them," Cathy said.

"Let's wait a few more minutes. Then off I'll go."

The smell of buttery popcorn filled the air along with the buzz of children. Puffy clouds had toned down the sun a bit.

"I wish I had brought some chairs," Cathy said, standing and shaking out her tired legs and feet.

Jamie cleared off a section of the counter, lifted her up with one fell swoop, and plopped her on top of the wooden ledge. She curled up her legs and got comfortable.

"Thanks," she said. "Great view from here."

"Glad to be of service," he said. "Shall I join you?"

The sun warmed Cathy's shoulders and for a moment she closed her eyes and enjoyed the moment.

"Jamie!" Pam's piercing voice cut the air. Cathy's eyes burst open to follow the voice. Jill was carrying Amber in her arms while Pam ran ahead.

Cathy gasped when she saw Amber's head covered in blood and tears pouring down her cheeks. Jamie went white and flew toward them. Cathy followed, her stomach lurching from the sight.

"What happened?" Jamie demanded.

Pam could barely get the words out between sobs. "Amber stood up, she wanted to see the train. I had her hand, I did." She was crying so hard she couldn't speak.

Jill grabbed a dishtowel and pressed it hard against the side of Amber's head. "The horse spooked and bolted and Amber fell off. We were walking by when it happened," Jill said.

"Let me have her." Jamie reached out.

Jill handed her to her dad and placed his hand on the now-bloody towel.

"It's okay, baby, Daddy's here."

Amber's cries settled into his shoulder, now also stained with blood.

Pam placed a hand on Amber's back. "She hit her head on a board. It all happened so fast."

Jill, always calm, who after four children was used to this kind of thing, stepped forward. "Let me have a good look." Gently, she lifted the towel and separated Amber's hair. "Small, but deep and near the back of the skull. Head wounds really bleed with kids, but I think a few stitches is all it needs to be good as new."

"No stitches," Amber wailed.

Cathy was relieved until she realized how far it was to the nearest emergency room. "Take her to Santa Rosa Community Hospital, just east of downtown."

Jamie's ghost-like face turned to Cathy, terrified.

"Go," she said.

He ran toward their car with Amber in his arms, Pam close behind.

"Call me at home when you can," Cathy yelled after them. Cathy's limbs were freezing, her hands shaking.

"She'll be fine. They'll stitch her up good as new over there."
Jill patted Cathy on the shoulder. "And we're here for you."

"Thanks," Cathy said, staring into space.

It was all clear now. With complete certainty she knew
Jamie would always choose his family first, as he should. Cathy
would always be left behind. As hard as it would be, Cathy
could stand alone. Pam could not. Cathy still had to be the
strong one and make the right choices

Chapter Thirty-Five

*C*athy watched Jamie hustle around the café chopping and prepping before he rushed off to Santa Barbara for his interview today. All the plans were in place. Pam and Amber, who now sported a bandage on the back of her shaved head after her trip to the emergency room, would drop Jamie at the airport and then head over to Oakland to see Pam's mother. This would be their last visit with her mom for quite a while if they moved to southern California. With Pam's mother hardly recognizing them, it might be time to say goodbye.

Endings were everywhere Cathy looked.

Jamie kept trying to talk to her, but Cathy avoided him. She couldn't look into his face or she'd lose it. The pain in her chest that kept her awake all night had now spread through her entire body. Why did it have to be this way? Why find the perfect person that you could love forever and make it impossible to be with him? Was life just cruel?

Cathy silently prayed he wouldn't get the job, and then hated herself for being so selfish. She prayed instead for the best outcome for everyone. It wasn't just about her. She had to let go.

The coffee filter fell out of her hands and wet grounds splattered everywhere. Jamie dropped down on the floor to help clean them.

"Those new filters are so flimsy," Cathy said.

Jamie held the dustpan while Cathy swept up the rest of the mess. He dumped everything in the trash, turned, and blocked Cathy's path back to the sink.

"We need to talk," he said.

"Do we?"

"Cat, please."

They walked into the back room and shut the door.

"This interview wasn't my doing," Jamie said.

"Really?" Cathy said, hating him at this moment but knowing he was telling the truth.

"Pam made all the arrangements behind my back too."

Cathy met his gaze. "I know."

Jamie hung his head. "I'm confused. Even about Amber falling off that ride. It feels like it was somehow my fault."

"If you'd been with them on the ride, it still might have happened," Cathy said. "It was an accident."

His face paled. "What do you want me to do?" he asked.

"Does it matter?" she said. What could he say? Yes, it matters but you are not my wife? Why was she making it more difficult on him when he needed to be his best for this opportunity? Cathy touched his arm. "I'm sorry. I'm disappointed, but also happy for you. You deserve it."

"Thanks, that means a lot," Jamie said. "I have to go, but I promise I'll be back. We'll straighten out everything then."

Cathy couldn't even think about the restaurant now; remembering to breathe was enough. She dreaded going home tonight and sharing the house with Pam.

Jamie ran his fingers across her cheek. She wanted to melt into his arms and stay there forever. Instead she opened the door and walked back to the kitchen.

The back door swung open and Jill walked in. Her eyes were all over them.

"Morning, Jill," Jamie said, taking some bags from her arms and placing them on the counter. "Thanks so much for the backup. I really have to get a shower and head to the airport."

"Good luck," she said.

Jamie took off his apron and headed for the door.

"They'll love you," Cathy yelled after him. Who wouldn't?

Jill's expression mirrored the sadness Cathy felt as she turned her back and finished prepping lunch.

Even though the kitchen was dead silent, Cathy could hear Jill's voice loud and clear in her head. "Let him go."

The day flew by and Cathy was glad to be home again. Pam's car was in the driveway, so it must have been a short visit with her mom. Cathy hoped it went well. She walked up the deck and hesitated at her front door. Little sparrows dipped their bills into the schoolhouse-shaped feeder hanging from the awning. Their lives were so simple. Sleep, eat, fly. Cathy wondered if Jamie had made it to Santa Barbara safely and how the interview went, but she didn't want to let on to Pam just how concerned she was.

She flung open the door. "Anybody home?"

Not a sound came back.

She walked to the back door and looked out. Pam and Amber were sitting on a blanket under an apple tree having a picnic. Cathy waved. "May I join you?"

"Yes," Amber said. "We have lots of cookies for you too."

Cathy sat between Amber and her Madame Alexander Doll and forced a smile at Pam. "Looks like a nice party. Any occasion?"

"Daddy called," Amber said, holding a cookie up to her doll's porcelain lips.

Cathy's breath caught. "And?"

"The interview in Santa Barbara went well." Pam grinned.

Was Pam going to make her beg for more? Cathy stared at her flower patch in full bloom and waited. The deep pink cosmos were radiant in the sun. Bees hummed around the new blooms then hopped over to the periwinkle-colored delphiniums and tall white daisies.

"They want him to work the dinner service tonight to help make a decision," Pam finally said.

"That sounds promising." Cathy took a deep breath. At least it was not a done deal yet. But once they saw how well Jamie worked, how he cooked …

Amber handed her a plate of cookies and Pam poured some lemonade in a paper cup. "We're going to have a big party when Daddy gets the job."

Cathy smiled. "What fun." She munched on the chocolate chip cookie and sipped her sugary drink. She probably wouldn't be invited to that party. The sun filtered through the branches, making patterns on the blanket. Three ladies having a tea party. Libby came over and rubbed against Amber, purring loudly.

"Can Libby have a cookie, Mommy?"

"Cats don't eat cookies," Pam said.

How does she know? Cathy thought. Perhaps at tea parties cats do eat cookies.

Cathy's mind drifted on the afternoon breeze. A going-away party?

"We'd better clean up now. Bedtime will be early tonight," Pam said. "Jamie's plane gets in tomorrow morning, so we'll be out the door by 8 a.m."

"You'll miss some of the traffic that way, too," Cathy said.

Pam started cleaning up the cookies as Cathy sat there immobile. She didn't want to go inside. She didn't want the day to end. She didn't want him to leave. She was acting like a pouty child.

"I think I'll stay out here a while," Cathy said.

"Whatever," Pam replied, taking Amber's hand.

Amber turned and ran back to her. "I want to stay with Auntie Cathy!"

"You can't, you have to come in for a bath."

"I don't want to," Amber said.

Pam pulled her toward the house. "You want to be clean for Daddy, don't you?"

Cathy kept her mouth shut and stayed out of it. Pam was obviously tired and impatient tonight. Cathy wondered what kind of mother she herself would be if she had the chance. To have a daughter like Amber seemed a dream come true. She lay back on the blanket and closed her eyes. Images of walking on the sandy beach with Jamie danced before her. His strong hands sketching the infinity sign in the sand, rowing the boat along the river, holding her hand. He would always be in her heart no matter what happened.

The sound of the phone startled Cathy. Her heart raced as she rushed into the house, where Pam was holding up the receiver. Amber was wrapped in a bunny towel, her hair dripping wet.

"It's for you," Pam said.

Cathy took the phone and heard Jill's voice.

"Any news?" she said.

Tears threatened. What a friend: Jill didn't approve yet she still cared. "We should know tomorrow. It looks good. Hope you're up to coming back full time soon," Cathy said.

"Are you okay?" Jill asked

"Of course."

"We'll talk tomorrow," Jill said reassuringly and hung up.

Jill's voice calmed her. Cathy wandered around the kitchen thinking about dinner, but nothing appealed to her. Amber and Pam were eating peanut butter sandwiches. She took out some Tillamook cheddar cheese, sliced some apples, and opened a bottle of chardonnay. Cathy poured a glass and planned to drink until she was ready to flop into bed.

Pam was watching her.

"Would you like a glass?" Cathy said.

"I sure would."

There was a time when drinking with Pam was something Cathy really looked forward to. Where did this friendship go? Cathy was not sure there ever really was one.

She handed Pam a glass. "I'll be out on the front deck if you want to join me."

"I'll put Amber to bed and meet you out there," Pam said.

"Goodnight, pretty girl." Cathy kissed Amber on the cheek.

Amber walked off with her mother, stopped, and blew Cathy a kiss goodnight.

Cathy caught it and put it in her heart.

Outside on the deck, evening was setting in and the last traces of a ruby and amber sunset were fading from the sky. A white egret flew gracefully over the trees leaving her with a feeling of peace. A few deer dotted the grassy hill in the distance. It was one of those moments when no matter what was happening in her life, time stopped and everything seemed perfect. For a second. Cathy rocked slowly in her chair and watched the cats chase some poor creature in the yard.

What did Pam want? Why did she all of sudden want to spend time with her? Cathy heard Pam's footsteps approaching and took a large gulp of the crisp, cool wine. Pam sat next to her on the carved bench and put the open wine bottle down on the side table. Cathy refilled her glass. Pam did the same. "To Jamie's success," she toasted.

Cathy had no idea what to say. Each moment of silence added to her discomfort that she was trying to wash down with more wine. The tart apple and cheese melted in her mouth. She really should eat something more if she was going to keep drinking like this.

"Bottle's empty," Pam said, pouring the final drops into her glass.

"I'll get another." Cathy rose a bit unsteadily and retrieved another bottle from the refrigerator. She gulped a handful of almonds and headed for the porch. On her way out, she checked on Amber. She was curled up like a kitten under the covers. Pam was right. Amber was not Cathy's girl, but it didn't keep Cathy from growing to love her.

Cathy took a wool throw from the couch and returned to the bench outside. She offered it to Pam, but Pam waved it away.

"The night breeze feels wonderful after the warm day," Pam said.

It did, and so did the wine. A pleasant numbness was setting in and Cathy's worries seemed further and further away.

"I think Jamie's going to get this job," Pam rambled on, a bit slurred. "We're going to stay at first with Caroline and her husband in their pool house."

Now it fell into place with a sobering clarity. Pam must have been calling Caroline all this time and telling her all her woes, and Caroline probably pulled a few strings to get this interview in Santa Barbara for Jamie.

"When did you decide on Santa Barbara instead of Sonoma?" Cathy asked.

Pam topped off her glass again. "Oh, you know, nothing was working out here and Jamie can make so much money in a place like that."

Did Pam even care about all the work and money Cathy had put in for the remodel? Or how much the Upstairs Café meant to Jamie?

"I know that job will pay more than I could give," Cathy said.

"Yeah," Pam continued, "and Caroline's husband knows so many rich people. Who knows where Jamie's career will go?"

Cathy could see that all the plans were already made. The interview was probably just a formality. Bile rose in her throat.

"How are the schools there for Amber?" Cathy asked.

"I'm sure they're the best. Everything else there is."

Cathy could see it now. Pam and Caroline sticking Amber in daycare and spending their days getting their nails done, shopping, hanging out in wine bars while Jamie worked. How did she ever like this person? In high school Pam was always there, someone to hang out with. But there was a good reason they had barely stayed in touch since. Maybe Cathy was wrong, but she doubted it.

"I'm sure you'll be happy there, Pam," she said without heart.

Pam looked at her with bloodshot eyes. "*We* will be happy there."

Breathe, Cathy told herself. She poured herself a little more wine. It was drink or kill. Maybe both.

"I know Santa Barbara is not your kind of place, Cathy," she said.

"What do you mean 'my kind of place?'"

Pam squirmed. "You know, it's not all back to the earth, natural and stuff."

"Oh, I see. So my place was second choice?"

Pam shook her head. "No, sorry, I didn't mean … I just thought there'd be more opportunity there, for Jamie."

"Sonoma is not Santa Barbara and I don't have a pool house."

Pam looked at Cathy like she was trying to figure out what Cathy had just said. "I know you don't have a pool."

Cathy waved her arms. "No, I don't, or a mansion in the hills or a rich husband …"

"You could have had one."

Cathy couldn't believe Pam said that. Did Pam realize how cruel that reference to Todd was? "I like my life just fine the way it is here," Cathy spit out.

"That's what I meant. You belong here," Pam said, her speech becoming progressively slurred.

Amber appeared at the screen door. "Mommy, I can't sleep," she said, rubbing her eyes. "Can you read me a story?"

Pam could barely stand and fell back down in the chair. "Go to bed, honey. Mommy will check on you later."

"I want Daddy," she cried. "He would read me a story."

Pam tried again to stand but slumped back into the chair. She waved at Amber, "Back to bed now, sweetie. I'll be in soon."

"Okay." Amber sighed and scampered away.

Pam mumbled, "It's always Daddy this and Daddy that, like I'm not even there."

Cathy remembered when she'd met Pam in sixth grade and how she used to walk around pretending her dad was coming back any day. Why couldn't she see how lucky Amber was to have a good father?

"She loves her daddy. What's wrong with that?"

"You had a great dad too," Pam said.

"That's debatable."

Pam laughed. "You all felt sorry for me 'cause my dad abandoned us. But you, you had the perfect dad … like Jamie."

Everyone had thought her dad was perfect. Pam had stayed in denial all these years. "Open your eyes," she said. "The perfect dad you thought I had, he was abusing my mom and me. Then he drank himself to death and left my mother nearly broke."

Pam covered her eyes with her arm. "I don't want to hear this," she said. "He was the nicest, kindest man, like Jamie."

Cathy raised her voice. "Didn't you ever wonder why I never asked you to spend the night? My so-called *nice father* drank himself crazy at night. He yelled at us, even hit my mom a few times. I had bruises down my arms. How could you be so blind, Pam?"

"How can you lie like that?" Pam glared at Cathy. "I'm not as blind as you think I am. You're just jealous because you don't have a husband like Jamie."

"You're right," Cathy said. "I am."

Pam grinned smugly.

Cathy wondered if Pam had ever really been a friend. Had she always had an agenda and being friends with Cathy was part of her plan?

"Why did you even come at the end after Todd left me?" Cathy asked.

"You'd had everything Cathy. And you lost it. After Todd left you, no one would talk to me either because I was *your* friend. You were so wrapped up in your own problems you never noticed that I was all alone too."

Cathy's head spun. Nothing made sense anymore. Friends or enemies, they were stuck together in this house until the drama ended.

Pam poured herself another glass and the second bottle was now almost empty. Cathy hoped she wouldn't have to carry Pam to bed.

Pam spilled the wine down her shirt and started to giggle. "Whoops!" She lifted her blouse in the air. "What's wrong with me?"

Good question, Cathy thought. For all of them. Cathy felt a bit woozy herself. "I think we'd better go to bed now."

Tears rimmed Pam's eyes then rolled down her cheek. "My dad never came back," she sobbed. "But I know Jamie will never leave Amber. He loves Amber."

Pam's body was racked with tears now. She wiped her nose and eyes with her arm. Cathy couldn't bear Pam's pain. She scooted in next to her and wrapped Pam in her arms.

"Everything is fine, Pam. Jamie loves you, Amber loves you … I love you."

Cathy realized she still had a place for Pam in her heart. Love, or perhaps pity, forged a strong bond. She thought of sweet Amber with her fragile little heart. A daddy's girl. She needed her dad by her side every day while she grew up. Her mom too. Cathy cleared her head and forced herself to stand.

She reached out her hand to Pam, but Pam fell back like dead weight. Cathy lifted Pam up under her arms to support her while she leaned on Cathy's shoulder, weeping softly.

"You always were a good friend, Cathy," she said, her words slow and drawn out.

It took all of Cathy's strength to drag Pam into her room.

"Time for beddy bye," Pam said, flopping into bed in her clothes. Cathy pulled the quilt up over her and set the alarm for 8 a.m. She could imagine the headache they both would have in the morning. Down the hall in the little room, Cathy double-checked and found Amber sound asleep with the doll tucked under the covers and the *Velveteen Rabbit* book on her nightstand.

"Good night, princess," she whispered, kissing Amber on the forehead.

Cathy tiptoed down the hall and turned off all the lights in the house. Finally in her room, she pulled off her clothes, slipped on a nightgown, and fell into bed. Sleep, sweet sleep.

Except it didn't come.

Eyes closed, she imagined Jamie beside her. His warm hands, moist lips, kind heart. He'd been coming through the fog to her for months in her dreams. Moving always closer, then almost out of reach, his penetrating blue eyes were all she could see. The dreams had stopped once he had arrived here.

He was The One. She'd known it the minute their eyes met over the injured dog on River Road that day. People said she'd know when the Right One came along. Was it just a bunch of romantic crap? If Jamie was her One, why was he with Pam?

Cathy never believed that existed. The one person that would fit, that got her, all of her, and still loved her. The one she would never forget, not in this life or the next. Jamie was it—her heart was sure. The world melted away when he was near. Everything was clear—pain gone, floating in bliss.

Danger zone. Stop. Do not enter. Too late, she was already there, indulging the fantasy. The sun shone, birds sang, Jamie and Cathy lived happily ever after in their cottage in the woods. A golden-haired little girl chased a little golden puppy through the clover.

Stop. Cut. Rewind. Who was she kidding? He may be Cathy's The One, but he was Pam's Husband.

Would it help anyone if he stayed in a marriage when he loved someone else? Was it fair? Fair should not be in the human vocabulary. Fair to whom? To Cathy's family when her father died so young and left them nothing? When her husband abandoned her? Or her unborn baby girl who died before her first breath?

Fair to herself to feel this way for someone she could not have? To do something that she could never live with herself for?

Fair was nothing more than a four-letter word.

Chapter Thirty-Six

The interview was over. As the plane took off from Southern California, Jamie looked out the window at the glistening Pacific Ocean below. He saw large mansions with pools in their backyards and sculpted lawns. Everything looked like it had sprung out of a designer magazine. Picture perfect.

Was that how their life would be if they lived here?

It was not the sprawling apple orchards that lined River Road, the green river curving its way to Jenner. He missed the red earth of Sonoma County, the open land and gardens. The old farmhouses with dogs out front and horses in the pasture.

He missed Cathy. His dreams waited for him in Forestville. The Upstairs Café, filled with customers eating local, healthy, gourmet food that he had created. A little house with a fenced yard for Amber, and a blue dog like Arrow.

The plane turned inland over the central valley and headed north back to San Francisco. His wife and daughter would be waiting for him there. Waiting for the news that Pam so longed to hear.

Chapter Thirty-Seven

Cathy had gone to the shop early to help Jill. They worked side by side prepping for lunch, just like it was any other Wednesday morning. They knew the routine well.

"Oh, by the way," Jill said. "Paula and Linda stopped by to see when you want to sample their wine. I've heard their little start-up vineyard here in Forestville produces some great wines."

"Did they leave a card?" Cathy asked.

"It's on your desk."

The Upstairs Café was still a darn good idea, whether Jamie stayed or went. If she hired a part-time chef and worked here herself, Cathy could get it off the ground. The recipes were ready, the furniture ordered. As she often said, why not? It would give her a place to bury herself, too busy to have to think. And possibly some money to pay off the debts from doing it in the first place.

Cathy glanced at the clock: 11:30. Again she wondered how his final interview went. Had they made a decision? She was dying to call home and see what the news was, but they wouldn't be home yet. Pam and Amber must have been at the airport by now to pick him up, and they would have to fight traffic on their way back.

"When you come back to earth, I need some more grated salad made up," Jill said.

Cathy tried to pay attention, finish the lunch service, and not chop off a finger. Brian arrived and lunch breezed by, even though her eyes were constantly glued to the clock.

Thank goodness her mind was on something else for a while besides Jamie. Pam and Caroline must have planned this whole thing. Betrayal stung. But who was betraying whom? Good karma or bad karma, they would all have to answer for it.

Cathy fought the nagging thought that she was not good enough for Jamie, nor her café. But even so, she just couldn't see Jamie with the Santa Barbara set. He could hold his own in the kitchen or anywhere else, but the people, the pressure, the image he would have to live up to. Pam, of course, would be in all her glory.

"The clock moves faster if you don't look at it every five minutes," Jill said, giving Cathy her raised eyebrows. "Why don't you just go home and find out what's happening?"

"Are you sure you don't need me?" Cathy asked, hoping she would say, "Go home."

"Brian's here, and remember, I used to handle this place most of the time by myself anyway."

Cathy nodded, her mind elsewhere.

"Scat, get out of here, will you? And let me know how the interview went."

It was obvious Jill had had enough of Cathy dropping things and getting in the way for one day.

Cathy took off her apron and washed her hands.

Jill stood behind her. "How are you doing?"

Cathy looked up. "I'm okay, for now."

Jill put her arms around her. "Be strong. We all love you here."

Cathy bit her quivering lip to hold back tears. There would be plenty of time for that if ... when they left. "Thanks, Jill, what would I do without you?"

"Probably close the shop," she said, eyes gleaming.

"Right," Cathy said. "See you tomorrow."

She packed up, exited the kitchen, and drove home. Butterflies did battle in her stomach. What if he got it? What if he didn't? What if he left? What if he stayed? She pulled in and turned off the car. When she saw their car in the gravel drive, she could barely face walking into her own house.

This was ridiculous. She slammed the car door and marched up the stairs. She was not some helpless twenty-year-old. She could take care of herself. Time to get real. No one ran to meet her at the door, but Cathy could hear chatter and laughter coming from their bedroom as she entered. When she reached the door to their room, Cathy couldn't believe what she saw. There were boxes and suitcases on the bed. They were packing. The scene faded, Cathy's breath stopped. She could feel the click of her heart going into lockdown.

Pam saw her first. "Cathy, we have good news!" She looked like a little girl telling her Santa had come.

"We have a present for you, too," Amber giggled.

Jamie stood up and the pain in his expression did nothing to reassure her.

"He got the job in Santa Barbara! Sous chef at the five-star Santa Barbara Inn with one of the best executive chefs in the nation! Can you believe it?" Pam was actually clapping her hands with joy.

No, Cathy couldn't believe this was happening. She finally managed to get out a word.

"When?"

Jamie stepped forward. "I start next Monday. We'll be leaving Friday."

"In two days?" Cathy's voice sounded like she was being strangled.

Pam took a handful of clothes out of the closet and began folding them and putting them in a suitcase. She was humming. Cathy was dying, and she was humming.

"I'm so sorry to leave you stranded like this," Jamie said. "I can work tomorrow, and I'll do everything I can to help get things in order before I leave."

"Can we give her the present now? Can we?" Amber said, moving from foot to foot in a little dance.

"Sure, honey," Pam said. "Let's go get it." Cathy watched them walk toward the laundry room and wondered what they put in there. Poison?

Jamie took her hand. "I'm so sorry."

Cathy pulled back. Her face must be a mess of emotions and she didn't want to break down. "All our plans ... now what?" she said.

He stroked her hair and for a second Cathy thought he might kiss her. She wanted to pound him and yell, "How could you?" She wanted to throw him down on the bed and make love to him.

"Look what we got you, Auntie Cathy!"

Cathy turned briskly to face the door.

Amber was carrying a white metal cage with a bright-colored little bird perched on a swing inside.

"A lub bird, for you," she said. "He can be your friend when we're gone."

The red-cheeked bird rocked back and forth. Pretty and alone. Cathy knew that love birds should always be bought in pairs. Or was that the plan? You, Cathy, are pretty, but when we are gone, you will be *alone.* She looked at Pam. Her face was a mask, but her eyes showed victory. Perhaps when they left, Cathy would open the cage and let her cats eat the bird. Of course she wouldn't. But she would certainly buy it a mate.

"Do you like it?" Amber asked.

Cathy kneeled down and hugged her. "It's a wonderful present, and I will always think of you when I see the bird."

And Jamie.

It was like a movie unfolding in slow motion. Amber packed her books, her cute clothes, and dolls. Cathy wanted to slam the suitcase shut and scream, "You can't go!"

Jamie was packing his cookbooks. "I wish I could give you more than two days' notice, Cat, but the owners were in a real jam and needed a chef to start immediately."

"I understand, Jamie, I do."

His smile was not matched by his eyes, which looked like those of a lost puppy. What else could he do? Throw away this incredible opportunity to stay out at the River with her?

"Tomorrow," he said, "Pam has to go back to Oakland and pack the rest of our stuff. I can work as long as you need me. As long as it takes."

"I appreciate that," Cathy said.

"I mean it." She knew right then that he did not want to leave.

"Mean what?" Pam said sharply.

Jamie rose to face her. "I mean I'm grateful for all she has done for us and I will help her any way I can."

Pam put her hands on hips and cocked her head. "Maybe you better think about helping your family first."

"I think that fact is obvious," Jamie said.

"And think about not having to raise Amber among all these hippies and gays here on the river."

Jamie put up his hand. "That is uncalled for Pam."

Hands on hips, Pam held her ground.

Cathy was uncomfortable and tried to break the stalemate. "So, Pam, is everything all right with your mother?"

Pam swirled around. "Why?"

Cathy touched Pam's arm. "I care. How is she doing?"

"Her doctor called. He'd like to meet with me tomorrow at three. We'll be stuck in rush hour traffic coming home, but it was the only time he could see us. Something about final arrangements before we leave." Pam's eyes wandered the room. "So, we have to finish most of the packing tonight."

"I see," Cathy said.

Amber's singing filled the air. "We're going to live at the beach and swim in the ocean with the fish."

Cathy pondered Jamie's words. Whatever she needed? I need ... *you*, she thought. But Pam needs you more. The war is over. Cathy never meant it to be a battle, but in the end, Pam fought for what was hers ... and won.

She couldn't watch this parting scene one more second and turned to leave. "I have some things to do. I'll be back soon."

"Don't rush. We'll just be packing," Pam answered.

Cathy found her keys and jumped in the car. She rolled up the windows and locked the doors, as if she could keep reality out. Her heart pounded in her ears. How dare they ... live here, eat here, be her friends, and then just turn around and walk out after all their plans? Remorse? Pam certainly had none, although Cathy couldn't really blame her. White country picket fences look good in the movies, but to Pam they were a prison. And there was the not-so-little matter of the chemistry between her husband and Cathy.

She backed out and drove slowly down her country lane to where it ended at the foot of a forest. Cathy stopped, rolled the window down, and yelled, "I don't need them! Go ahead and go."

She sounded like a crazy woman. This was *not* her. She didn't want to settle down and play house. She'd be fine. Better without them. Back to her routine. Everything was great until they came along. Who was she kidding? Certainly not herself anymore. She didn't want to go back to that lonely, bitter recluse she'd become. She'd put the fear behind her. She'd loved and been loved. Nothing would ever be the same.

Chapter Thirty-Eight

When Cathy walked out of her morning shower toward her bedroom, Jamie handed her a sealed envelope. Grief lined his face like a dry, cracked riverbed. She could barely keep herself from pulling him into her arms. Cathy locked herself in her room and ripped it open. It was dated that day: 7/7/77.

Cat,

One look at your face when Pam announced we were leaving and I almost told her everything right there and then. I wanted to reach out and hold you in my arms, whisper your praises as I pulled your body into mine. How can I leave you? I am, for the first time in my safe, comfortable life, completely and ecstatically happy. When I'm with you, time disappears and it is only you and me. Your caring heart holds me, and my heart knows only you.

I recall the first time I saw you. Sun glistened on your auburn hair. When you looked at me, everything else faded from view and you alone radiated in full color. Every night since we arrived, I listen to the creaking sounds of the old house as it settles and force myself back to earth. Knowing you are near,

*sleep eludes me. Often my mind races over the job interviews
and the importance of securing my family's future. I tell myself
to keep my mind on my goal and my feet on the ground. But
every smell, every texture, every taste reminds me of you.*

*Tomorrow we are leaving, a thought I cannot bear. I
look at Pam and guilt washes over me. But I can't imagine
my life without you.*

Always with you,
Jamie

The letter drifted to the floor. What was she suppose to
do now? Run out there? Tell him she felt the same way? Beg
him to stay? Say, "Forget Pam and your darling little daughter?" Maybe he just wanted her to say, "Everything is all right.
You just go ahead and leave. I'll be fine."

Silently Cathy pulled a sundress over her head and slid
into her Birkenstocks. Work could not wait, especially today.
She had to go.

She picked up the letter and held it to her heart. Neatly,
she folded it up and put it in her jewelry box before heading
to the kitchen.

She boiled some water on the stove and pulled out a bag
of Mo's 24 tea. The blend always calmed her and she loved the
sayings. She steeped the tea bag and turned over the tag. It was
a William Blake quote and it sent chills through her body no
matter how hot the tea was. She placed the cup in the sink and
joined Jamie in the car.

"Just drive," she told Jamie. Her emotions were in her
throat and she did not want to say the wrong thing.

They drove silently to the café, entered, and started work.
He kept trying to be helpful. How was she going to make it

through this last day? If Jill didn't have a doctor's appointment, she would have told him not to come in. Just as well, Cathy wanted to make sure they had plenty of time to go over the Upstairs Café plans and decide whether or not to cancel it all.

The tofu was soaking in soy sauce and garlic, to be grilled later for their tofu tostada special. Cathy started chopping tomatoes and cilantro for the salsa.

She sensed his body next to hers.

"Yes?" she said, keeping her back to him.

"I'm leaving you this folder of all the recipes. Just call me if you have questions, or need anything at all," Jamie said.

"Set it down. My hands are full at the moment, as you can see."

His hands were on her shoulders. Jamie gently turned her to face him.

"You're trembling," he said. His hands moved up and down her arms, soothing her. "Cathy, I meant every word I said in the letter."

Her face remained hard as she choked down her emotions.

He tipped her chin up to look at him. "If only circumstances were different, nothing could tear me away."

The misery in his face reflected her own. She did not want to be the cause of all this pain. Only dangling threads of her pride remained. Love took no prisoners, no matter what the circumstances; it broke open the heart with no regard for consequences. For him, for all of them, this had to be resolved.

She turned and washed the tomato mixture off her hands. He stood patiently beside her, waiting.

"Jamie, let's just finish with lunch now. Afterwards we can go over all the figures and decide a direction that makes sense for the café."

He sighed and turned back to the stove. The oil in the frying pan crackled in readiness for the corn tortillas.

Lunch was a blur for Cathy. Like a robot, she took and filled orders, but she was not really present. Her body was there, but the rest of her was floating safely off to the place where there was no pain, only happy thoughts. Voices blurred, dishes clanged, doors slammed in a distant universe where her body made sandwiches. A building pressure clutched at her, forcing her to look up. Jamie was watching her expectantly. She thought he'd just said something.

"Cat, do you want to sit down and go over everything now?"

She looked around and the café was empty. Jamie had cleaned the kitchen and Tim was alone up front in the store counting receipts.

"Sure," she said, pouring a glass of iced lemonade.

He spread the order forms and menus across a round table in the dining room. When she saw the Sunday brunch sample menu she remembered their plans for linen tablecloths and fresh flowers, the dishes they'd picked out, the logo with the line drawing of a dining room hanging in the treetops over a river.

Jamie went on and on about why Cathy should keep the restaurant plans in motion. He offered ideas, but none of this would mean anything without him.

Jamie stopped suddenly. "I'm a coward. I'd rather stay and follow our dream. But what I want has always come second." He paused. "My wife is happy. Caroline and her husband have helped pave the way for my career success. It seems like the right thing to do."

Neither of them spoke. Cathy stared out the front window to the empty street. There was not a soul in the shop. Tim caught her glance and waved as he walked over to the table.

"Not to bother you two, but how about I close up a little early? I'm meeting someone at the Rusty Nail and could use a shower."

"Hot date? Sure, get out of here." Cathy thought she should probably leave too.

Tim hugged Jamie. "Good luck to you, man."

"I'll miss you guys," Jamie said.

"Catch you on the flip side," Tim said with a wink.

Cathy watched Tim put the closed sign out and lock the door behind him.

Jamie's hands were on hers. "Will you ever forgive me, Cat?"

She met his hopeless gaze.

"I know I should go," he whispered, "but everything in me wants to stay."

And everything in me, Cathy wanted to say, but the words would not come.

He squeezed her fingers almost painfully. "I did the right thing marrying Pam. Was always taught to do the right thing … what everyone else thought was best."

Jamie looked like a lost little boy. She wanted to take him in her arms, rock him, and tell him, "I love you."

"I do care for Pam," he said, "in a different way. And Amber is my sunshine, everything to me. But …"

Cathy wanted to draw her hands away and cover her ears.

"Other than choosing chef school, I've never gone after what I've really wanted. When I'm around you, passion overrides my mind, floods my heart. For once, why can't I have what *I* really want?"

A tsunami of pain slammed into Cathy's chest. She couldn't look at him. She tried to get up, to get away, but she could barely move. Then she pushed the chair aside and stood, praying she would not cry. But a rogue wave forced its way out through tears that streamed down her cheeks.

He held her in his arms and she dissolved into him.

"Cat, what should we do?" he whispered, his warm breath caressing her neck.

They fit so perfectly together. If she kept her eyes closed, perhaps he would never let go; he would never leave.

Cathy gazed up into Jamie's stricken face. She pulled away, fled up the stairs, and slammed the guest room door of the Attic Room behind her. She heard his footsteps approaching and considered jumping out the second-story window.

Instead she opened the door. Neither of them moved.

"Jamie," she whispered.

He swept her up into his arms. "My Cat." His kisses trailed up her cheeks, tasting her tears.

When his lips finally reached hers, she was taken to another world, completely at the mercy of sensation. Breathing was impossible as she floated with him through time and space.

Gently he laid her across the bed. His eyes, glazed with passion, sought hers for permission. Cathy reached up, beckoning him to join her. Her fingers caressed his silky curls as his lips roamed her neck. Their bodies locked together, every corner and angle complementary. Together they were falling into an abyss of sensation, dissolving into each other, unable to tell where one body ended and the other began. His hands moved up inside her dress, stroking her thighs. She raised her arms and he slipped the dress over her head.

"You take my breath away, Cat."

Cathy was hopelessly paralyzed as she watched Jamie remove his shirt and lay his body across hers. It had been a long siege, but she surrendered to his touch. Like chocolate over a warm flame, she melted into his warm skin, wrapped her arms around his neck, and breathed his delicious scent into her being. His kisses moved up her neck, tasting, probing, finding their way to her lips. She wanted him. All of him. It was not too late to stop, but she no longer wanted to. Not now, not ever. He brushed the sweat-moistened hair from her face, and the fresh smell of strawberries lingered on his fingertips.

"Jamie," she said breathlessly.

He peered down at her. She could barely see the blue encircling his huge black pupils.

"My love," he said.

She wrapped her legs around him, pressing closer, and pulled his mouth to hers. His probing kiss was long and deep and she could hear herself moan as he unhooked her bra and stroked her breasts. Cathy quivered as he nibbled her neck. His hands were everywhere, setting her skin afire. Like a healer, every touch melted away the stored memory of pain. Every hurtful word lodged in her muscles dissolved into his tenderness.

Jamie's body moved rhythmically over hers, igniting a fire she never knew was possible. Burning, she dissolved into flames. And in that moment, everything was all right, and there was only love.

Weightless and filled with light, Cathy floated on brilliant-colored clouds. Perhaps she was on the other side of the rainbow, or cloud nine! She giggled softly. She loved the whole world and everyone in it. This must be how it felt to be loved enough to be Real.

The wispy sound of sleep-filled breath became louder as she floated back into her body. Cathy's eyes blinked open. The white linen curtains caught the breeze and their lacy border reached out to her as the pine-scented air filled the room. The cool air caressed their hot skin. Jamie's arm encompassed her and he buried his head into her shoulder, still half asleep.

"Jamie," she whispered, knowing she must be in a dream. But his eyes flickered open and his penetrating look captured her.

Jamie drew Cathy into his lean body. His fingers roamed up her back, sending a chain reaction tingling down her limbs.

"My love," he whispered, his lips lingering at her ear. He propped himself up on an elbow and looked into Cathy's eyes. "Are you okay?"

Okay? She was so far beyond okay, she wanted to scream. She was ecstatic, heavenly, blissful! "Most definitely. You?"

He sighed. "I'm always happy when I'm with you."

Cathy wanted to lose herself in his arms again. But something was calling her back. The late afternoon sun was fading from the window and suddenly it hit her just how late it must be. The bedside clock said 5 p.m. and Cathy pushed herself up with a gasp.

"What's wrong?" he asked, true concern in his eyes.

"Jamie, it's five o'clock."

He stared at her like he had absolutely no idea what that meant.

"Pam," Cathy managed to say, " … and Amber must be almost home."

Emotions raced across his face. "I don't want to leave you, Cathy."

She leaned over and brushed her lips over his. "Neither do I, but …"

He kissed the words away and Cathy lay back, fighting the sensation to wrap herself around him and never let go. But Amber's innocent face, the memory of her little body running through her yard calling, "Daddy, Daddy!" made the next decision very clear.

A sickening feeling welled in her stomach. It took everything in her to push him away. With a heartbreaking moan, he leaned back. His eyes were moist. Cathy winced at the thought of what must be going on in Jamie's mind.

"I love my daughter, you know I do," he said so softly she could barely hear him.

"I know," she said.

"I'm a good husband. I always try to do the right thing, but now …"

He looked so forlorn; Cathy took him in her arms, stroked his hair and shoulders, and held his trembling body. "I'm here."

"If only I'd met you first," he said.

Cathy sat up in the bed. "Jamie, I wasn't ready back then."

"And you're ready now?" he asked.

She stared at this man in front of her and knew he was the only man she'd ever loved and probably ever would. But what Cathy said now could throw all of them off axis, and it was in her hands where they fell. A battle raged in her mind. How she wanted to tell him, "Yes, I will run away with you and we can leave everything behind."

"The minute I met you, I was ready," Cathy said.

He buried his face into her hair. "My Cat, I love you."

Tears ran down Cathy's cheeks. She clung to him. Perhaps if she held him tight enough, the moment would never end and tomorrow would never come. But the William Blake saying displayed on her tea tag this morning rang in her head: "He who bends to himself a joy doth the winged life destroy, but he who kisses the joy as it flies lives in eternity's sunrise."

She knew that one move, one sign from her, and he would never go home tonight. All of their destinies were in her hands. One by one, she lifted her fingers from his back. Love, she reminded herself, cared enough for the happiness of others to let go.

"Jamie," Cathy said with all the force she could fake, "get up and go home. I'll follow later."

He searched her eyes. Cathy watched his shoulders drop. Then his expression changed into resolve and his coat of honor slid back into place. He slid his legs over the side of the bed, exposing his bare back to her. She longed to run her tongue up his silky skin and lure him back. After what seemed like hours, he stood, gathered his clothes from the floor, and walked toward the bathroom. Cathy heard the shower running and envied the water glistening down his body.

Every cell in Cathy's body sparked with new life. She turned her head into his pillow and inhaled his musky scent, then held the pillow to her heart. She would never wash these sheets. The minutes clicked by as he washed their lovemaking from his skin. The shower water stopped. Cathy perked up the feather pillows, propped them behind her, and pulled the covers up to her neck. Her teeth dug into her bottom lip as she waited to see his expression.

Jamie emerged, wet hair hanging over the collar of his shirt. He looked just like he did a few hours ago, if you didn't look into his eyes. He sat on the edge of the bed with a deep sigh.

"You should go," Cathy said.

"I know." Jamie ran his fingers through her auburn hair and studied her face. "I love everything about you."

"And I you," Cathy said.

She could see their life together flash before her. Days, months, years. The vision did not stop at this life but moved out to infinity.

"Cathy, this is madness. I want to stay with you."

She squeezed his hand. "It couldn't last. We both know it." Cathy willed herself to think of the love he had for Amber, the commitment to Pam. "Don't you think I want you to stay?"

"Then why not? Somehow we can make this work for all of us."

Cathy wished it were true. There was no way not to hurt someone. "Jamie, if you stay, it might be wonderful for a while, but sooner or later, our guilt would suffocate us."

He looked angry and Cathy wanted to cry. She had to be the strong one. She knew what pain love could bring and the damage it could cause. She had to do the right thing for both of them no matter the cost to herself. To his core, Jamie was a man of honor; his heart was betraying him.

Jamie stood. Cathy's heart broke, spewing pieces into the air.

"Are you sure?" he said.

With regret that she knew she might never recover from, she said, "Yes."

He just stood there.

"Jamie, don't make it any harder, please."

"Cat, I'm so sorry. Now I've made a worse mess of everything and made it harder for you."

She took his hands in hers. "It's no one's fault."

"I love you," he said, slipping his hands away. "Don't ever forget that."

With a deep breath, he moved to the door. He turned and touched his heart. "Always."

"I love you," Cathy said as he stepped out and closed the door behind him. He was of her flesh, her heart, her soul. Even death would have no hold on their bond.

Heart pounding, she considered calling to him. But true love let go. It took everything in her not to run after him. She heard his footsteps descending the oak stairwell.

He was gone.

Chapter Thirty-Nine

The breeze coming off the river moved across her skin and the prickle of goose bumps raced up her body. Cathy dragged herself back to the bed, pulled the chenille blanket off the floor, and cocooned into it. Sensations of love washed over her as she remembered his kiss, his touch, his love. Her heart raced with no finish line in sight. How was it possible to feel blissful and suicidal all at the same time?

Enough! She threw off the covers, stripped the bed, and removed the evidence. Cathy yanked off the pillowcases but did not have the heart to wash them. She took one last whiff, savoring the memory, before wadding them into a ball and hiding them under the bathroom sink for now. His wet towel and the sheets went into the washer in the hall.

Out loud she told herself what to do. "Turn on the water. Get in the shower. One step at a time." The hot water stung her already sensitized skin as she let it wash away her sins. How could she do what she had done? How could she not? Cathy scrubbed away the scents of love before stepping out to dry. Could betrayal of a friend be justified for love? For happiness? Was honor just a five-letter word?

She must leave looking like she had just come home from a normal day of work. She blew her hair dry, staring herself down in the mirror. Her eyes were shining and an unmistakable glow surrounded her. Afterglow. Pam would know if she saw her like this after a day of working with Jamie. Guilt snaked up from the pit of her gut and Cathy dreaded going home. She did not want to hurt Pam any more than she already had. Cathy was hurting enough for all of them. But she wouldn't think about that yet. Her dress looked a bit disheveled. She smoothed it out, pulled it over her head and slipped into her sandals.

One last look at the room, now filled with memories, and Cathy shut and locked the door. At some point she would clean the room. Next month it might be a dining room filled with patrons. She floated down the stairs two at a time. Cathy sank into the front seat of her car, leaned her head back, and remembered his touch. "Love Is in the Air" played on the radio. She hummed along with it for a moment before pulling out. She could stop somewhere for dinner, but she had no appetite.

She glanced at the clock on the dashboard. Jamie should have had plenty of time by now to greet his family and finish packing. Fatigue set in and Cathy removed the subtle grin that hadn't left her face since Jamie left. By the time she walked in her front door, shoulders slumped; she was ready for the charade.

No one was around, but Cathy could see the light was on in the bathroom. She tapped on the door. Pam was bathing Amber. She could hear Amber moaning about getting her hair washed.

"We'll be right out," Pam said.

Cathy walked into the kitchen and filled a glass of water. She sensed Jamie behind her. She turned and faced him, lost in his gaze. He moved closer.

"Daddy, Daddy, Daddy," Amber squealed as she turned the corner into the kitchen and ran to Jamie. She was wrapped tight in a bath towel and her soaking wet hair was dripping down her face.

He lifted his daughter into his arms. "Are you all fresh and clean now?" he asked, kissing her cheek. Cathy saw the look of pure love in his eyes and remembered again why they could not stay together.

"Amber, come back here right now." Pam, hands on her hips, wearing a wet shirt, grabbed for Amber. "She's not dry yet and I need to get her ready for bed."

"Looks like you gotta go with Mommy for a while."

"Do I have to?" she said, her blue eyes pleading up at Jamie.

He looked to Pam, who shook her head vehemently. Her eyes left no room for any other answer.

Jamie put Amber down with a bounce. "Go on now. I'll be right in to kiss you goodnight."

Pam took Amber's hand and looked up at Jamie. "We need to get an early start tomorrow and there's still more to pack." She yawned. "And I'm exhausted."

"I know, Pam, I'll be right there."

Cathy waited a few beats before she whispered to Jamie, "Did Amber see us?"

He shook his head no. "There was nothing to see." But they both knew how close they had come and how bad that would have been.

Cathy heard Pam and Amber back in the bedroom. She moved closer to Jamie and took his hand.

Cathy paused, getting the courage to say what she must. "If we stayed together, you could never look into your daughter's face again without feeling guilt. Or Pam's. How long would it be before you would never be able to look into mine?"

He dropped his eyes. He was a good a man, and it tore Cathy's heart out to look at his expression.

"Jamie, we can try to be friends."

"You're right," he said, "but you deserve so much more."

Cathy looked up into his beautiful face. "So do you."

"Jamie, I need you," Pam yelled from the bedroom.

True words indeed.

Cathy tossed and turned and finally drifted off to sleep. A clear, dark sky beckoned her. Two dim stars rotated through space, caught in each other's gravity. Intense color and light blended as they struck in midair and molded into one radiant luminary. The new star moved through the heavens, beautiful and whole, until a blazing comet struck and tore it in two. Each half whirled out in an opposite direction through an ever-expanding universe. Each still carried with it a part of the whole. Each was forever changed. And the call from the other an infinite, receding echo.

Her eyes opened. Cathy focused back into her dark room. The stars were gone, but the message was clear. The room slowly stopped spinning as her body reconnected to real time. It was 3:02 a.m. She closed her eyes and imagined Jamie beside her and drifted in and out of sleep. Another hour crept by. Cathy focused on the beautiful days she and Jamie had spent together. Some people never knew this kind of love, and even if their time together was limited, it was worth it.

Dim light from the start of a rising sun was chasing away the darkness. She could hear the robins singing, welcoming the day. She waited until she heard Jamie in the shower, then threw on a robe and headed down to the other bathroom. As Cathy passed the guest bedroom, she saw Pam helping Amber get dressed.

"Morning," she said, continuing down the hall. It was time for them to leave. And now she was ready.

She brushed her teeth and threw cold water on her face in hopes of waking up. Her hair responded to the brush and almost fell into place. She would go to work today. Her life would go on. She returned to her room and threw on some jeans and a T-shirt. Sadness rattled deep in her bones; it was a familiar feeling. But with it now was an afterglow that spurred her on.

Jamie was in the kitchen putting coffee in a thermos and toasting whole-wheat bagels to be smothered in cream cheese. Amber ran out, followed by Pam, both in matching sundresses Pam had sewn.

"I'm ready, Daddy," she said, holding a little pink suitcase.

He scooped her into his arms and kissed the tip of her head. "Good job."

"Jamie, we need you to finish packing up the car and we can be off," Pam said.

"What can I do to help?" Cathy asked.

Jamie nodded at the bagels popping up in the toaster.

"Cream cheese it is." Cathy was relieved to be doing something.

Pam poured orange juice and sat down with Amber at the table. Cathy brought the bagels over and served them.

"Don't you want one too?" Amber asked.

"It's too early for me, sweetie," Cathy said. "I'll eat later."

Cathy watched Jamie pack an ice chest of sandwiches for the drive, just like when she was a little girl and her dad packed them up for a road trip. Only the ice chests back then were filled with beer.

"I'm taking some stuff to the car," Jamie said. "Be right back."

Amber chewed her bagel and took turns dropping little pieces of cream cheese down to the cats and giggling. "Auntie Cathy, will you be coming to my birthday party still?"

Pam played with her napkin. "I'm sure Cathy would like to come, but she's very busy with her business."

Cathy looked Pam in the eye. There was no love between them, and whatever had kept them together in high school was long gone. She turned to Amber. "I'll probably miss your party, but I'll give you your birthday gift early."

Amber smiled.

Jamie walked back into the kitchen and packed up the drinks from the refrigerator. He snapped the lid closed and headed outside. Cathy rose and went to hold the door open for him. She stood on the deck and watched him place it in the backseat.

Amber passed her coming down the steps and into the yard. She was running around, arms out, being an airplane. Pam brought out the last of their boxes and placed them on the porch. Cathy did not offer to carry them.

"This is it," Pam yelled to Jamie, pointing to the boxes.

Jamie was slow today. It looked as if it took everything in him to continue moving forward. Pam, now giddy and rushing around, seemed oblivious to his threatening undercurrent. Jamie lifted the final boxes and Cathy purposely avoided his gaze. As long as she didn't make eye contact, she could hold it together just a bit longer until they left. As Jamie loaded the last of their things, Cathy's heart threatened to betray her.

Cathy ran back into the house. Waves of nausea made her dizzy. When was the last time she ate?

"Auntie Cathy, where are you?" Amber's voice brought her back.

"I'm here," she said from the couch.

Amber scooted up to Cathy and threw her arms around her.

"My sweet Amber." Cathy hugged her back. She stroked Amber's silky hair. Amber looked up at Cathy with her bright blue eyes. "I love you."

"I love you too," Cathy said, squeezing her. "Ah, silly me, I'd better go get your birthday gift for you." Amber followed Cathy into the bedroom and hopped up on the bed. Cathy pulled the wrapped gift down from her closet. "Here it is."

Amber ripped open the paper and pulled out the stuffed rabbit.

"My own Velveteen Rabbit! Thank you, thank you," Amber said, hugging the rabbit to her chest.

Pam's voice trailed in from the living room. "Amber, where are you?"

Amber sprinted out of the room with Cathy behind her.

"Look what Aunt Cathy bought me, my own rabbit."

"That's nice," Pam said. "You can hold him all the way to Santa Barbara in the car."

Jamie walked over and put his arm around his daughter. "That's a very nice rabbit." He petted the rabbit on the head. He looked up at Cathy. "Thank you for the gift. It means a lot."

Squeezing the rabbit to her, Amber smiled at Cathy. "I will love him sooo much," she said, kissing him on his nose.

"I know you will," Cathy said. "Love him until he is Real."

She beamed at Cathy and took her dad's hand. "I will."

"Okay. C'mon, let's go." Pam said.

Jamie held his ground. "In a minute," he told her. "You can go wait in the car if you want."

Pam tapped her foot on the floor impatiently.

He faced Cathy. "Thank you for everything." He shook her hand, squeezing it for several seconds.

Cathy nodded.

Amber was at his side now. "It's time to go, little one," Jamie said. "Better say goodbye."

The lovebird was chirping in its cage. Even he was sad. Cathy must remember to buy him a partner soon. No one should be alone.

Cathy followed the three of them out on the porch. Pam said nothing, just walked to the car with Amber. "

She stayed planted on the steps and watched them get seated in the station wagon. Amber was in the backseat, rolling down the window. Pam had buried her face in a map. Cathy waited for the sound of the ignition but there was none. In slow motion, Jamie rested his head on the steering wheel and Cathy's heart stopped. For a split second, she imagined him running back into her arms. Then he turned and looked out the window at her. Cathy could see Pam's face register anger. In the backseat Amber waved frantically out the window. "Goodbye," she yelled, waving the bunny.

Cathy backed up toward the door, praying to hear the car start, praying not to. The engine finally turned over and she exhaled. Ever so slowly, the car backed down the gravel drive. Through the driver's window she could see Jamie raise his beautiful hand and wave. Cathy's arm was waving but her heart was breaking. Her knees buckled. She sat down in the rocker and watched the car move out the gravel drive and down the same lane they arrived on several weeks ago. The tires stirred up the dirt, leaving behind only dust floating on the wind.

For a flash second, the pain was unbearable. A thousand years of parting ripped through her soul until nothing was left. Libby jumped into her lap and Cathy buried her face in the soft black fur. Tears flushed every hidden corner. This was why she didn't want to love again. But even as she thought it, she knew that Jamie's love was a precious gift.

The lava cooled. The eruption was over. Cathy opened her blurry eyes, everything looked the same, and her life would move on. A white egret swooped past the porch, heading to the river. Perhaps it was a sign, that she was now free to be herself.

Epilogue

THE SUMMER of 2017

Sonoma County, Forestville, CA

The piercing blare of a siren woke Cathy with a start. Disoriented, she took in her surroundings. A medic was adjusting an IV in her arm, as pain forced its way up through the surface of her mind. She'd just been on her porch enjoying the afternoon breeze as she'd done for over forty years.

"Where am I?" she managed to get out.

"You're in an ambulance," his voice calm and even. "We are taking you to Memorial Hospital."

Cathy tried to sit up, but he gently held her down. "Just rest," he said. "Your daughter is following us and will meet you there."

"But how?" she asked. The last thing she remembered was being alone on the porch, her daughter had left, the blinding light … and Jamie. A warm sensation of wellbeing washed over her, as if he was sitting right beside her.

"You're a lucky woman. Your daughter forgot something and when she returned you were unconscious. She called 911."

Cathy fought off the drowsiness, trying to stay alert, watchful of what was happening. The ambulance slowed before coming to a stop. Doors flew open and she was being rolled on a stretcher through more doors into a hospital. In a stark room, filled with the stifling smell of antiseptics, nurses and doctors surrounded her, their words buzzing around in a distant haze. The incessant sound of monitors drowned out almost everything else.

Suddenly everything started to fade. The rhythmic beeping of machines stopped and a profound sense of peace filled her. Cathy was floating, free from pain, hovering above her body, watching everyone trying valiantly to revive her. There was no attachment to her body below, just a sense of wonderment as moments of her life flashed before her eyes. The doubled-over memory of losing her first child was balanced with the adoption of sweet Annie. The heartbreak of her divorce from Todd was overshadowed by the precious years with her husband Alan. She could see Alan showing up the first day to help remodel the Upstairs Café, and although her heart had once been locked closed, it was no longer. Her love with Jamie had paved the way for a contented life. Like a perfect tapestry, flawed but beautiful, each piece had been necessary to weave the whole.

Time and space no longer existed as she drifted into the bright light. Jamie's beckoning hand reached out, and took hers in his. His eyes met Cathy's, like they had so many times before. Jamie gazed at her the same way he had that day in the Cottage Room, when she had been loved into Real. And like eternity, she realized love had no beginning and no end.

More from Andrea Hurst

The Guestbook, Book One in the cozy Madrona Island Trilogy
Available now on Amazon.com

Everyone remembers their first love, but sometimes it's the second love that lasts.

"Evocative and heartfelt, The Guestbook is the profound story of one woman's journey toward hope, renewal and a second chance at love on a lush Pacific Northwest island. Curl up with your favorite cup of cocoa and enjoy."

~Anjali Banerjee, author of Imaginary Men and Haunting Jasmine said about this women's fiction romance

Other books by Andrea Hurst

Tea and Comfort, Book Two in the Madrona Island Trilogy

Island Thyme Café, Book Three in the Madrona Island Trilogy

Madrona Island B&B, Prequel to the Madrona Island Trilogy (a standalone story)

Christmas on Madrona Island, a holiday novella reprising Madrona Island

Acknowledgements

I want to extend a special thank you to all the people who acted as readers, editors, and supporters to help make this book the best it could be:

To Cameron Chandler for his exceptional edits on the revised edition, Cate Perry for her developmental edits on the first edition, to Audrey Mackaman for her skillful copyediting services, and to Natasha Brown for an amazing first edition cover design. To Jean Galiana for her valuable insights, reading every version of the manuscript and always being a friend.

To the valuable readers whose feedback polished the story:

Anjali Banerjee, Ashley McConnaughey, Cameron Chandler, Cherise Hensley, Karen Brees, Katie Flanagan, Laura Whittenburg, Maddy Bullard, Michaelene McElroy, Natalie Carlisle, Rebecca Berus, Ron Wilkinson, Rowena Williamson, Siri Bardarson, and William Dietrich. And a thank you to all of my ARC readers for stepping up.

To my river friends, without you there would be no story: Barbara, Paula, Linda, Steve, Jesper, Ruth, Susan, and Mark.

Thank you to Tracey Garvis-Graves, Melissa Foster, and Bharti Kirchner.

And to Justin and Geneva for believing in me.

To everyone at Just Write at Local Grown, where most of this book took form, thanks for being there.

Author Bio

*A*ndrea Hurst received her BA in Expressive Arts while living on the scenic Russian River in Sonoma County. She is author of *The Guestbook*, the first book in the Madrona Island Trilogy. Her passion for books drives her to find and write stories that take readers on a journey to another place and leave them with an unforgettable impression. She lives in the Pacific Northwest, on an island much like the fictional Madrona of her bestselling series, with all of its natural beauty and small-town charm.

To learn more about Andrea and her books, visit www.AndreaHurst-author.com or www.andreahurst.com.

Join her on Facebook www.facebook.com/andreahurstauthor

68974306R00209

Made in the USA
Columbia, SC
14 August 2019